# SHE'S GONE

# ALSO BY DAVID BELL

# SHE'S GONE

# DAVID BELL

sourcebooks
fire

Published by Sourcebooks Fire, an imprint of Sourcebooks
P.O. Box 4410, Naperville, Illinois 60567–4410
(630) 961-3900
sourcebooks.com

Cataloging-in-Publication data is on file with the Library of Congress.

Printed and bound in Canada.
MBP 10 9 8 7 6 5 4 3 2 1

For Molly

# VIDEO #1

I PUSH THE RED RECORD BUTTON.

I've never made a video like this, never tried to talk so openly to strangers. Icy sweat trickles down my back. I don't know what to say or how to begin.

My face beams back at me, pale and thin from the time I spent in the hospital. I wear a small white bandage on my forehead, and I'm still feeling the effects of the concussion. Bright lights make me wince like a vampire exposed to the sun. If I move too quickly, I get nauseated, and my ears won't stop ringing.

It's time to talk. My phone is recording, and I can't just sit here staring.

I almost turn it off—shut it down.

But I need to talk. I need to get this out.

"Hi," I say, before realizing how simple that sounds. "My name is Hunter Gifford. I'm seventeen years old. A senior. I don't know, maybe a lot of you already know who I am. I guess everything that happened has been in the news. That's why I've stopped looking at my phone. Or talking to anybody. Or maybe they've stopped talking to me. I'm not really sure. But it has the same effect. Normally, I like to write things down to make sense of my life, but I haven't been able to write since the accident. I just stare at the blank page and nothing comes out. So I decided to give this a try."

I clear my throat and watch the red light. My face looks even whiter than when the video started…if that's possible.

I remind myself to keep talking.

"I'm making this video because of all the things that happened that night. Because of the accident. And because my girlfriend, Chloe Summers, hasn't been seen since then. A whole week ago. She was in the car that night, but no one has seen or heard from her since. I guess I should back up. I *think* she was in the car that night. She should have been. We've been dating. We went to homecoming together." I try to swallow again, but I can't produce any spit. "We went everywhere together. So I assume we left the dance together, but I don't know for sure. Because of the accident, and what happened to my head…"

I see myself point to the bandage. My movements look awkward, but I don't want to stop and start over. If I stop, I may not start again.

"I don't remember the accident. I don't remember much of that night. There are holes—blind spots I just can't see. And that means I don't know what caused the accident. Or what happened to Chloe. The police told me we drove into a tree in Dad's

Charger, and somehow I ended up at the hospital. The truth is, no one even knows how I got there. The police think a Good Samaritan found me dazed, wandering on the side of the road, and dropped me off. But Chloe was gone. Everything she had with her—her purse, her phone, even her shoes—was still in the car. But no Chloe. Gone without a trace. That's what they keep saying on the news."

My mouth is dry, and my lips look like cracked pottery, but I need to finish.

"So I'm hoping someone out there knows what happened. To Chloe, I mean. Everyone is worried. Her parents. Her friends. Her teachers. Me. If you know, just call the police. Or message me. Or tell a teacher or somebody. Because she's somewhere, right? And she might be hurt. She might not remember anything just like I don't. And she's probably scared or confused or cold or completely out of her mind."

The next part makes me nervous. I've thought about leaving it out. It's really personal. Everyone thinks people my age just spill everything all over social media, but I'm not like that.

But it feels right. It does.

"And, Chloe, if you're seeing this...well, I don't know what happened that night. I don't remember. I really don't. But I remember that I love you." I pause. I don't even try to swallow because I can't. "And I want to know where you are and that you're safe. I just want to know that more than anything. Even if you don't want to see me or date me, I need to know you're safe."

I take a deep breath. The red light blinks back at me.

I should probably smile. My whole life, people have told me to smile more. Smile when I have my picture taken, and smile when I meet a stranger. But I don't like smiling that way because it feels weird and fake.

My skin feels itchy, my limbs stiff. I don't want to smile, but I want to look concerned.

Worried. Or whatever I'm supposed to be.

But I don't know how to do that, either, so I end my spiel.

"Just let me know, okay?"

I push the red button to stop recording.

# ONE

THE ALARM RINGS, BUT I'M ALREADY AWAKE.

I slept maybe an hour, and my eyes burn like they've been scoured with bleach.

I groan, a noise full of desperation, and pick up my phone to silence the screeching alarm. The concussion effects make it sound ten times louder.

My screensaver taunts me. A photo of Chloe and me taken on a day we spent at the lake during the summer. We're both smiling, and a burst of sunlight pops over her right shoulder. Like she's glowing. Her eyes are bright blue.

During the brief time I slept, her face filled my dreams. She was alive and by my side. I reached out to touch her, to take her hand. Contact with her skin always sent an electric jolt through my body, and every cell in me jangled with energy when we were close.

But then I woke up and landed in reality with a cold splash. I groan again. No words, sounds, or thoughts are enough to sum up everything that has gone wrong. Chloe is missing.

My head hurts, a constant reminder of the crash. I take in the familiar surroundings of my bedroom, the things that used to make me feel at home. A shelf full of science fiction and fantasy novels. The covers worn, the books well-read. A poster of the movie *Dune*—the original—that Mom bought years ago. A cactus Chloe gave me that she named Harriet after her favorite book, *Harriet the Spy*. A few of the soccer trophies and ribbons I still display.

My phone tempts me. I posted the video last night, and then checked the page about fifty times a minute.

Big mistake.

The number of views was nothing to write home about. But the comments...

You killed her.
You know the truth.
You're a liar.
Memory loss. Right.

But I kept looking, hoping for the one person who might have posted something helpful—the one person with the missing piece of the puzzle. But it never came. I finally put down the phone around 4:00 a.m. and tried to sleep. I closed my eyes, but it didn't help. Awake or asleep, I only see Chloe's face, the wrecked car, the lonely spot by the woods on County Road 250. Chloe was there that night when the car crashed...wasn't she?

*Where is she now?*

Water runs in the bathroom down the hall. My sister, Olivia, getting ready for school. I know where I have to go today. I just don't know what lurks ahead.

The rumpled covers and the soft pillow tempt me to stay in bed, but if I do, I'll only think about Chloe *all day*. I'd stare at photos and texts *all day*. I'd start to read the hateful comments again, the conspiracy theories and accusations. The stories claiming Chloe was taken into the woods by Satan worshippers. I know I'd give in to it all.

I've been hiding in my room for almost a week, ever since I came home from the hospital. The therapist said to go back to school, return to my normal life.

*Routine is therapeutic,* she told me.

I grab the jeans I threw over a chair last night. A shirt from the closet. Socks and shoes. I'll give her advice a try, even though I don't believe for one minute anything will be therapeutic. And nothing will ever make me feel normal again.

# TWO

IN THE KITCHEN, A BIZARRE SIGHT GREETS ME. DAD stands at the stove holding a beat-up wooden spoon, stirring something in a pan. Whatever it is appears to be smoking and smells like hot tar on a summer day. I gag.

Dad is dressed for work. Tan pants, olive green sweater with the sleeves pushed up. He smiles at me, but it's forced. The way you'd smile at someone you feel sorry for.

"I'm making oatmeal," he says. "I thought…well, this is what you eat in the morning. Right?"

"I usually have cereal."

"Oh, I thought…not oatmeal. Are you sure?"

"I'm sure, Dad."

"Do you want me to…" He points at the refrigerator. "I can make the cereal."

"I can make cereal," I say.

"Okay. I mean, if you're sure. I just wanted to…"

Dad teaches history at the community college. He's always

reading something or grading papers. His words frequently trail off in the middle of sentences. People who've taken his class tell me it's so inspiring how much he loves history, that when he lectures about some important topic like D-Day or the Civil Rights Movement, he goes on and on until one of the students reminds him the period is over.

When I ask if they've ever gone to his office hours, they say, "I've never done that. He's not really the kind of professor you go talk to."

I always want to tell them, *He's not that kind of dad, either.*

Which is why the oatmeal is so weird. Dad last made breakfast…*never.* At most, he points to the coffee he brewed or the loaf of bread for toast before he rushes out the door for his way-too-early office hours.

He hands me the wooden spoon like it's a fragile ancient artifact. "Here you go. If you put some cinnamon in there…the burning taste or whatever."

"Thanks, Dad."

Since he's made the effort, I grab a bowl, slide the pan off the burner, and scrape out some oatmeal. Dad just stands there by the table, holding his coffee mug like he has all the time in the world. Like a guy trying to show no sense of urgency. And utterly failing.

This is about me going back to school. I can feel it.

"I'm okay, Dad. I can handle it."

"I know, I know. I don't doubt that." He takes a loud sip of his coffee. "It was on the news this morning that the latest search didn't come up with anything. They're not…not sure when they'll do a big search again."

"Are they giving up?" I ask.

"Not that," he says. "It's just…to get that many volunteers out."

"People have short attention spans."

Dad nods. He has as much faith in humanity as I do.

His overstuffed messenger bag and his laptop sit by the door. He taps his foot against the tile, shifts his weight.

Dad is almost fifty but still thin, not like most dads. He rides his bike on the weekends, rarely overeats. Once a month he sits in the backyard looking at the stars and smoking a cigar that smells worse than the burnt oatmeal. He must think about Mom on those nights, but I never ask.

"You see, Hunter, people can be…cruel. They can say things. You've been in the news, and some people always think the worst about the boyfriend when something like this happens."

"I know, Dad."

"I'm just saying…"

The spoonful of oatmeal nearly chokes me. It tastes scorched, like he stirred ashes into the pot as a seasoning. I don't want to hurt his feelings but…

"I'm just saying that if you want to stay home today, or if you just don't…I mean some kids get homeschooled. I can certainly help with that. And my colleagues on campus can help, too."

Mom died of breast cancer a year and a half ago. Since then,

Dad has pretty much had to do everything. He works a lot and pays the bills. He drove us around everywhere until I got my license. He tries in his own weird way to be both parents, even though it's not his strong suit. Things are always a little awkward with him.

Tears form in my eyes. I stare at the gross oatmeal like it's the most important thing in the world. Like black tar breakfast is my absolute favorite. I can't look at him. Not now.

"It's okay, Dad," I say. "I'm ready. I need to do it sooner rather than later. Besides, it's better than sitting around the house just… thinking."

"And your head, it's… Is it feeling better? The nausea?"

"No nausea," I say. *Unless I eat more oatmeal.* "Just a little headache. It's getting there."

Dad nods. Maybe he even looks a little relieved. He wants me back in school, getting on with my life. And he hates having his routine disrupted.

He finishes his coffee and sets his mug on the counter with a little thump. "Well," he says.

One of our awkward silences descends on us. He's ready to go but doesn't know how to leave.

And I don't have anything else to say to him. As usual.

Olivia clomps down the stairs. She comes into the kitchen like a miniature hurricane, her phone clutched in her hands, her eyes and mouth wide.

"Oh my God, you guys," she says. "Did you see this?"

# THREE

"SEE WHAT?" DAD ASKS.

He looks like a poisonous snake has just curled up next to his foot. His son is a murder suspect, and he can't handle any more bad news.

Olivia is holding her phone like it's a holy book she's about to read from. She's fifteen and dressed in her usual outfit: combat boots, tight jeans, black T-shirt, flannel shirt tied around her waist. She has a new streak of color in her brown hair. Purple this time. Last week it was pink.

Dad is about to get blindsided. He would have told me not to do it. To keep my mouth shut and put my head down until everything blows over. As if it ever will…

"Hunter made a video," Olivia says. "The quality is terrible. He should've picked a different background. It's like some low-budget terrorist group made it." She looks up from her phone. "You should have at least sat in front of your bookshelf. That would be interesting. Here you just look really pasty and pale. I mean I know you're hurt and everything."

"What video?" Dad asks, pushing away from the counter and moving toward Olivia.

"Why did you put this on YouTube and not TikTok?" Olivia asks.

"It's not really right for TikTok—"

"Oh, I see," Olivia says. "You shared this on the creative writing club channel. Ex Libris. Clever. Then people at school can see it and start to share."

"What video?" Dad asks.

"You should at least do a TikTok telling everyone you posted on YouTube," Olivia says. "Although the comments tell me people are seeing it already. Yikes."

"What is this video?" Dad asks.

"It's about Chloe," Olivia says. "What else?" She hands her phone to Dad and pushes the play button for him because he pretty much can't do anything on his phone without help.

My voice comes across the kitchen, tinny and small.

*Hi, my name is Hunter Gifford...*

Dad watches with an open mouth and Olivia turns to me. "Have you read the comments?"

"Some."

Oliva makes a face. "Nasty. People are so rude. They get online and totally stop acting like human beings." She breezes across the kitchen and peers into the pan on the stove. "Blech. Who made this?"

"Dad did," I say, pushing away my bowl.

"*Dad* made it? Professor Benjamin Gifford *cooked*?"

We both look at him as the video ends. Dad takes a deep breath. He hands the phone back to Olivia like it's a dead bird. He goes over to his bag and picks it up. Dad doesn't like conflict, and he never tells us what he's feeling. We just have to guess when he's unhappy with us. And it's pretty obvious he's unhappy right now. All the goodwill that went into him trying to make breakfast and offering to homeschool me seems gone.

"This is a mistake, Hunter," he says, his voice level. For him this comment amounts to the Gettysburg Address.

"I'm trying to find Chloe," I say. The ache in my head gets more intense.

"Things just started to quiet down a little," he says. "The crank calls. The dog crap on the porch. We just got some peace."

"You said they're done searching," I say. "Maybe this will motivate them to try again."

"It's a mistake. The lawyer told you to keep a low profile when you left the hospital. And you posted that on a school channel?"

"Dad—"

"It's not a school channel," Olivia says. "It's a club channel. Hunter and Chloe created it, and this livens it up a little. Usually, Ex Libris posts boring poetry readings. Snooze."

"Oh, jeez," Dad says, shaking his head. "Okay, I'm late. Are you sure you're okay to drive to school?"

"The doctor said I could."

"Okay. Just be safe."

And then he goes to the door without looking back.

"What are you so pissed about, Dad?" Olivia asks.

"Livvy, it's okay," I say.

"No," she says. "He's trying to help find Chloe. He has the right to do that, even if his presentation is ass."

Dad stops in the open doorway. He doesn't go out and doesn't come back in. He just stands there, a man caught in-between. He doesn't look over his shoulder when he speaks. "The cops said to keep a low profile. There are a lot of raw emotions. People get…" He pauses and lifts his free hand to his forehead. "Hunter's going back to school today and that…It's going to be tough."

"What if the video helps us find her?" Oliva asks, her voice rising.

Dad stands in the doorway a few moments longer. He looks like he's going to say something but stops. Then he says, "Just be careful driving, okay? And if you don't feel well, go tell the nurse."

And he's out the door and off to work.

Olivia throws her hands in the air in an overly theatrical gesture. She wants me to be just as outraged. Which I am, in a way, but I'm also trying to understand. Dad doesn't like talking about things. He doesn't like emotions being on display.

As Chloe used to say, "The apple doesn't fall far."

*Used to say?* No. *Says.* Chloe *says* that about me.

"It's okay, Livvy. Maybe I shouldn't have made it. Maybe it's just going to make things worse. All the things people will say… all the things they're posting."

Oliva stares at me with her mouth wide open, her braces gleaming beneath the kitchen light.

"What people say? What people say? Is what people say or post worse than the fact that nobody knows where Chloe is? Or people harassing us by smearing dog shit on the porch? Or knocking over the trash cans? Come on, Hunter. Think. Is that stuff worse?" She stomps off, but as she goes up the stairs, her voice floats back to me over the sound of her heavy steps. "I think it's beautiful how much you love Chloe, Hunter. I really do."

And she's right. I do love Chloe.

And I love my lunatic sister, too.

# FOUR

DAD WOULD BE HAPPY. I DRIVE SO SLOWLY IT FEELS LIKE the car is standing still. Old ladies in giant cars pass us—that's how slow we go. I barely notice my headache.

The accident on homecoming night is still under investigation. They tested my blood, and they know I wasn't drunk or high. The police say it's possible another car might have been involved—either accidentally or on purpose—because otherwise how did we just randomly plow into a tree?

They checked both our phones, so they know we weren't texting. They took paint scrapings off her dad's nearly new Charger to see if someone else rammed into us. Why they think someone would do that, I have no clue.

Even though it was her dad's car—which is nicer than the gray 2010 Corolla I drive—it appears I was driving, and Chloe was in the passenger seat. Her shoes, phone, and purse were found on that side. My blood was on the steering wheel. A trace of Chloe's blood was on the inside of the passenger door. They have a whole team of cops trying to figure it all out.

Since I can't remember a single thing about the accident, I'm not any help. But the police turned my life inside out. They took hair and saliva samples. They went all through my room—my closet, my desk, my computer. They took the clothes I wore that night and went through my locker at school. If I had any secrets, the cops know every one of them now.

The lawyer Dad called—a middle-aged woman who looks more like a librarian—allowed the police to do those things, and then privately told me I'd be fine as long as I told the truth.

But it all raises the question—why would someone want to run us off the road?

And if it was just an accident, why did they leave the scene? And take Chloe?

And why did I wander around until someone found me? Why didn't I stay?

Why didn't I try to help Chloe?

Maybe my head was too messed up. Or maybe…that's where I start to look suspicious.

It turns out the hospital has security cameras outside the emergency room doors. No car dropped me off that night. I just came wandering up. The cops showed me the grainy video that looked like something from a found footage horror film, and I saw myself stumbling to the door, my hand held to my bloody forehead. I look like the guy in the movie who brings the virus into the hospital. Either someone dumped me in the lot and stayed out of sight. Or they didn't want their car to be seen for some reason.

Or maybe I faked the whole thing. That's what some people say. I drove into a tree and bashed my own head and did something terrible to Chloe. Then walked five miles to the hospital in the dark. With a concussion.

As we make the drive to school, my hands grip the wheel tight. This is only the second time I've driven since...since that night. I stop extra long at every stop sign. I look both ways even when a light turns green. I'm wrong to make fun of the old ladies. Their behavior makes sense to me now.

Olivia is in the passenger seat, texting away, her feet tucked underneath her. She's clearly not worried about my driving. Her thumbs move over her phone like a video in fast-forward.

She spends every ride to school texting this way. But I want to talk. Maybe I'm more anxious than I realize. Maybe dad is right. Maybe I should lay low. After those comments on YouTube, who knows what people will say in person?

"Aren't you going to see Gabriela in less than five minutes?" I ask.

"I need to plan *where* we're meeting. I haven't seen her since yesterday."

"Wow. So long."

She lowers the phone to her lap. "Oh, shit. Am I being an asshole for texting Gabby while Chloe's missing? I'm sorry. I'll stop."

"I wasn't saying that." And I wasn't. "I was just teasing you. You know, the way I always do."

"Are you sure? I'll stop."

"You don't have to stop. I'm glad you have Gabriela. You're lucky."

"I know," she says dreamily. "And it's almost our three-month anniversary. So let's talk about something happy." Olivia turns and looks out the window. We're driving through a neighborhood near ours. Rows and rows of brick ranch houses that Chloe called midcentury modern. The yards are full of leaves, and a lot of the porches have been taken over by pumpkins and cornstalks and plastic skeletons. "Look at all the Halloween stuff. Isn't it awesome? Gabriela and I are taking her little cousin trick-or-treating. Did I tell you that?"

"No, you didn't. Or maybe you did, and I can't remember."

"No worries. We're all going to dress like zombies. You know, all pale and deathly and shit."

Pale and deathly. That makes me think of something...

"Livvy, about the video..."

"Don't worry about Dad, Hunter. He can be such an asshole sometimes. It's like when I try to talk to him about Mom, and he's all like, 'I just don't want to think about that, Livvy.' Can you believe he says that to me? By the way, I told him fifty times to stop calling me Livvy. I'm not a little kid."

"I call you Livvy all the time."

"*You're* allowed to. You're my brother, and I give *you* permission. But not Dad."

"Give him a break. He's just...private."

"I hate that word. Private. 'It's private, Livvy.' 'Some things are meant to be private, Livvy.' Mom never said that shit to me."

"Is the video bad?" I ask. "I mean, people are already saying shit in the comments. Will it get worse?"

Olivia takes her time answering, which is rare. Usually she fires from the hip, the words flying out of her mouth like missiles. But she's looking back out the window now, her fingers twining through the purple streak in her hair.

"Your intention with the video is really sweet," she says finally. "I know how much you care about Chloe. And *I* love her to Jupiter and back. I mean, she's way better than Hannah. I don't know how you could stand her. I know Chloe can't stand her."

"They basically can't stand each other. And I dated Hannah two years ago."

"Okay. But I love Chloe, you know? I really do."

"I know."

Olivia stops twirling her hair. She raises her hand to her eyes and touches each of them gently. Everything makes Olivia cry. Movies, puppies, songs, babies. They all make her cry. She's seriously missing Chloe, too. Chloe is an only child, and Olivia doesn't have any sisters. Olivia always told me I could never break up with Chloe because if I did, she'd disown me and claim Chloe as her own.

"But people *are* going to say shit," she says. "In person, and not just in the comments. They've already been harassing us. Dad didn't want to tell you, but somebody let the air out of his tires on campus a few days ago."

"They did?"

"Yeah. He had to call a tow truck to come and fill them up so he could drive home. People are assholes, Hunter. It's like Shark Week. A little blood in the water, and they go wild."

"I wish Dad had told me," I say. "Have people been bullying you?"

"I'm fine," she says. "People have said some things when I walk by. Cowards. Every once in a while, somebody says some bullshit about Gabby and me. I can handle it. I mean... I know why you made the video. And I know you were feeling some real shit when you made it. But some people might not get it. You're kind of like Dad in that way. People don't know what's really going on inside. Maybe you should have just written something. Video is kind of...you know, unforgiving. And it looks like it's already spreading around the school. Maybe you *should* stay off TikTok."

"Are you saying the video makes me look fake?"

The school comes in sight. Rows of yellow buses, the endless procession of student cars. I used to pick up Chloe and drive her to school. She and Olivia would text jokes back and forth while I drove. They'd laugh and laugh and sometimes not let me in on it. Then we'd park in the lot, and Olivia would sprint into the school looking for Gabriela while Chloe and I walked together holding hands.

I wish I could hold her hand again. Like in the dream. Like we used to do walking into school. Just hold her hand...

I find an empty spot, aware that Olivia still hasn't answered my question.

"Well?" I ask.

Olivia is staring straight ahead, but then she whips around to face me. "You look stiff. Like in school pictures. You always look like you're sitting on a nail or something." She takes a big breath, her shoulders rising and falling. "Like I said, I know who you are. But all these people who don't…and, my God, Hunter, a lot of people have probably shared it now." She gestures to the parking lot, the school, the town beyond. "I'm afraid they're going to think you look guilty."

# FIVE

OLIVIA STAYS GLUED TO MY SIDE AS WE WALK TOWARD
the school.

"What are you doing?" I ask. "Aren't you meeting Gabby?"

"Yeah."

"So why are you here? With me?"

"Because I want to be."

We join a stream of students. Kids from every one of the
four grades, kids from every social background, kids from every
race. Garrett Morgan High is a big school because our small
city in Kentucky just keeps growing. There are two other high
schools out in the county, and there's talk of a third, but Garrett
Morgan is the biggest with almost two thousand kids. I try
not to dwell on the irony of going to a school named after a
Kentuckian who patented the stoplight because he witnessed a
horrible car accident.

"You can go on," I say to Olivia. "I'm fine. I'm just going to go
to class and blend in. And try not to look guilty."

"I never should have told you the truth," she says.

"You've never not told the truth in your life. Go find Gabriela. Go be sickeningly cute together. I'm okay."

Once she's gone, I continue my slow walk into the building—past the display case full of trophies won by the football team, past the giant painting of Abraham Lincoln, past the grinning, cheesy portrait of the current president—and begin to feel like everything might be okay. The online trolls don't represent the rest of the world. People post things online they would never have the guts to utter in real life.

Dad always says no one under the age of forty follows the news anyway. Maybe they don't know I'm a suspect. Maybe they don't know anything.

The voices around me hum, a dull murmur punctuated by the occasional shout. The odor of disinfectant reminds me of my nights in the hospital, some toxic liquid the maintenance crew smears all over the floors to make them shine. My pulse slows to a normal rate.

I take the stairs, two at a time, to my locker on the second floor. There are fewer kids there, less noise pollution. I'm a week behind. I tried to keep up while I was home but didn't do nearly enough. That's another reason to come back. I need to get back to work, to have something to throw myself into. I can't control much of what is going on around me, but I can control how hard I work in school.

College applications loom. My grades cannot slip. Maybe I can even write something again.

I want to feel normal, even as my healing mind tells me I can't.

A couple of faces I don't know turn to gawk at me as I head to my locker. I'm still wearing the bandage. It's smaller but it's there. When I feel their eyes on me, I unconsciously reach up and touch it. I consider going to the bathroom and ripping it off. If I want to blend in, why did I wear an ugly sign on my head?

*Because the doctor told you to…*

Maybe they weren't looking at me because of the accident. Maybe they were just looking.

A couple more kids turn and stare, and my skin itches the way it does when someone wants to take my picture. Like ants crawling right below the surface.

I quicken my pace. I just want to get to the locker, lean inside, shuffle my books around, and pretend to have something to do. Then I'll go off to class when the crowd thins.

But the door of my locker—number 209—has something on it.

It takes me a minute to figure it out. It looks like a Halloween decoration. Did Olivia put it there to welcome me back?

It's a dangling rubber skeleton, tied to the locker with a length of string.

Somebody lets out a loud laugh behind me. But I don't get the joke.

A piece of paper is pinned to the skeleton. A note, printed in a creepy, Gothic font.

Only two words: CHLOE KILLER.

# SIX

MORE LAUGHTER BEHIND ME. MORE AND MORE.

My hand swings like an axe, grabbing the skeleton, yanking with all my might to pull the string loose. It breaks off in my hand, and I stumble back.

And then someone says, "Damn."

I slam the skeleton and the note onto the floor and grind it under my sneaker. I grind and grind, hoping it will all disintegrate. But the skeleton is rubber, and it just rolls around under my foot. The note slips away, landing face up, taunting me.

CHLOE KILLER.

I come back to myself. People stream past me. Slowly. They're studying me, wondering if I really am batshit. And wouldn't a killer rage and throw things around?

My reaction is exactly what they want. They can all text their friends and say, *That dude who killed his girlfriend went nuts in the hallway. He was flipping his shit.*

I take a deep, centering breath. The kind Mom told me to take when I was scared of the dark. I kick the skeleton aside with my foot and leave the note where it is. Who cares, right? The online trolls have already crossed over into the real world. The calls. The junk on the porch. Dad's tires. Ignore them.

But my hands are shaking and my heart rollicking as I open my backpack and take out my books.

"Yo, Hunter."

Before I turn, Chad is next to me, his long arm draped over my shoulder.

"Dude, you're back."

He pulls me close and then lets me go. He smells like toothpaste and shaving cream.

"Thank God," I say.

"What's that?" He points at the skeleton on the ground, sees the note. "That's bullshit. Total bullshit. Hey!" He yells at no one in particular and starts to look around the hall, searching for a guilty face. "Did you do this?" He points at random people. "What about you—"

"Chad, it's okay. It's okay. Just ignore it. It's okay."

There's one kid holding his phone, filming me. But he scoots away. Everyone else moves on.

"You sure?" Chad's three inches taller than I am, which is why he's the starting goalie on the soccer team. That's how we met as freshmen. He's thin, but not weak, with hair that flops over his forehead. He wears a flannel shirt with the sleeves perfectly rolled to the elbows and carries a single textbook and one new folder. "You don't need to take this crap."

"I'm just glad to see someone normal. I know you came by the house."

"Little Livvy said you were asleep both times. I was starting to feel hurt, like maybe you didn't love me anymore." He nudges me with his elbow. "It's cool. I know you weren't feeling well. But you're back now." He places his hand on my shoulder. "Seriously, man. You doing okay?"

"I am. Maybe. Trying to."

"Good. We've got a lot of talking to do. And my mom wants to have you over for dinner."

The first bell echoes through the halls like a warning. We have four minutes to get to class.

"What do we need to talk about?" I ask.

Chad looks at his phone, shifts the book and folder in his hand. "I wanted to tell you at your house. That's why I came over. And I wanted to see if you were okay. But I didn't want to text you. I mean you are a suspect and everything, and I heard the cops are digging through all your shit. At least that's what's on the news."

"What did you not want to text me?"

"No time now." He pats me on the back. "Lunch, okay? And, seriously, I'm glad you're back. Everybody wants to see you, man. Lunch, okay?"

"Okay. But, Chad, what is it?"

He pauses, scratches the clean-shaven chin where one large pimple has sprouted. "About homecoming night. About the night Chloe disappeared."

His words jolt me, and he pats me on the back again and then he's gone.

I kick the skeleton one more time. It grins at me from the floor. Stupid, mindless. Dead.

# SEVEN

EITHER NO ONE WANTS TO TALK TO ME. OR NO ONE KNOWS what to say.

I can't decide which.

I slip into my first period class—pre-calc—and head for my seat near the front of the room. I have friends in this class, people I talk to on a regular basis. But everyone turns away from me and grows quiet, the chattering voices shutting off like someone hit the mute button. If this had been any other day, I'd have sworn that I'd walked into the room with no pants on or with a note scrawled on my face. That's how quiet it is.

Church quiet. Funeral quiet.

I slide into my seat and pretend to look at something in my textbook. A heavy pressure settles on my neck and shoulders, an invisible weight. The silence is a force pushing against me. The skeleton dances in my mind's eye, the ignorant note. Did someone in this room let the air out of Dad's tires? I want to tell them all to fuck off, but I sit, staring at my book.

I risk one look up and see Mike Basher, the quarterback on the football team. Everyone likes him even though he's really a terrible football player, and the fans groaned two weeks ago when the starter broke his collarbone and Basher took over for the rest of the season. He also used to date Chloe. They were a thing for about three months at the beginning of junior year, even going to the previous homecoming together. And apparently Basher and Chloe's dad, Scott, both share an interest in old cars. About a month after Chloe and I started dating, I went over to her house and found Scott and Basher in the detached garage, bent over the open hood of the '75 Mustang Scott was restoring. When I asked Chloe, she just rolled her eyes and told me to forget about it. The next time I went over, Mike was in the hallway when I went to the bathroom. Basher apparently walked around their house like he lived there.

Then in the second week of this semester, in creative writing class, Basher wrote a poem about a girl he was in love with, calling her a queen. And the description of the girl in the poem sounded exactly like Chloe. At first, Chloe didn't think it was about her, but when I went through it line by line with her, she started to come around. Finally, she went to our teacher, Mr. Hartman, about it, and while he listened sympathetically, he said he didn't think Basher meant any harm.

"It's his artistic expression," Mr. Hartman said. "An intense feeling given voice. I'd say there's no real malice there."

Chloe felt like I had pushed her to say something when her gut told her not to.

"Now Mr. Hartman thinks I'm a freak," she said.

A couple of weeks before the accident, Chloe told me she wasn't going to ask Mr. Hartman to write her a letter of recommendation for college. I asked her if she didn't want to ask because she still felt weird about the whole Basher poem thing, but she didn't answer me.

So it's no surprise when Basher blankly meets my eye that morning. My stupid jealousy flares, even though Chloe claims he's a bit shallow.

Then Basher does something. He nods his head subtly and gives me a quick thumbs-up.

I don't know why Mike did that, but he lifted my spirits. Maybe things won't be so bad. Maybe I can make it through this.

Then our teacher comes in. Mr. Berning. He's a giant guy, well over six feet tall with bulging biceps and a military haircut. He used to coach the basketball team but stepped down a few years ago after three straight losing seasons. He still teaches though, and the guy is all business. He never smiles at anyone, never cracks a joke. All the students hate him. If his wife disappeared and *he* made a video, everyone would think he was guilty. No doubt about it.

But maybe Mr. Berning is a really nice guy at home. Maybe he calls his wife silly names and makes dumb jokes that he laughs and laughs about. Maybe he slips little notes under her pillow for her to find when she wakes up. I've never thought of Mr. Berning that way, but I understand him a little better now that I don't want people making cruel assumptions about me. Maybe he has layers we can't see.

Chloe and I leave notes for each other like that. We write silly things on scraps of paper—*I love you! I miss you! You're the sexiest!*—and then try to leave them where the other person will find them later. Stuffed into books or the pockets of our jackets. Placed under the windshield wipers on the car. Chloe once left one that said *Kiss Me* in the medicine cabinet of our bathroom, and my dad found it while looking for a razor. We laughed a long time at his confused response.

Berning jumps right into graphs and functions. The stuff made zero sense to me before the accident, and it's no fun studying math with a throbbing head and a missing girlfriend. In fact, the math stuff makes me think of Chloe. She always helps me with my calc homework. She wants to major in chemistry in college, maybe go premed. She has always gently mocked my inability to grasp mathematical concepts right away, and then when I figure it out, she kisses me and says, "See, it's not so hard." My mind spirals into images of her until a voice interrupts.

"Attention, please. May I have your attention, please."

It's Berning—he's caught me spacing out. But the voice comes through the loudspeaker above the whiteboard. Berning rolls his eyes and caps his marker. He crosses his massive arms and stares out the window at the changing trees.

"Pardon me for interrupting class time with this important announcement."

It's the principal. Dr. Jackson. She almost never speaks to the school over the PA unless it's something serious. Usually the assistant principal, Dr. Whitley, makes the everyday, mundane announcements in his soft, Kentucky accent.

So why is Jackson on the PA today?

"As you all know, our school community and the community of Bentley have suffered a horrible tragedy—the disappearance of Chloe Summers."

My mind swirls. Those eyes study me again. A thousand eyes pushing against my back. Basher's face is blank again. No nod. No thumbs-up. Maybe he's thinking none of this would have happened if he and Chloe were still together. Berning turns away from the window. His eyes look like a shark's. Cold. Distant.

The worst crosses my mind—why is any announcement being made at all? Everyone knows Chloe is missing. What could Dr. Jackson have to say that hasn't been said?

Have they found her? Is she dead? Is that it?

"Tonight, we are going to gather as a community in a show of support for Chloe's family and friends. At seven o'clock, we will assemble on the football field for a candlelight vigil. This vigil has been organized by the student government committee and is the students' way of honoring Chloe. We in the administration support and applaud that effort. Everyone in the community is invited to attend. Please spread the word to your family and friends. It is vital in times of tragedy that we remember our ties to each other. Information about the candlelight vigil will be posted on the school's website and social media outlets. Remember, unity is strength. Thank you, Garrett Morgan Bobcats."

The PA clicks off. The room is still.

I wait for someone to say something, to acknowledge what's going on.

Berning steps forward and says, "Okay, about this $x$ coordinate. It's a tricky one, and you guys just aren't getting it no matter how many times I try to explain it…"

# EIGHT

THE MORNING DRAGS. THE HANDS ON THE CLOCKS IN every classroom move like they're in slow motion. People still stare at me. Others look away. Like there's a target on my back.

Something changes after the principal's announcement. Voices in the hallway are more hushed. Classroom chatter is more muted. Everything feels muffled. Even though the sun shines brightly outside, it feels like one of those long, rainy days that never end.

It's a relief when I finally make it to lunch, to our usual table, the one where we've been sitting since we started high school. My friend group changed that year. Soccer was a big part of my life growing up, and when I came to Garrett Morgan and made the team, I started hanging out with the other soccer players. My grade school friends faded away.

For a couple of reasons, I'm not on the team anymore. I twisted my knee pretty bad during practice sophomore year and missed most of the season. And Mom was first diagnosed the summer before that, and her illness pretty much took over our lives.

That's also when I first took a creative writing class and joined Ex Libris, the creative writing club. That interested me more than soccer.

And Ex Libris changed my life because that's where I met Chloe.

The first time I saw her, we were workshopping our stories and poems. I turned in a science fiction story I was very proud of, something certain to make me the most famous fifteen-year-old writer in the United States. But Chloe calmly and clearly picked apart some of the science in the story, and my face flushed with embarrassment and disappointment. I decided to quit writing altogether.

After the meeting, Chloe texted, telling me that she really liked my story, and if I ever wanted to talk to her about the science, she'd be willing to help. I'm sorry to say I didn't take her up on it, and it was a year and a half before we started dating. But I never forgot how smart she was. How confident. And also willing to help someone she barely knew.

I'm also not as good as the other guys on the soccer team. I was probably going to get cut junior year. No, not probably. I was. Rather than go through that torture, I tried other things. But my friends are all still playing.

Hector and Cameron are already at the table. And Cameron's girlfriend Natasha. They all look up. They all texted me right after the accident. They all came by the house while I still felt pretty sick from the concussion and couldn't really talk to anyone.

The sight of them lifts my spirits.

Hector smiles. "He's back," he says, chomping on a carrot stick. He always smiles, even with carrot pieces in his perfectly straight teeth. "The prodigal friend."

"I guess you're not dead," Cameron says.

Natasha nudges him, gives him a warning look. But I don't care. That's how Cameron deals with things. A morbid joke. A dig. When he says *I guess you're not dead* he means *Good to see you.*

"Not yet," I say.

"Well, I'm happy to see you," Natasha says. "These guys are animals. They don't know how to express themselves in a thoughtful way. But I'm glad you're back."

Natasha likes the grand statement, the big gesture. She likes to pretend she's more mature than the rest of us, and we let her. Her parents went through a nasty divorce when we were still in middle school. Bottom line: the whole town knew her dad left her mom for the twenty-one-year-old babysitter. Natasha acts like nothing bothers her, so maybe she can give me tips on dealing with public humiliation.

Chloe admired the way Natasha took what people in town dished out and just kept right on going. Chloe always wished she could worry less about what people thought of her.

It's just good to be around friends who give a shit about me.

"Where's Chad?" I ask. I take a bite of the PB&J I packed

the night before, but it tastes unappealing. My appetite has been weak. I feel like I shouldn't be enjoying anything if Chloe isn't around. "He said he had something to tell me."

"He's with Hannah," Hector says.

"When isn't he?" Cameron says.

Hector shrugs. He refuses to say anything bad about anybody. Ever. That's just Hector.

But then an awkward silence settles over the table. Everyone keeps talking and eating around us. Dishes clatter. People shout and laugh. The smell of fried food fills the air. But at our table, it gets quiet. It kind of pisses me off, because I want to think this is the one place things can feel normal.

All three of them eat slowly but don't speak.

"What?" I ask.

Hector looks away. Cameron takes a bite of his ham sandwich.

Only Natasha turns to me. "Well, we were just wondering if you're going to the candlelight vigil tonight."

I stop chewing. It tasted crappy anyway.

Hector looks away. Cameron takes another bite. He'd keep eating if the cafeteria were being shot up. He'd dive for cover or jump out a window with the sandwich in his hand.

"I thought about it all morning, but it just doesn't seem right. People are saying a lot of shit. Why would I want to subject myself to that?"

Hector nods like he agrees. But then again, he agrees with almost everything anyone says to him.

Cameron kind of shrugs. "Well, we have practice. State is coming up."

Only Natasha maintains eye contact. She's honest. She's willing to say what's on her mind. That's something she has in common with Chloe, which is why I can't believe Chloe ran away like some people are saying. How could Chloe have a problem so big it would make her want to run and I wouldn't know about it?

"What?" I ask Natasha because she is the most likely to respond. Maybe that's something girls do better than guys. They actually talk about important shit.

"Well," she says, "we all saw your video, Hunter. It's spreading around school."

My shoulders drop. The video. *Why did I do that again? What made me think that was a good idea?* "And?" I ask.

"If you don't go to the vigil, then people are only going to know what they see in the video. And on the news. And the video is kind of, well, it kind of makes you…"

"Look guilty?" I ask. "Is that what you're saying? Look guilty?"

Hector and Cameron look up in unison, like they choreographed the move. That word. Guilty.

*Guilty.*

Natasha doesn't flinch. "Yes, Hunter. It totally does."

My mouth starts moving. It feels disconnected from my brain, and the words just fly out. Maybe this is how Olivia feels all the time…

"How can one video do that? How can one video cancel

everything Chloe and I did together? Like the time we went to her grandparents' cabin by the lake? Or the hours we spent talking? The time she sat up all night with Livvy and me when our dog died? The fact that we…that we had started…"

Their faces stare back at me. Hector. Cameron. Natasha. All looking, mouths open. Concerned. A little freaked.

And a couple of people at the table behind us have turned around to gawk as well.

I lower my voice.

"How can anyone know what goes on between two people? It's none of their fucking business."

My friends' faces are full of pity. No one wants pity. Not at all. And I don't feel any better after my little rant. I feel worse.

At that exact moment, Chad comes walking up with Hannah. As usual, he looks happy and carefree. And for no good reason I'm mad at him, probably because he wasn't there when this whole conversation started. So as soon as he reaches the table, I say, "Where the fuck have you been? I thought you had something important to tell me."

Chad keeps his cool. Only Hannah's face shows any surprise. Her mouth opens, and she looks at me and then at Chad, her blond hair pulled back off her rosy cheeks. But she doesn't say anything. And no one else does, either.

It's Chad who finally speaks. "Okay then. Why don't you and me take a little walk?"

# NINE

WE WALK OUT OF THE CAFETERIA SIDE BY SIDE, BOTH OF us as quiet as monks.

I'm quiet because I owe Chad an apology. He's quiet because he knows me well enough to know he just has to give me a little space sometimes. He's one of the few people who gets that. Olivia does, too.

And so does Chloe.

Outside it's sunny enough to make me squint. There's an area of picnic tables and benches where we're allowed to hang out when the weather's nice. That's pretty much where Chloe and I started dating. We'd known each other through Ex Libris and had even been talking and texting for weeks. But I saw her out there one day, sitting alone, reading *Macbeth* for class, and I walked up and said, "Spoiler alert, it's not a happy ending." And, thankfully, she laughed. We went to Blue Door Coffee after school the next day, supposedly to discuss our Ex Libris submissions, but we talked about everything else. Our families, our dreams, what it would be like to do something other people couldn't forget. That was pretty much that. I didn't want to be with anyone else.

In the distance, a group of guys is tossing a football around. It doesn't really feel like fall yet. No cool weather. No frost. Chad and I walk in the direction of the football players, sticking near the trees that border campus. A couple holding hands passes us. A kid staring at his phone almost walks into us. Three girls talk animatedly but grow silent when they see us. Three sets of eyes trail toward Chad, and the bravest one says hello to him.

"Hey," Chad says, before the kid and her friends walk past us, laughing and whispering.

I break the ice. It has to be me. I'm the one who fucked up.

"I'm sorry," I say. "I don't want to be a dick."

"It's cool. It's a tough time."

"Well, still. I shouldn't…"

"It's okay. I saw that note on your locker. I heard the announcement about the vigil. It's a lot."

"Yeah. Well, I'm still sorry."

"We're cool."

My thanks stick in my throat. The branches and leaves on my right swing in the breeze. Someone lets out a triumphant yell on the football field, and one of the guys jumps around like he's just won the Super Bowl.

"But I do want to tell you something," Chad says. "About Chloe. About homecoming."

Another word sticks in my throat. But I force it out. "Yeah?"

"Yeah." He points to a weathered bench. I know what he means—we should sit. That's how it is with Chad—he points or says one word, and everyone knows what he means. And they follow.

So we sit on the rickety bench and hope it doesn't collapse under our weight. No one is around. The football game continues in the distance, but the jumping and yelling have stopped. We have about twenty minutes until classes resume.

Chad takes his time before speaking. Those few bites of peanut butter and jelly have settled in my gut like bricks. My mind goes in two directions. On one hand, I want to know what he has to tell me. On the other...

"This is why I came by your house when you were out of commission," Chad says. "To tell you what happened on the night of the dance. Hannah saw Chloe crying in the bathroom. She was really upset about something. Hannah talked to her for a while and got her calmed down. Did you know that?"

I did but only because when the cops talked to me in the hospital, it was one of the things they asked me about over and over—did you know Chloe was crying in the bathroom on the night of homecoming? And I told them I didn't know. *Over and over.*

Chloe almost never cried. Not at movies. Not at sappy songs. Not when we disagreed or fought. Pretty much never.

Then the cops came by the house two more times, asking me more questions. The same things, like a song on repeat: *Do you remember anything else? How were things between you and Chloe? Would Chloe ever run away? Did you break up? Did you have a fight? Did you ever hit her? Were you cheating on her? Was she cheat-ing on you?*

And then the big things they asked: *Were you having sex? Is it possible Chloe was pregnant?*

Super fun stuff to talk about with your dad in the room. And your little sister eavesdropping from upstairs.

They got the truth. Chloe and I had sex for the first time—and I mean the first time for *both* of us—one month before she disappeared. It happened to be our six-month anniversary. Everyone—including Chad—said the first time wasn't going to be great. And they were right. It wasn't.

But my first time was with Chloe. That mattered to me more than anything else.

Chad goes on. "I figured you knew about her being upset. Even if you didn't remember it all. Hannah told the cops about that."

I only knew because the cops told me.

But I also remember that Chloe wasn't herself in the weeks leading up to the dance. She'd been distant. Short-tempered. Not as warm. Not all the time. Not every day. But more than usual. And when I asked what was going on, she claimed she was stressed out by school. An AP Chemistry test she needed to ace. Her work on student council. College applications. Her parents were totally *obsessed* with her college applica-tions. They acted like the fate of the free world hinged on her getting into a good private college, preferably Ivy League. They always applied a lot of pressure. About her grades. About her future. But the college applications brought their intensity to a new level.

And we didn't try to have sex again. There was no second time. Chloe didn't seem interested in anything physical, and I chalked it up to all the weirdness in her life. We'd figure it out sometime in the future, when life was quiet again. Actually, I was secretly hoping we'd finally try again on the night of homecoming.

The cops seemed to listen when we talked, but there was one thing I struggled about telling them. I went back and forth about it in my mind but finally brought it up.

I told them Chloe kept a journal. Handwritten in a leather notebook.

Why the struggle over whether to tell them?

Mainly because it had taken Chloe so long to tell *me*. She'd only mentioned it at the beginning of the school year, after we'd been dating for close to five months. She brought it up in passing in the creative writing club one day. When we were alone later and I asked her about it, she said it was no big deal. It was just something she'd started doing the previous spring because our teacher, Mr. Hartman, recommended it.

But she never offered to show it to me.

She said she kept it hidden in her room in an out-of-the-way place. Her parents knew she kept it, and she worried they—especially her mom—might snoop.

Since the police went all through their house, and removed

computers, phones, hair samples, fibers, and everything else, they must have found the journal. Right?

"Before the cops told me, I didn't know she was crying on the night of the dance," I say to Chad. "Or if I did know, I don't remember now. A lot of that night, ninety percent of it, is just a blind spot. I remember going to her house. I remember all of us going to Hannah's for dinner. I kind of remember walking into the gym. The music was terrible…"

"It was."

"And that's about it. The rest is just…nothing."

"Remember I got that concussion against Morgantown last year? When I collided with that big dude? I didn't know my own name when I came off the field The trainer asked me the date, and I said it was 1972. So it might come back, right? It did for me."

"The doctor says it could. There's no way to predict. But the more time passes…" I wonder if this is what my grandpa felt like as dementia passed over him like a dark cloud. Did more and more of his life just disappear? It scares the shit out of me to even think about, losing that night forever. "But you didn't just want to tell me that, did you?" I ask. "What's really on your mind?"

Chad nods. In profile, he looks like a guy everyone would want to vote for if he ran for class president. But outside of soccer he's barely involved at school. He's definitely a person who charts his own path and doesn't care what anyone else thinks.

He turns to me. "Hannah saw Chloe a little later that night.

They were out in the hallway by the big trophy case. Chloe had calmed down. She wasn't crying. But she told Hannah she had a bigger problem to deal with, more than whatever had been making her cry earlier."

My knees wobble. "What was it?"

We face each other. A small gnat floats between us, dips and dives in the bright sun.

"Chloe told Hannah you were very angry that night. At the dance. That you were madder than she had ever seen you before. And she told Hannah she wanted to leave the dance before you did anything stupid."

# TEN

IT'S ALMOST TIME FOR CLASS, AND CHAD TELLS ME HE can't be late because he has a test in AP Spanish. As I follow him toward the building, I consider what he just told me—that I was angry the night of the dance, angry enough that Chloe wanted to leave before I did something rash.

Was it the possibility of me wanting to have sex again that put Chloe on edge?

Did that upset her?

A cloud slides in front of the sun, casting a shadow across the school grounds. Everyone files back inside, including the sweaty football players who jostle each other, their carefree fun irritating me way more than it should.

Is it possible Chloe and I fought, and I just don't remember? Is it possible the fight was so bad—and I was so angry—that she felt scared?

What's the alternative? That Chad is lying, feeding me a story to take advantage of my wrecked memory?

"Hey," Chad says as we approach the glass door. "We'll figure this all out, Hunter. Really, we will."

"Do you think Basher could have done something to Chloe?" I ask. "First, he gave me a friendly look in calc this morning, but when the vigil was announced, he looked really blank. His look was cold, like he hated me. And hated everything."

"Basher? The world's worst quarterback?" Chad laughs. "The guy can't even read a defense. Do you think he could hatch a plot like this?"

"He could be jealous. Want her back. I told you he still hangs out at her house with Chloe's dad."

"Forget him."

"Hold on," I say.

He waits, arms crossed, face expectant. "Now what?"

I choose my words carefully, fully aware that I might piss off one of the few friends standing by me. "Okay, Hannah told you all this, right? I can't remember any of it... Did anyone else see it?"

"They were alone. The girls' bathroom. The trophy hallway."

"I know. It's just...Hannah."

Chad rolls his eyes. "You're going to go there? Seriously?"

"This is important, Chad."

Here's the thing—it's flat-out weird sometimes with Hannah and Chad. Weird because Hannah and I dated for a few months sophomore year. It felt more serious than it was because it was the first time either one of us had a real boyfriend or a girlfriend. When I see Hannah now, I know she's pretty, but her looks are nothing compared to Chloe's natural beauty.

"You don't trust Hannah. She lies, right?" He's shaking his head. "Look, I know you're freaked out and everything, but you can't just start lashing out and doubting your friends. We're on your side."

"Yeah, but…"

There's the way it ended with Hannah and me.

Hannah went to Destin, Florida, on vacation with her family and made out with another guy. Not just once—they had some kind of vacation fling. Hannah told another friend, who told me. The betrayal felt like someone had cut out my heart.

Hannah always tends to stretch facts. A lot. She'd exaggerate how high of a grade she earned on a test. How much money she made babysitting. How much land her parents own at the lake.

"Look," Chad says, "it's the truth. And Hannah can tell you herself if that's what you want. But don't lose your faith in everything and everyone who cares about you."

I'm not sure I won't, so I remain silent.

And I'm really not convinced Hannah is my friend. I'm not sure of anything about her.

Chad claps me on the back and takes off for his test. I think about heading to the nurse's office and telling her I'm too sick to stay at school. I can claim a relapse of my concussion symptoms—headache, sensitivity to light. Blank memory. I have a ready-made excuse.

But then I remember why I wanted to come back to school. Routine. Being normal. But I also thought being here would help me learn something about what happened to Chloe. I wasn't accomplishing anything sitting at home feeling sorry for myself. Do I want to go back to that shit?

No, and Chloe wouldn't, either. Whatever went down that night, she'd want me to be out, engaging with the world. She wouldn't want me to quit, so I resolve to stay.

That's when I see the kid filming me again. He stands in the hallway just inside the glass door, tracking only me and none of the other students streaming by like minnows. It's the same kid as this morning, the one who had his phone out documenting my reaction to the skeleton and the note. Because of the phone in front of his face, I can't tell who he is or if I know him. He wears a Western Kentucky University cap, red with white stitching, and a gray hoodie. He's short. A freshman maybe?

"Hey!"

The lines of students part as I dash for him. What must I look like, going after him like this? Lately it seems like I'm doing a lot of things I don't normally do.

But this kid doesn't flinch. He keeps filming even as I push his phone down, resisting the urge to smack it across the floor, slam it to the ground, and stomp on it.

Like the stupid skeleton.

"Oh, hey, Hunter."

He's no freshman. He's a senior with familiar features: the

nose with a tip like a bulb, the freckles, the big round eyes that look almost childlike.

"What are you doing, Daniel?" I ask. "Why are you filming me?"

"Oh, that." He looks down at the phone in his hand like it just materialized out of thin air. "Well, it's an interesting story if you want to hear it."

"I *do* want to hear it."

The bell rings. We all have four minutes to get to our next class. European history for me.

"It's going to take more than four minutes," Daniel says. He smiles like we're in on the same joke, like we'll both find this exchange amusing. "But I think you'll want to know what I have to say."

I doubt it. I've known Daniel since kindergarten. From grades four through eight, we were the very best of friends. We did everything together. We watched movies, traded comics. We rode our bikes all summer and went sledding on Hospital Hill on those rare days when it snowed here in southern Kentucky.

Even though we weren't close anymore, he came to Mom's funeral and told me to let him know if I needed anything.

And, yes, we made stupid little videos together. The kind you make when you're twelve featuring army men and dinosaurs and Matchbox cars.

But we drifted apart once high school started. My group of soccer friends—Chad, Hector, Cameron—came along. Daniel went another way. Chess Club. Dungeons and Dragons. When we were best friends, I couldn't imagine not seeing or talking to Daniel every day. But standing there in the hallway, I can't remember the last time we really talked. We just didn't know each other anymore. It's as though I'm staring at a big chunk of my childhood that's drifted away. What could *he* possibly have to tell me?

"Well, please stop filming me, okay? It's...creepy."

"I'm not a creep," he says.

And the way he says it tells me people have called him that before. He's the kind of guy who lives on the edges of our world, a moon orbiting far away from the center of high school gravity.

"I didn't say you were. Look, just don't film me, okay? I've got enough troubles right now. And I'm going to be late for class."

"I saw your video this morning. It looked like you were kind of laying everything out there."

"That video...big mistake."

"No," Daniel says. "It was real. Authentic. Maybe people don't understand that, but I do."

"Yeah, okay. Thanks." And I know what he means. He means—I know who you really are. Better than most people. And maybe he's right. Maybe we haven't drifted as far apart as I think.

"Are you going to the vigil?" he asks.

"I guess so. Maybe. Yes."

"Can we talk there?"

"I don't know. There are going to be a lot of people."

"I'll find you," he says.

He doesn't say those words by accident. We used to say that to each other—*I'll find you*. When we were younger, we'd make plans to meet and before we'd hang up the phone one of us would say it to the other. It was our way of saying we understood each other so well, we were so in tune with each other's thoughts, that we'd always manage to track down each other.

Hearing him say that jabs me in the heart. It's been five years or more since I'd heard those words.

I kind of smile, and I kind of want to cry.

He smiles. Knowingly. He got me. He knows that.

"Okay. At the vigil," I say.

He nods his head and walks off. He looks so much like the Daniel I used to be friends with that it feels like I've gone back in time. Except I haven't.

Chloe is still gone, and I still don't know what happened that night.

And tonight, I have to face the crowds at the vigil.

# ELEVEN

THE REST OF THE DAY PASSES IN A BLUR. I GO TO CLASS, but I'm not really there. My mind trips over everything—the looming vigil, the video, Chad's info about the night of the dance. Basher. Even Daniel. Halfway through the afternoon in physics lab, I realize that having so much to think about has really helped me ignore the stares and the whispered comments.

Between the last two periods of the day, Olivia approaches me in the hall. When she started at Garrett Morgan, she complained—*loudly*—to anyone who would listen, that I acted like I didn't know her. Yes, I drove her to school in the morning, but she claimed I practically pushed her out of the car while it was still moving in order to avoid being seen with my tagalong little sister.

It was an exaggeration, of course. But there was some truth in what she said. Mom died when I was fifteen and Livvy was twelve, so Dad asked me to do a lot. I've cooked for her, watched over her, walked her to the bus stop, taken her trick-or-treating.

And I hoped when she reached high school, she'd blossom a little, come out of her shell and assert her independence.

I didn't need to worry. Her personality grew like a balloon expanded to its breaking point.

So when I see what she's like now, I feel a little lift. And also a sense of pride. I didn't do all the work of raising her—Mom did a heck of a lot before she died. And Dad, in his own way, is a rock we can always count on. He may be a little clueless, but he's completely dedicated. He's barely socialized since Mom died. He's home with us night after night after night. But still…Olivia wouldn't have bloomed like an overwatered weed if it hadn't been for me. And it's not a one-way street, either. It hit me in the last year that Olivia is about the best younger sister anyone could have, and the past week has truly confirmed that.

We make eye contact. She smiles, and I feel better than I have all day. She's holding hands with Gabriela, but Olivia breaks loose and runs over to me. She throws her arms around me and gives me a hug right there in front of everybody.

"What's that for?" I ask.

"For you. Just because you look like you need a pick-me-up."

"Okay. Thanks."

Gabriela joins us. She has jet black hair past her shoulders with a purple streak that matches Olivia's. Gabriela doesn't talk nearly as much as my sister, but when she does, she exhibits a wisdom beyond her years. It seems like Gabriela is really a thirty-year-old posing as a teenager. Dad says her unflappable maturity comes from being the child of immigrants. Gabriela came to America from Mexico when she was five and didn't speak a word of English. Now, she's the top reporter on the school paper and writes more clearly than most of our classmates.

"I don't need a ride home," Olivia says.

"Are you two doing something?" I ask.

Gabriela rolls her eyes and looks away. She taps her foot.

Olivia just shrugs. It's the rarest thing of all for her to not speak when asked a question.

"What is it?" I ask.

"She has detention," Gabriela says.

"What for?" I ask.

"Just a stupid misunderstanding," Olivia says. "And not very fair. I was fully justified in everything I did. I might write a letter to the school board. Or Gabby might do an exposé for the paper."

"I'm not doing an exposé," Gabriela says.

"What did you do?" I ask.

Olivia looks at her phone. "I'm going to be late."

"Livvy," I say, "you're always late."

"Just forget about it, Hunter," she says.

Gabriela is still tapping her foot. She shrugs and says, "So here's the thing, Hunter. Liv punched a guy in study hall. He was talking shit about you, calling you a murderer, so she decked him."

The knuckles on Olivia's tiny hand look raw and red. She hides it behind her back. When Olivia was in kindergarten, she once punched a boy who was bullying another student. But there's been nothing like this since then.

"Who did you hit?" I ask.

"Some meathead from the lacrosse team. A freshman. He had it coming. And anyway, I just grazed him. No blood or anything. But he looked scared, didn't he, Gabby?"

Gabriela rolls her eyes again. "Uh, the guy's two feet taller than you, and he thinks you're a psychopath. Everybody does now."

"Good. Let them. But I got three days' detention." She lifts her hand, placing her index finger under my nose. "Don't tell Dad. He has a lot on his mind already. Besides, I don't need to hear shit from him, too. He's so clueless he won't figure out I'm getting home late."

"I'm going to the library while she's in jail," Gabriela says. "My mom will pick us up."

The visual pops into my head. My tiny sister, all five feet nothing of her, hauling off and punching a lacrosse player to defend my honor.

A laugh rises inside me and bursts out of my mouth. A real, genuine laugh. It feels really, really good, like letting out a long-suppressed sneeze.

"Oh, Livvy," I say, "you're such a little nut."

I give her a hug and continue to laugh on my way down the hall. And more people gawk. What are they all going to think of our family now?

# TWELVE

SINCE I'M NOT DRIVING OLIVIA HOME, I STOP BY THE
English department, which is on the second floor near the gym.
Before I get there, I hear voices raised, commotion, and laughing.

At the entrance to the gym, there's a giant landing with trophy
cases that display prizes from way in the past. A tarnished victory
cup from the team's lone state basketball championship in the
1960s, old and wrinkled jerseys that belonged to former players
who are most likely dead, and yellowing newspaper clippings for
games no one remembers. This is the spot where Chad told me
Chloe and Hannah talked on the night of the dance.

Students are all over the hallway. Some are dancing around
on one side of the landing while another films them. A few more
stand off to the side in a group of four. They all hold phones,
gesture wildly, and laugh. They're part of school's new TikTok
Club. They meet after school once a week and post videos they
hope will go viral. A month ago, a freshman uploaded a video of
her dancing with her eighty-year-old grandfather, and the thing

took off. Millions of views. Now it seems like every kid in the school wants to make something like that. The club is officially sanctioned. It even has a faculty sponsor—Mr. Williams, who teaches journalism and new media.

They ignore me—even the kids I know—because they're too busy to notice anything. At least that's how it looks until someone in that group of four sees me. They all grow quiet and stare at me, and two of the kids who were dancing like maniacs stop moving and look as well.

Why are all eyes on me? Am I really such an object of fascination that even the inane TikTok Club comes to a halt when I walk by?

When no one says anything and when they don't go back to filming, I lift my arms. "What?"

They continue to stare, like I'm a piece of furniture that suddenly started talking.

I give up and turn around, heading back toward my original destination, the English department. I want to see Ron Hartman, who teaches creative writing and runs Ex Libris. Ron is the real deal. It seems strange to see the TikTok kids meeting so close to his office since he detests social media, cell phones, and anything that goes viral on the internet. He's a poet, even published a book twenty years ago. He says he wants to write more, but teaching takes too much time and energy. The rumor is he used to teach at a college in Colorado but got fired or left because he thought the higher-ups were too uptight. He taught for a while in Europe, too, and then came to Bentley because his grandparents were from here.

Chloe and I both belong to Ex Libris. Even though Chloe plans to study chemistry in college, she's always loved to read and write. That explains the journal, and it explains why she joined the club sophomore year when Ron heaped praise on every poem she wrote. I didn't know Chloe very well then. I knew who she was—a beautiful, unattainable girl way out of my league. Obviously, we never hung out, and whenever Ron praised her writing, I felt a sting of jealousy deep in my chest.

But the jealousy didn't last. She *is* that good. And poetry isn't really my thing. Verse and meter confines me, and my free-verse poems turn into stories and just keep going and going. Ron says to accept who my identity as a writer and move on. Ron—he lets us call him "Ron" when we meet in the club—says prose writers make more money than poets anyway. He always laughs to let us know he isn't really serious. He encourages his students to write what we want.

"Let's face it," he said once, "the world is full of rules and expectations. Just let your imaginations run wild wherever you can."

The office is mostly empty. Mr. Feltz and Mrs. Paine are there, each with their heads bent over their computers, tapping away. Feltz has been at Garrett Morgan for over forty years. He has a thick gray mustache and a bulging stomach. He looks up and leans back in his chair, which creaks beneath his weight.

"Looking for Hartman?" he asks.

I took Feltz's class, *Reading American Authors*, last year. He was good, but a little scattered. He spent too much time talking about his stint in Vietnam. His war stories were fascinating, but a lot of students fell asleep. He knows my role in Ex Libris—I'm the president this year—so I'm always coming by to talk to Ron. Sometimes Chloe comes with me, although lately she's been busy with her college applications, and I've been coming alone.

"Is he around?" I ask.

"He's out today," Feltz says, brushing crumbs off his shirt. His gut makes a shelf where they land.

"Sick?" I ask.

"Likely," Mrs. Paine says without looking up. "Or he ran off to join the circus."

Feltz chuckles. Mrs. Paine teaches drama, and her hair is the color of a fire engine and flows down her shoulders like a flaming waterfall. Chloe says it's a wig.

"Nothing serious?" I ask.

Feltz shakes his head, tapping a red pen against his thigh. His fingernails are thick and yellowed, and his hands look like they could crush rock. An image of a younger, thinner version of him slinking through a Vietnamese jungle, M16 in hand, pops into my head. He must look at all of us kids with our medications and our anxieties and viral videos and worry for the future.

"You've been in the news a lot," he says. "And you're a video star. I guess one advantage of Hartman being a Luddite is he won't see you shared it on the Ex Libris channel."

I remember my manners, the ones Mom taught me. And given his military experience…

"Yes, sir. I was just trying to do something to help…"

"Chloe took my class sophomore year," he says, still tapping the pen. "A bright girl. Very promising. I hope they solve the case soon. And with a positive result."

"Me too." I feel like I'm disturbing them…

But Feltz keeps talking, like the pen is a metronome keeping the beat for his words.

"You know, Ron is incredibly distraught over her disappearance and the accusations coming your way. We were talking about it on Friday, and he wishes he could do more to help. We all do, I suppose."

"I don't know what anybody can do," I say.

"I learned at a very young age there are some things well beyond our control. We have to learn to accept them and make the best of things. It's like when I was—"

"Don't scare the boy with the 'Nam stuff, Henry," Mrs. Paine says, still not looking up. "He has enough on his plate."

Feltz smiles beneath the big mustache. He stops tapping. "I guess you're right. Ron will be back, Mr. Gifford, don't worry. He's rather resilient, our Ronald."

# THIRTEEN

THE HOUSE IS QUIET. AND, THANKFULLY, NOTHING appears vandalized or out of place. The odor of burnt oatmeal lingers like a fog.

Olivia is in detention. Dad is still at work. It's times like these I miss Mom the most. After school, she'd always be here, working on a freelance project or baking. She'd stop and talk to me about my day, and do the same thing with Olivia, and sometimes Mom would push aside her graphic design work and the three of us would watch a TV show together or play a board game before we had to start our homework. An hour or so would disappear faster than I could imagine.

The memories make the house feel emptier. If only...

Before I left school, Hector and Cameron had tracked me down and invited me to hang out for the hour before they had practice. We often went to get something to eat or to Cameron's house and played Xbox. But today I'm tired, and my eyes feel heavier by the moment.

The doctors told me the concussion would make me sleepy, and they encouraged me to take naps if necessary. Is there any better prescription for a high school student than naps? I collapse onto my bed, sleep deeply for ninety minutes before my eyes pop open. It's the first time since the accident I *didn't* dream about Chloe. She's been so alive in my dreams, it feels like someone punched a hole in my heart when I realize her face wasn't there.

The silence remains. Dad still isn't home. No surprise. He likes to stay on campus late, attending meetings and getting ready for class. And if Olivia was home, she'd be playing music loud, dancing in her room like a tornado. She likely went off with Gabriela somewhere. Gabriela's mom likes to feed Olivia, and Olivia likes to eat. She gets tired of our steady diet of spaghetti, sandwiches, and delivery pizza.

I check my phone.

A few of my friends have texted asking if I'm still going to the vigil.

I don't write back right away. I wait.

And think.

Maybe it's wrong to go. What do I hope to accomplish there? More gawking? More comments? Wouldn't it be better to stay at home and fly under the radar?

But what about the video making me look guilty? Won't staying away make me look more guilty?

What's right?

I text back: Yeah, I guess so. Maybe. I'm not sure.

Cameron responds first: Text me or Hector when you get there.

Then five minutes later,

Chad writes: Cool. See you there.

So then—I guess I'm going.

I pick up a book, one of Mom's favorites. It's a story collection by Ted Chiang that I started before the dance, before the accident, and I haven't tried to read any of it since. I was in the middle of a story called "Division by Zero," but I don't remember the characters or the setting, so I flip back, trying to find something familiar, going almost to the beginning until things start to make sense, which only reminds me of the blind spots about the accident and the dance.

The back of my neck prickles with cold. The book shakes in my hand.

The doctors promised things would come back, but how do they know? And that scares the shit out of me. Big-time. It makes my insides turn to Jell-O and shake. It's like a horror movie where the main character's own brain turns against him and he can't stop it. I spiral, wondering if all my other memories will start to disappear. Not just things relating to the night of the accident but everything else—Chloe, Mom, my friends, my childhood…

Is that why Chloe was missing from my dreams today?

What if the time comes when I can't remember her at all?

My eyes squint shut as I conjure that day at the lake just to prove I can do it, just to make sure she remains three-dimensional in my mind. Chloe's hair blows around her shoulders, and a spray of freckles dots her nose. Her eyes are blue but flecked with little spots of gold when the sun hits them. The water was freezing, but she waded in, turning over her shoulder and looking back at me, waving her hand, wanting me to join her.

"Are you a chicken?" she asked. "Are you afraid of a little cold?"

I wasn't afraid. I watched her because she looked so amazing, her arms and legs muscular, her skin flawless.

She bent down, cupped some water in her hands, and threw it my way.

"Come on," she said. "I need you to keep me warm."

And that was when I jumped up off the towel and followed her, splashing my way into the water and taking her in my arms...

But seeing her again is like ripping open a scab and making it bleed. The sweetest most twisted pain imaginable. And yet, as difficult as it may be, I'll take that pain forever if that's all there is.

"Just come back," I say to no one. "Just come back, Chloe."

At that second, my phone chimes.

Ron is right about social media—as he is about everything. Everyone would be better off without it. I'd deactivate my accounts, but what if Chloe tries to reach me? What if someone sends me a tip or a piece of information that tells me where she is?

My phone chimes again.

Olivia, probably texting from Gabriela's house.

So you saw it?

What are you talking about?

Olivia tends to do that. She starts speaking or texting as though we're in the middle of a conversation. This time her mind is moving faster than her hands.

The video.

What video? She can't mean the one I made…why would she ask if I'd seen it? So, what video is she talking about?

Oh, she writes being as cryptic as possible.

Oh, what? What video?

Three dots appear, and they sit there a long time, taunting me. Is she composing a novel or a text?

Olivia? What is it?

Her message finally arrives. It's a link to a video.

Posted on TikTok.

Dread fills me, like water filling my throat, cutting off air. But I can't look away…I can't…

Once it plays, I get why the TikTok Club acted so strange earlier.

# FOURTEEN

IN THE VIDEO, A GUY AND A GIRL—I DON'T KNOW EITHER one—sit on chairs next to each other. The girl has blond hair and wears a formal dress. The guy has hair the same color as mine and he's wearing a white shirt and a poorly knotted bow tie. They both have large sunglasses on, so it's tough to see their faces. But the guy is holding a toy steering wheel, the kind that makes an annoying horn sound every time a little kid presses it.

They sit next to each other and, using perfectly coordinated movements, smoothly and gracefully reenact a car accident. They sway to one side and then the other, their mouths opening wide, miming fear, the girl's hair flipping to the left and then the right.

A familiar song plays, sung by a guy with a high, overly dramatic voice. It's something Mom always listened to when she was in a funk. It kind of sounds like the singer is mocking the very words he's singing.

*And if a double-decker bus / Crashes into us / To die by your side / Is such a heavenly way to die*

At the end of the video, after all the choreographed gyrating and swaying, the girl simply disappears from the frame, leaving the boy there alone. The whole thing takes about ten seconds.

Over and over again, I play it. Olivia keeps texting, but I ignore her.

How could these students be so clueless? How could they do this when Chloe is missing and in danger?

How?

Then again…the pranks, the comments. The skeleton on my locker.

It's all the same. It's blood in the water.

Olivia writes again, and this time I read her text.

I thought about not telling you but everyone's going to be talking about it at school. Maybe even at the vigil. Sorry.

Do you know these kids? I write.

No. But I'll find out.

Forget it.

Skip the vigil, Hunter. It's fine.

The vigil. A bunch of people who don't really know Chloe

standing around pretending like they care. Most of them will be there just to be seen. Or to take photos they can share on social media.

My thoughts about it jumble again...

But one thought keeps cycling through my mind.

It'll look worse if I don't. Like I don't care. You said the video made me look cold.

Forget I said that Hunter.

I'm going.

I check the time on the phone. 6:27. Olivia keeps texting while I get ready.

Gabby and I will be there no matter what. Meet us there.

I text her a thumbs-up. I've started a message to Chad, asking him to pick me up, when the door swings open. It's Dad, brief-case in hand, filling the doorway so I can't get out.

"I think we should talk," he says. "About tonight."

"Okay, sure," I say. "You mean the vigil, right?"

"I do."

"Well, Dad, I've decided to go. I don't know if that's the right thing or not. In fact, it's likely wrong for me to go. And I know you said to keep a low profile, and you're probably right. Most of the time you are. But…it's like this, Dad, I just think I have to go. I have to show my face. And I've been going through hell at school and everywhere else, and if I want to go and prove they can't get the best of me, then I'm going to do it. Okay? So can you just let me do what I want to do even if I'm wrong?"

Dad just stands there, looking at me. I haven't raised my voice to him in…ever. No one raises their voice in our house. Just Olivia when she's excited about something. But no one really yells *at* anyone. No one gets too worked up. Certainly not Dad. He barely cried when Mom died. When he came to the hospital after the accident, he looked at me like I'd skinned my knee.

He puts down his bag. When he's angry he goes all silent. Or maybe he wants to lecture me.

He clears his throat. "Are you finished?"

"I think so."

"I was going to say I'd like to go with you," he says. "I don't think you should go to something like that alone. Is there time for me to run to the bathroom? I left campus in a hurry to get here on time."

I'm too shocked to speak, so Dad brushes past me for the bathroom. Mom always said people can surprise you.

I wonder if she had Dad in mind when she said that.

# FIFTEEN

THE VIGIL IS ON THE FOOTBALL FIELD BEHIND THE school. By the time we arrive, the parking lot is almost full, and people are streaming into the stadium. Four news vans hum off to the side, and a reporter in a suit stands practicing before a camera.

The sun is disappearing, and the stadium lights are on, casting a hazy, white glow over everything. A half-moon rises over us, and the air is cooler than it's been all week. A light breeze kicks leaves across the lot, pushing them against buildings and light posts.

Dad parks away from the crowds. Good move. Either he and I are more alike than I realize, or he's reading my mind.

Before we get out of the car, I say, "You know, I kind of want to…you know…"

"We can stand near the back. Or off to the side."

"Right."

"We don't have to go in at all if you'd rather skip it."

"No," I say. "I think it's good for me to go. If I don't, it could be worse."

Dad pushes open his door, and we walk together, keeping our distance from the main crowd of people. A lot of students walk with their parents. Kids carry homemade signs and balloons and stuffed animals. Can I just say right here that Chloe hates stuffed animals? I take a deep breath and remind myself that people are just trying to be nice. They've seen other people bring stuffed animals to a vigil or a scene of a tragedy, so they do it, too. Chloe would rather receive a book or a gift card to her favorite sushi restaurant or advice on getting into medical school, but you can't really show up at a vigil with those kinds of things.

We enter through a gate on the side of the stadium where a couple of volunteers hand us candles. One of them, a girl about Olivia's age, does a double take. Her eyes get wide, but she doesn't say anything. She'll now have a story to tell her friends. Another volunteer directs us to a box full of matchbooks. Dad grabs a pack, and we stop at the back of the south end zone and try to blend in. Now that we've settled on a spot, I text Olivia, Chad, and Cameron to tell them where we are.

A temporary stage has been erected in the middle of the field, right over the spot where our mascot, Billy Bobcat, is painted onto the grass. It's the same setup they used to announce the king and queen after the homecoming game just over a week ago. The night before the accident and Chloe's disappearance. A group of us went to the game together, and Chloe, even though she hates football's brutality, painted a blue "GMH" for Garrett Morgan High on her cheek. She always says there are worse things than sitting outside on a fall night, watching young men try to kill each other.

We lost the game, 42–10. Chloe laughed when Basher threw his third interception of the night, and we all mocked her for having dated such a terrible quarterback.

"Are you jealous?" she asked.

"No," I said. "I just wanted to see us win our homecoming game *once* before I graduate."

Tonight, all the school and town big shots are on the stage. The principal, Dr. Jackson, is next to the assistant principal, Dr. Whitley, and the superintendent, Dr. Olsen. The mayor is there, too, in a black skirt and white shirt, tapping away at her cell phone.

And Chloe's parents at the end of the platform, holding hands.

Her parents—Scott and Laura Summers—always seemed to like me. Sure, it was low-key awkward when Chloe and I first started dating, and they'd have me over for dinner, and we'd have to stumble through those weird conversations parents always have. *How is your dad doing? How is your sister? Where do you want to go to college? Did you know Chloe has plans to go to medical school? What do you want to do, Hunter? Oh, you want to be a writer? Isn't that interesting…*

But things with them got easier after a while. Her mom hugs me when I come to the house, and it feels nice to have some version of a mom back in my life. Even if she isn't my mom, Laura is very cheery—sometimes more than I can stand, although it all seems to come from a good place. She rides Chloe about her grades (which are always good) and her weight (Chloe is thin without trying too hard) and even her clothes (Laura thought Chloe's dress for the dance was too short. Not me, no way.).

Chloe told me her parents tended to be overprotective. They're a few years older than my parents and struggled to have Chloe. Laura had two miscarriages before Chloe was born, and they'd always worried they'd never have a child. Then, after Chloe was born, they couldn't get pregnant again. Chloe said those miscarriages explained a lot about her parents' overprotectiveness.

But they're not all about being uptight. Chloe and Laura also take the occasional girls-only shopping trip up to Louisville, and they spend a lot of weekends bingeing Netflix when her dad is out of town for work. I've told Chloe more than once I'm simply jealous that she has a mom. Silly maybe, but it's true.

Scott is harder for me to figure out. He's the human resources manager at the automotive plant north of town where they make SUVs that get shipped all over the world. When he's not at work, he spends a lot of time hanging out in the detached garage, building tables and birdhouses and shit or working on his prized Mustang. Sometimes he's just out there sweeping with a giant broom. As far as I can tell, he seems to be *really* into sweeping the garage. My dad does nothing mechanical. At all. He usually makes me or Olivia change light bulbs when they burn out, and he calls a plumber if one of our sinks gets backed up. Mom used to fix some of that stuff herself, but not Dad.

At first, I thought Scott didn't like me because he didn't talk much and sometimes gave me that look that said, *I know what you want to do to my little girl*. Chloe told me he was just quiet, an introvert who took a while to warm up to anyone. It turned out to be true. About the fourth time I was at their house, he made a dry joke. Laura asked him if he wanted a little wine with dinner, and Scott responded by making a whining noise.

"There you go," he said. "A little whine with dinner."

Turns out he'd been making jokes all the time. I just didn't know it.

I started laughing at the silly things he said, and he seemed to appreciate me after that. And now, when I go over to pick up Chloe, he sometimes invites me into the garage and shows me the Mustang he's working on or the table he's stripping and restoring. I pretend like I'm interested even though the smell of gasoline and polyurethane is thick enough to choke an elephant. But I know what I have to do.

But here's the problem: I haven't spoken to her parents since the accident. I want to—I really do—but there hasn't been a chance. They're all over the news on Twitter and YouTube, and they look absolutely shook. Lost. Adrift. Which is about how they should look given what's happened. But I kind of came to the vigil because I thought maybe I'd get a moment with them, just to see how they're doing. We're all going through the same thing—aren't we the three people who care most about Chloe?— but for some reason we haven't talked. It feels like there's a hole, like a tooth has fallen out and needs to be replaced.

Dr. Jackson taps the microphone a few times. Feedback screeches over the field and everyone winces as they look up. The murmur of conversation dies as Jackson clears her throat and announces that we're going to begin.

She starts talking about the order of events, and that's when Chad, Cameron, and Hector appear, looking freshly showered. They each pat me on the back and say hello to Dad, who solemnly shakes their hands like we're all at a funeral.

Jackson tells us she's going to speak first and then the superintendent. And then maybe Chloe's parents. She doesn't add, "If they're up to it," but she doesn't need to.

"And then we'll conclude by lighting our candles and offering up our thoughts for Chloe's safe return."

Someone moves closer to me. Is it Olivia and Gabriela, coming to offer moral support? But it's Daniel, holding his phone in front of his face again.

He must see the irritation on my face, because he lowers his phone, smiles, and kind of looks sorry. Then he nods at Dad.

"Dr. Gifford," he says, holding out his empty hand.

It takes Dad a moment, but then a genuine smile crosses his face. "Is that Danny?"

They shake hands and lower their voices because the principal is speaking.

"Been a long time," Dad says. Another dad might pat Daniel on the back or even hug him, but Dad keeps a safe distance between them. He never gets too close. Dad always liked Daniel.

Or "Danny," as no one has called him since he was seven. Dad always thought Daniel was a smart kid, which he was, and encouraged our video projects because they kept us out of trouble.

Daniel faces my soccer friends. They all nod at each other but don't speak. When Daniel turns toward me, Chad rolls his eyes a little in a shitty way. He's always had a bad attitude toward Daniel—*there's the freak who used to be Hunter's pathetic BFF.*

"I'm filming the vigil," Daniel says to me. "In fact, I'd better get this." He turns away from me and aims his phone up at the principal. I think—*hope*—he's done shooting me. But before the principal gets too far into her speech, he turns around and speaks in a voice that's a little too loud, "Is tonight a good time to talk? After this?"

A few people glare at us. The last thing I need is for word to spread that not only did I kill Chloe but I also talked through her vigil, so I whisper, "We'll see."

I nod toward the stage, trying to get him to be quiet.

Daniel lifts one finger to his lips, indicating silence, and turns back to filming. But he looks over his shoulder one more time. "You're going to love what I have to show you."

# SIXTEEN

DR. JACKSON GOES ON. AND ON.

Someone comes up behind me, puts their arms around me, and squeezes tight. Tiny hands with raw knuckles, dark blue nail polish, silver rings. Olivia. Gabriela gives me a hug as well, and a real smile spreads across my face.

Olivia's mouth falls open when she sees Dad. She's frozen like that for moments, perhaps the longest stretch of time she's ever gone without speaking in her life. Finally, she asks, "What's this?"

"He wanted to come," I say, talking about Dad like he's not right there. Which we do sometimes when he's absorbed in something else. "He drove me."

Olivia goes to hug Dad.

Dad does this thing where at the most he gives only half-hugs. He uses one arm and puts it around you and then pats you on the back. It bothers Olivia that he can't bring himself to give her a full hug. It's not something I've had to deal with very often, because Dad's maybe hugged me twice in my life—at least that I can remember. Once in the hospital when Mom died. The other when I was nine and cut my knee on the school playground and bled all over the place. Dad had to pick me up because Mom was at a conference, and I was so afraid of getting stitches that he gave me a hug in the waiting room. The hug stunned me so much, I stopped crying and went with the nurse without looking back. They probably could have put the stitches in without anesthetic.

Dad gives Olivia a half-hug now, but she doesn't seem to mind. She leans against him, and Gabriela goes to stand by her. They hold hands while the superintendent goes on about how wonderful Chloe is, but it sounds pretty fake because he doesn't know her, and he clearly just asked people what to say about her. When he's finished, he glances toward Chloe's parents and raises his eyebrows. The silent question: *Do you want to speak?* Apparently, yes, because he goes on to introduce Chloe's parents and waves them up to the microphone.

The whole thing is pretty awkward. More awkward than one of Dad's half-hugs.

For one, when someone is introduced at a big event, people usually clap. But the whole crowd seems weirded out about clapping for the parents of a missing girl. So everyone gets even quieter than they already have been.

Chloe's parents step forward, holding hands, each looking scared and shell-shocked. They blink into the TV lights like actors who don't know their lines.

Basher and the guys he usually hangs out with stand thirty feet away. They're not all football players, but they're big guys who always talk loud, joke loud, and drive loud. They're laughing about something, nudging each other. They don't see me watching them.

On the stage, Chloe's dad, Scott, nods to the crowd as he steps up to the mic, which screeches from feedback again when he touches it. He pulls back his hand and offers a little smile, but it looks strange and forced. Inside my chest, it feels like my heart is folded in half. They're both devoted to Chloe and not just because she's their only child. And if I thought it was the worst thing ever to lose my mom when I was fifteen, I really can't imagine what it's like for them to not know where their daughter is.

"Thank you. Thank you all." Scott's voice is low. He clears his throat and steps closer to the microphone. "Thank you for all of your support. On behalf of Laura and me, we just want to thank you for the kind words and the support and the prayers. We just want to say that…well, we know Chloe's out there. And we want her to know we love her…and we miss her so, so very…"

His voice cracks, and his chin quivers. He scrunches his eyes shut, and Laura reaches out and rubs his back.

Sniffles fill the air around me. Olivia. Gabriela. Hector. Everyone. Even Cameron looks serious, which he almost never does. Chad has his head down, staring at his feet.

My eyes fill with tears, and I lower my head as Gabriela reaches over and squeezes my arm.

I want to thank her, but if I open my mouth, I might vomit. And it's not just the remnants of the concussion. It's everything. All of it. So I close my eyes and just stand still.

Scott's voice comes back over the speakers. "That's all we're going to say right now. It's tough to talk, so we won't say much. But we appreciate everything. We do. Laura wanted you all to know that..."

And a few people do applaud, a scattering. And someone shouts, "We love you, Scott and Laura."

And someone else shouts, "We love you, Chloe."

And I whisper the words to myself so no one hears: "I love you, Chloe."

The only thing left to do is light the candles, but Scott speaks again. And what he says makes me open my eyes and look up.

"Hold on just one minute," he says. "Laura does want to say something. I thought she was too...but, well...if that's, if you're sure...okay. Honey?"

# SEVENTEEN

LAURA MOVES TOWARD THE MICROPHONE, BUT WITH
every step, she steals a look over at Scott, who is nodding, encour-
aging her to keep going. She wears a Garrett Morgan High
sweatshirt that looks kind of tight. It must be one of Chloe's. She
also has a yellow ribbon pinned on her chest. She looks ten years
older, and Scott steps forward and takes her hand as she reaches
the microphone.

She looks out over the crowd, which has again fallen into a
hushed silence. Then Laura just stands there, her lips pressed into
a tight line. A few people applaud. And someone shouts encouragement, telling her to take her time and speak her truth.

Laura's face changes. The look of stunned grief she's worn for
the entire evening slides away, and her features start to harden.
Her lips remain tight, and her eyes narrow. She keeps one hand
in Scott's and with the other grabs the microphone, but the way
she holds it reminds me of the way someone would take hold of
a club just before swinging it at someone's head.

Gabriela and Olivia shuffle their feet and move closer together. Olivia leans toward me and says, "She looks kind of freaked. Is she okay?"

"I don't know. I really don't."

"Scott's right," Laura says. "We do thank you." Her voice sounds rock steady. Steadier than Scott's. "And I know you all join us in praying for Chloe. We all miss her and would do anything for her."

Scattered voices yell their support.

*"Yeah."*

*"That's right."*

*"Chloe."*

"But, you know, there is one person who doesn't seem to want to do anything to get Chloe back. There's one person who won't cooperate with the police. Who won't help us at all."

A murmur ripples through the crowd. Scott shifts his weight from one foot to the other on the stage.

My back stings. Like someone has slipped a long, cold needle between two of my vertebrae.

"And his name is Hunter Gifford," Laura says.

Heads in the crowd turn, looking around. Trying to spot me. A few nod my way, and I wish for a cloak of invisibility.

Laura goes on. "He says he can't remember anything from that night. Nothing. And he was the one in the car with her. He turned up at the hospital, and he's okay, but Chloe is nowhere to be found. And how did he get to the hospital? Who knows?

There was no car on the security cameras. I don't understand that. Do any of you?"

A few people shout back. "No!"

More heads turn toward me, faces finding me in the crowd. People nudge each other and point at me, like I'm a display at the zoo. My cheeks flush like every set of eyes pointed my way is giving off heat. Basher and his friends have all turned my way as well. They glare, and one of them yells, "No!"

"What the hell?" Olivia shouts. She drops Gabriela's hand and steps forward, like she's going to break through the crowd, jump up on stage, and take Laura on.

But Dad places a restraining hand on her shoulder. "Easy, Livvy."

Her face is flushed, too. Gabriela takes her hand again and whispers something I can't hear.

Chad is shaking his head, telling me to be cool, to not let this get me riled up. Cameron and Hector have their mouths half-open like they can't believe what's being said.

"It doesn't make sense," Laura says. "Not if he loves her like he says he does. And then, to add insult to our injury, he makes that video. That damn video. It's all over school. Do you know he wants to be a writer? Isn't that convenient? He makes a video that everyone is talking about. It's just a story to him. I think—"

Scott steps forward and whispers something into Laura's ear.

"I'm almost done," she says to him. "Just a minute."

Someone shouts, "Let her finish."

But Laura doesn't need any encouragement. "He wants to

be a writer. That's what he always talks about. Do you think he wants to write a book about Chloe? Do you think he wants this video to go viral or whatever and then write a book about her?"

The murmurs grow louder. More faces turn, more eyes burn into me like lasers. I feel like a rabbit with the blades of a lawn mower churning my way. I want to run. But something keeps me frozen in place.

"I think he knows more than he's letting on," Laura says. "A lot more. I think the police need to sit him down again and get him to talk. He's the boyfriend. The boyfriend always knows."

"He's here!"

This voice is close. Very close. A guy in a flannel shirt and a Tennessee Titans cap points my way. I've never seen him before. He's got to be close to forty, maybe somebody's parent. He points at me, his hand rising above the crowd because he's so much taller than almost everyone else.

"He's here," the man says again.

"Easy, man," Chad says to the guy.

And I don't want Chad to get into a fight with the guy over me. Unlike me—and my other friends—Chad isn't opposed to fighting. It's only happened twice since I've known him, and only when he thinks he's been disrespected.

The murmurs from the crowd on the field turn to shouts. And now it seems like every face is looking my way. Not just a few.

*Everyone.*

You could sear a steak on my face, it's so hot with embarrassment and fear. And, yes, anger.

I told the police everything I knew.

Don't they know how much I want to remember? How desperate I feel? That for Chloe's sake I want to remember everything from that night?

Dad is next to me. He has his hand on my upper arm, his grip like steel bands.

"Let's go," he says, his words clipped.

"Bullshit, Dad. I want to tell them the truth. I want to go up there—"

"We're going."

Chad jerks his head toward the parking lot.

Dad physically moves me away from the crowd. As we head off toward the car, people are hissing and booing and shouting things.

Olivia and Gabriela follow behind us, and my sister lifts both hands in the air, flipping off the entire crowd, which probably helps my cause about as much as when she punched the lacrosse player in the face.

Behind Olivia, Daniel films everything. My former best friend.

Something comes flying from overhead and splats onto the field between Dad and me, sending up a spray of liquid that hits our pants and shoes. A giant soda from McDonald's. Then a rock the size of a baseball flies past us, skidding across the ground.

It's bad. It's dangerous.

We're out of the stadium and halfway across the parking lot, but the voices from the stage still reach us, rolling across like thunder.

"Look. He's running away," Laura says. "It's not that he can't remember. It's that he just doesn't want us to know the truth."

# EIGHTEEN

WE RIDE HOME IN AWKWARD SILENCE, EXCEPT FOR THE satellite radio, which, as usual, Dad has tuned to the '80s station. It's the music he and Mom listened to when they were in school. As if things couldn't get any weirder, the song from the TikTok video comes on. Now I know the name of the song. "There Is A Light That Never Goes Out" by The Smiths.

I smack the power button. "Can we just…not?"

Chad texts me: That was a shitshow. Need anything?

With dad. It's cool.

Dad keeps his eyes on the road. Olivia and Gabriela are in the back seat, and Olivia starts going.

"That was such bullshit back there," she says. "How can that woman say those kinds of things about Hunter? In public? *Public*? She basically accused him of murder in front of the whole town."

Dad speaks in a steady voice. "Grief is difficult. It makes people do strange things."

"You're making excuses for her, Dad," Olivia says. "I want to fight back. Hunter is being bullied at school." She must not be wearing a seat belt, because she leans so far forward her voice is right in my ear. "Did you tell him about the video?"

"My video?" I ask.

"No. The TikTok."

"What is all this?" Dad asks.

"It's nothing," I say.

"It's not nothing."

"Livvy, why don't you sit back?" I say. "Put on your seat belt."

Olivia throws herself back in the seat and makes a loud groan of frustration. She speaks to Gabriela as if we're not there.

"Can you believe these two?" she asks. "All hell is breaking loose, and they just want to sit there and do nothing. People are harassing us. And they do nothing. Can you believe it, Gabby?"

"I should stay out of it," Gabriela says.

"Stay out of it?" Olivia asks. "Is that really what you want to do?"

"Oh, look, it's my house. Thanks for the ride, Dr. Gifford."

Dad eases the car to the curb, and Olivia and Gabriela whisper their goodbyes to each other. They make it sound like they'll never see each other again, even though they'll be texting the rest of the night. But maybe I'm a fool to judge them for their sappy, heartfelt goodbyes. What wouldn't I give for one more chance to tell Chloe how I feel? Maybe everyone should say goodbye that way every time they part. Even if it's just for a night.

When we get to our house, I expect Dad to head to his study, but he stops in the kitchen and says he'd like to talk to me.

Olivia stops, too, and leans against the island with her arms crossed. She's clearly still pissed. She doesn't want to let go because she thinks she hasn't been heard. And she wants action taken. Now.

I try to give Laura the benefit of the doubt and think about it the way Dad explained. *Grief makes people do strange things.* Olivia should know. The night Mom died, Olivia came home and smashed her favorite dollhouse—one my grandfather had built for her. I mean she stomped on it until it was unrecognizable. I asked Dad to do something, to stop her, but he just let her get it out of her system. Which she did. She smashed the dollhouse until she ran out of energy, and then she slumped to the floor, sobbing. Dad calmly picked her up and carried her to bed. She didn't smash anything else after that.

"Go on up to your room, Livvy," Dad says. "I want to talk to your brother alone."

Olivia starts to protest, jutting her chin out like a boxer stepping into the ring, but then some of the iron goes out of her body. She sighs and turns for the stairs, clomping all the way.

As she goes, she mutters, "It's not right. She can't say that shit about Hunter. She can't…"

Dad rolls his eyes a little and points to the kitchen table. Livvy deserves a break. She just cares about me. Dad and I sit, scraping our chairs against the tile. He looks tired, and his eyes are kind of sad. But they're always kind of sad.

He drums his fingers against the table a few times. "I feel like I should offer you a beer or something."

"I don't want a beer. It's fine."

"I was just kidding…kind of."

"I know, Dad. What's on your mind?"

He nods. "I don't want to keep you from your homework. I know you're still getting caught up. But…well, what's going on at school? What's this video Livvy is talking about? Is something wrong?"

"It's nothing, Dad… It's just…bullshit."

"Is it? Do you want me to call the school? I can't really control what Laura says, and I'm trying to give her the benefit of the doubt, but if someone is bullying you…"

"I can handle it, Dad."

"I meant it when I said you could be homeschooled. We could work that out. You're graduating in six months or so. You're an excellent student."

"I don't… Thanks, Dad. But I don't want to…"

"Give them the satisfaction?"

"Exactly. I just don't. Chloe wouldn't want me to quit. She wouldn't quit if things were reversed. I'm not going to, either."

Some of the sadness goes out of Dad's eyes to be replaced by…admiration? Pride?

"Fair enough," he says with a nod. "But if you change your mind, or if you want me to call someone…from the school…"

"I'll let you know," I say.

We sit there staring at each other while the refrigerator hums. We rarely talk about anything real, and when we do, neither one of us ever seems to know how to end it. So we tend to stare at each other in awkward silence before someone gets up or goes to do something else.

"Well," I say, trying to push things along.

"You know," Dad says, "when your mom died, I didn't really talk to anyone about it. I thought…well, I thought I had to be strong for you and Livvy. I focused on the two of you, which was the right thing. But I guess I'm asking you to make sure you take care of yourself."

The clock on the wall ticks, and the second hand swings around. Music starts to thump from upstairs as Olivia deals with her frustration.

"Dad?" I ask.

"Yes?"

"Do you think Chloe is still alive?"

Dad doesn't hesitate. "Until we know otherwise, there's always hope."

There's no awkwardness between us now. He said exactly what I wanted—and needed—to hear.

"Okay," he says, standing up. "Make sure you get a good night's sleep."

And he's off to his study before I can respond.

# NINETEEN

MUSIC BLARES FROM OLIVIA'S ROOM. SHE'S MAD AT DAD
for not pushing back against Chloe's parents or our other tormen-
tors. And she's probably mad at me for not lashing out.

Olivia tends to see things in black and white. If we let her
cool down, which she normally does pretty quickly, she'll be on
to something else by the time we ride to school in the morning.

A text arrives from Daniel:

Hey! That's shitty what happened at the vigil. Remember I
said I had something to show you. See you soon?

Did he say that? He filmed me in the hallway at lunch and
then filmed me again at the vigil, acting like he was the second
coming of Quentin Tarantino. He expresses understanding now,
but his camera rolled while my family slinked away. While people
threw shit at us.

Another text appears:

You're going to want to see this. Srsly.

He did say he had something to show me, right before Laura named me public enemy number one.

Even when we were kids, he always had a camera in his face. He never really got that it wasn't polite to go around filming people without their permission. When we were ten, Daniel filmed an old guy in the park who had tattoos of anchors and airplanes up and down his arms and was feeding birds on a park bench. The guy—who looked to be about a hundred—saw him and came over, moving faster than either one of us could despite his age. He knocked the camera out of Daniel's hands and gave him a lecture about privacy. The old guy even threw in that he hadn't landed on Iwo Jima so young shits like us could film him whenever we wanted.

The guy terrified me. Daniel laughed it off, relieved only that his camera had landed in the grass and wasn't broken.

But, while it's true that Daniel didn't understand boundaries, he never lied. Ever. If he tells me I'm going to want to see something, then he really believes I'm going to want to see it. But is he thinking of the twelve-year-old version of me he knew better than anyone else or the seventeen-year-old version he barely knows at all?

My mind flashes to Daniel and Dad shaking hands and how happy Dad looked. That moment took me back to being a kid, when Mom was alive and the only thing to worry about was getting chewed out by an old guy in the park. It feels simple by comparison.

And after hundreds of eyes turned to look at me with disdain and throw rocks at me, it wouldn't hurt to know someone else is on my side.

Sure. Be there in a few.

Dad's sitting at his desk in the study, glasses pushed up on top of his thinning hair, a stack of essays spread before him. He looks highly skeptical when I say I want to leave until I mention Daniel's name, and then his face brightens.

"Okay, sure," he says with a nod. "But not too late."

"I won't be."

"Are you walking?" he asks.

"Yeah. I've always walked to Daniel's."

"You were fourteen the last time you did that. You didn't have much choice."

"I still remember the way."

Dad's face looks pinched, like he's stubbed his toe.

"What?" I ask. "I just want to get out of the house and hang out with an old friend."

"I know. It's just...look, someone might have hurt Chloe. And if that person is still out there, I don't want you or Livvy wandering around in the dark alone. Plus...people are clearly unhappy with us. I can drive you or..."

"Okay, I'll drive myself. It's a ten-minute walk on a nice night, but I'll drive."

Dad looks relieved, like the pain had miraculously evaporated. "Thanks," he says.

"Sure."

"And text me when you get there," he says.

"I'm not twelve."

"I know that. If you were twelve, I wouldn't let you leave the house at all."

He pushes his glasses down and goes back to grading.

# TWENTY

DANIEL LIVES ONE NEIGHBORHOOD OVER FROM US. EVEN when we were kids, I understood the differences between our families. Daniel's father left when Daniel was five. And he pretty much never came back or had anything to do with Daniel. Maybe that's why Daniel was so sympathetic when Mom died. He'd already lost a parent. He'd already been though all those emotions.

Daniel's mom, Elizabeth, is a nurse. She worked a lot of nights, because those shifts pay better. My mom always admired the way Elizabeth kept it together after her husband left. But Daniel spent a lot of time alone, and he definitely had more freedom to come and go than I ever did. What do they call that? A free-range kid?

The familiar boxy ranch house looks a little dingier than I remember. Daniel greets me at the door, wearing basketball shorts and a hoodie. After five years, everything inside looks the same and smells the same, right down to their now ancient cat, Roscoe, who yawns from his perch on the end of the couch. The feeling of déjà vu is so intense, it's like stepping into a time machine.

"Roscoe's still alive?" I say.

"He's sixteen. We think he's immortal."

"Almost as old as we are."

Daniel leads me down the hall to his bedroom, the last door on the right. There's one change—Daniel has a slick new laptop open on his desk. An expensive camera sits in the middle of a tangle of wires, and it looks like Daniel could run his own TV studio.

"Nice laptop," I say.

"My grandparents got it for me."

"Sweet."

"My grandpa died six months ago. There was decent life insurance or something…"

"Shit. I'm sorry."

"It's cool." Daniel starts fiddling with the laptop, tapping keys and minimizing windows. He speaks to me over his shoulder. "If you want something to drink, you know where it is."

He says this like I was just there yesterday.

"I'm okay."

"You're going to love this." He sounds as enthusiastic as the twelve-year-old I used to know. Totally geeked out over whatever he has to show me. "Seriously. You will. You'll trip."

"You keep saying I'll love it, but I don't even know what *it* is."

"Okay." He finishes tapping and turns to face me. The harsh glow of the light shows scraggly whiskers above his lip. His eyes glisten with the kind of joy normally reserved for Christmas morning. "You know I want to be a filmmaker. What am I saying? Of course you know. You've known that since we were five. Well, anyway, I've been working on a project the last week or so, and it's really pretty amazing."

"The last week…"

"Yeah. Think about it, Hunter." He speaks with his arms spread wide, like a politician asking for my vote. "This is a once-in-a-lifetime chance for me. I mean I watch these movies, these documentaries that are streaming, and I think—wait, I better stop. I better say something else."

"Say what?"

"I should say I'm sorry about Chloe. About what happened to her. You know she and I took trig together last year. We didn't talk to each other for, I don't know, like the first two months of the year. Then one day Mr. Klems came in, and he was wearing two different shoes. One was black and one was brown. Same style of shoe but different colors. We started laughing together, but no one else noticed. And then we just starting talking a lot before class. She just…well, not everyone in school is nice. You know, just decent. And Chloe always was. She treated everyone well. She must have told you we had class together."

"I don't think she did," I say. "She knew you and I were friends."

"Hmm. How does your head feel?" He studies me. "You've got a nasty bump there."

"It's better." I reach up and gently touch it. The bandage is gone. "Still hurts. My neck and shoulders hurt some, too. But I'm just glad I'm not nauseated anymore."

"That's the worst."

"Yeah. My memories haven't come back."

"That's freaky. To have all those blanks."

"Yeah, it is. I don't know what I did that night."

"Well, I just want to say I'm sorry. And it's shitty the way some people are treating you. Tonight, at the vigil, what her mom said was totally out of line. I mean total bullshit. And people throwing stuff. It's not right."

"Thanks. Did the police talk to you? They're pretty much talking to anybody who remotely knew Chloe."

"They talked to me at school. I think they just went through the rosters and pulled every kid out who was in a class with her."

"What did you tell them?"

Daniel pauses for a moment. He seems like an actor, drawing out a scene for dramatic effect. "That's kind of why I brought you here. It will all be explained. See, tonight at the vigil, I couldn't really say anything to help you or stop the camera. You know? I have to get the story down objectively."

"What story?" I ask, and something starts to dawn on me. "Are you talking about—"

"*This* story," he says, jabbing his finger toward the laptop. "My movie. That's what I was starting to say earlier. What's the hottest genre right now? Movies, podcasts, everything?"

It's like he's giving me a pop quiz. "I don't know. Horror? It sure as fuck feels like I'm in a horror movie."

"No," Daniel says with a little impatience in his voice. "True crime. It's everywhere. *Everywhere*. And do you know how lucky I am to have this story fall right in my lap? Most filmmakers have to go out and find a story. They have to move somewhere and track it for years. This one is happening right here in Bentley, in our backyard. Do you see what I'm saying?"

And I do. I clearly do, but he says it anyway.

"I'm making a true crime documentary, Hunter. About Chloe's disappearance. This is the big break I've been waiting for, and I want you to see it." He points at the laptop again. "Or at least see what I've got so far."

His words stun me into silence. *This* is what Daniel wanted to show me. The floor shifts beneath my feet, like we're having an earthquake.

"You're making a movie about Chloe?" I ask. "That's *wrong*. You can't just make a movie about people. Are you serious?"

Daniel nods, his head bobbing like an enthusiastic puppy. "I'm *very* serious."

"No. No, no, no. That's a fucking terrible idea. You can't put me in it. And you can't put Chloe in it, either. You can't put that stuff you filmed earlier. I didn't give you permission—"

"Hunter, Hunter. Wait." He holds his arms out, pleading with me. "Will you just wait and listen to me?"

He seems sincere so I stop and listen. I owe that to someone who used to be my best friend.

"I want you to see this," Daniel says. "I haven't showed it to anybody else. You're the guy I always made movies with and now I'm making this one, and it's the first time it feels like I'm doing something adult. Something important. Not just…goofy kid stuff. Will you please watch? It's really rough. Really, really rough. But I think you'll appreciate what I'm doing and where I'm heading. I really do."

Daniel's invocation of our childhood moviemaking adventures has the intended effect. I give him the benefit of the doubt. It's a small benefit, maybe about five minutes long, but I'm willing to extend it to him.

I let out a long-held breath. "Okay. I'll watch. But just a little."

Daniel claps his hands together. "I knew you would. And guess what? You're not going to be disappointed."

He turns back to the laptop and starts tapping away. Then, with a dramatic flourish, he hits the play button. And his movie begins.

# TWENTY-ONE

IT TAKES A MOMENT.

Then some cheesy and ominous music starts playing. It really does sound like a low-budget horror movie, the kind that are all over Netflix.

"The soundtrack isn't great," Daniel says, his eyes still on the screen. "I'll have to pay somebody to do something better. I just goofed around on the piano in the other room."

Images start flashing across the screen. A baby. A child with blond hair. An older child with two missing teeth, smiling at a fair.

Chloe. They're photos of Chloe.

There's an image of Chloe standing in between her parents at a church, all of them grinning.

"Wait," I say. "How did you…did her parents…"

"Instagram, man. Or Facebook. I'll have to get their permission later, of course. This is just a rough cut."

The photos of Chloe's life move forward chronologically, including ones that start to show her and I together.

I've spent a lot of time over the past ten days looking at photos of Chloe online. But seeing them in Daniel's room, filtered through his perspective, somehow makes them even more poignant. The stream of photos makes the magnitude of her disappearance more real.

A pain grabs me in the center of my body. It's like someone's twisting a corkscrew into my chest.

A voice comes from the screen.

"On October 7, seventeen-year-old Chloe Summers disappeared from the small, bucolic town of Bentley, Kentucky, where she lived with her parents."

*Bucolic?*

It's Daniel narrating. His voice is thin, reedy, nothing at all like the kind of voice that would ordinarily narrate a documentary. He sounds like he's twelve years old.

As if reading my mind, he looks back at me.

"Yeah, I need to hire a narrator. If someone buys it, they can get a famous actor to do it. I was thinking someone like J. K. Simmons. You know?"

But my eyes are on the screen, and I'm not thinking about Daniel's pipe dreams.

It's the site of the accident. County Road 250, a stretch that runs through a heavily wooded area north of town. The images of the road and the trees make me shiver. The camera zooms in on one tree in particular. The bark is shredded, a big gash in the trunk. The tree we hit…

"On the night of her homecoming dance, a night that should have been filled with fun and laughter, a night that should have been exciting and joyous, Chloe Summers was traveling on this lonesome road, nestled in the car with her longtime boyfriend, Hunter Gifford. Two young people with not a care in the world. Two young people with their entire lives spread out before them like an inviting buffet of possibilities. All of it shattered in just one sudden, tragic instant."

The camera zooms in even closer to the tree. Candles, flowers, and stuffed animals are scattered around the scene. A few handwritten notes are visible. The camera moves in on shattered chrome and glass. A black streak on the tree from the Charger.

"All of it leaves a devastated community with one heartbreaking question that there is not yet any answer to: *Where. Is. Chloe?*"

The piano chords ring like the most solemn church bell. It's so loud they vibrate through the floor.

The scene shifts to downtown Bentley. A row of shops. The square.

"Who in this sleepy southern town knows the truth about what happened to Chloe? Who has the key that can unlock this darkest and most terrifying mystery?"

The shot lingers on the square for a long time. Too long.

The large digital clock across the room reads 10:15. I need to get home. And the movie seems so cheesy that I don't want to have to give Daniel my honest opinion. And I don't want to have to lie.

"Well, thanks for showing me that, Daniel. I think you're off—"

"No," he says, pausing the movie. "You can't go. We're not to the part I want you to see yet."

"But I have homework to do. I'm still behind from the hospital."

"You said you'd watch it, Hunter. Remember?" His voice drops lower as he turns back to the screen, so I have to strain to hear. "I think it's the least you could do for an old friend."

"Well…sure…."

"I saw the way Chad looked at me tonight. Like I was the biggest loser on the planet."

"Okay, I'm sorry."

His guilt trip works. He is an old friend. My oldest. And maybe now I need all the friends I can get.

"Okay. But is it coming up soon?"

"Soon," he says, brightening. "And it's the part that'll totally blow your mind."

# TWENTY-TWO

SHOTS OF THE SCHOOL FLASH ACROSS THE SCREEN. Students driving their cars into the parking lot. Students walking the halls. Dozens of faces I recognize, but the shots linger too long, and the cuts are jumpy and unprofessional. The music remains dull and repetitious.

My mind drifts. What will school be like tomorrow?

It was shitty enough today with the stares and the comments and the skeleton on the locker. Now that Laura has publicly accused me of withholding information, it will only get worse. Maybe Dad's offer of homeschooling would be better. My own pace. Maybe I'd even have more time for college applications.

But my mind can't get all the way there. What if I miss something by not being there? Aren't the chances pretty good that someone at Garrett Morgan knows something?

The sound of my name brings my eyes back to the screen.

Daniel is trying to get my attention. But it's the movie. It's Daniel's voice saying my name on the screen.

It's a photo of Chloe and me taken the night of the accident, one she uploaded to Instagram while we were at the dance. We have our arms around each other on the dance floor. I've seen the photo on her Instagram page since the accident. I've looked at it many times since that night, but I don't remember it being taken. I've tried and tried to conjure that moment, which is likely one of the last meaningful ones we had together, but I can't. I've searched my memory until my head starts to thump, but I still can't locate it.

The photo lingers on Daniel's screen, with the droning piano music and Daniel's squeaky narration, and I again notice Chloe's smile.

It's not right. It looks…I don't know…forced. Strained. And not in the way people look when someone sticks a camera in their face and says, "Smile!" and they want to tell whoever is taking the picture to fuck off.

No, it's not that kind of forced smile. Not a mildly irritated one. Chloe actually looks…unhappy. Shaken would be a better word. And I don't understand why.

If I see that look maybe other people will, too. Maybe her mother has seen it. Maybe that's why she threw me under the bus.

"…the last person to have seen her alive. And has naturally became the object of much suspicion. According to the National Crime Prevention Council in Washington DC, the overwhelming majority of murders are committed by someone who knows the victim."

The photo from the dance remains on the screen, but the camera zooms in. Closer and closer to my face until it almost blurs. The music slows, distorts. It drones deeper than before.

"What does Hunter know? What has he told the police? Can we believe him when he says he doesn't remember the details of the accident? I recently spoke with a doctor of neurology—"

I lunge forward and start hitting keys on the computer until one stops the video.

"What are you doing?" Daniel asks.

"What am I doing? What are *you* doing? Damnit, Daniel, do you know what this makes it look like? It makes it look like I killed Chloe."

"We're not to the part I want to show you."

"Delete it," I say. "Just get rid of it. I can't have people seeing this."

I peck around on the keyboard again, trying to find the Delete key.

Daniel stands up from his chair, and as he does, he places his hands on my upper arms, pushing me away from the computer. We're face-to-face, almost nose to nose.

"Hunter," he says, "you can't just destroy my movie. You can't. It's not finished."

"You're making me look guilty. Why don't you look into someone else? Someone like Basher."

Daniel lets go of me and steps back. His cheeks are flushed. "Hunter, you have to see the whole thing. That's the point of a true crime documentary. To introduce the suspects, to make people wonder. I have to do that to build suspense."

"But *I'm* the only suspect. And this confirms it. If people in town see this…"

Some of the anger drains out of me. I feel tired. Frustrated and tired.

"Just forget it, Daniel," I say. "We're not even friends anymore. Why would I expect you to be on my side?"

I storm out of his bedroom and toward the front of the house. I wish I hadn't said that about not being friends. But I'm also so mad about the movie, about the suspicion he's casting on me, that I can't bring myself to go back and apologize. So I just keep walking and yank open the front door.

The door opens behind me. And then Daniel's voice.

"Hey! Hey! Hunter!"

I stop in the middle of the yard and turn to face him.

He walks up to me, and in the dark, the whites of his eyes are the only prominent thing about him.

"Hunter, that's a shitty thing to say to me. About being your friend. You're the one who stopped hanging out with me. You're the one who found your new soccer friends. Guys who look at me the way they did tonight."

"We were kids, Daniel. Lots of people get new friends. It's not some big personal thing."

Daniel stares at me, his lips parted. "Not personal? What else could it be? We were best friends. We did everything together.

And then…I thought the movie…we used to make those movies together, so I thought you'd appreciate it. I thought maybe we could, you know, reconnect over something."

"Over a movie that says I'm guilty of killing Chloe?"

"Okay, fine. Go back to your new soccer friends. But I'm going to finish that movie." He points back to the house, which looks dark and small under the stars. "That's my thing. I haven't stopped making movies. And I never will. I thought I could interview you, get your side of the story. But if this is the way you want it, fine."

He turns and storms across the yard, his shoes brushing across the dewy grass.

His name forms on my lips.

But I don't say it.

He goes into the house and slams the door. There's nothing left to do but turn around and go home.

# TWENTY-THREE

I CAN'T SLEEP.

Again.

The argument with Daniel loops through my mind. Was I right to lose my cool? Should I have said those shitty things?

Three times I reach for my phone and start to text him, apologizing. And every time I don't. Would he believe me? Do we have any friendship left worth saving?

And do I even owe him an apology? He's the one shooting a documentary that makes me look guilty. Don't I have the right to be pissed? It's my life. And Chloe's life. Do I need an amateur filmmaker using a bad voice-over and clichéd music to turn everything upside down?

The last time I pick up my phone, just before midnight, it chimes. A text from Daniel. No words, just an embedded video. It's the movie. It's the last thing I want to watch. The anger surges all over again, so I ignore the message.

I fall asleep and manage to stay under more deeply than I

have in a while. When I come to and look at my phone, it's 4:17. My eyes are so tired, they burn. The house is quiet. Dad and Olivia sleep without trouble. If Mom were here, would she sit up with me? When I was a kid and got sick, she'd sit by my bedside all night checking my fever and bringing me water or a cold compress for my forehead.

But she's gone. And I love Dad and Livvy more than anything, and I know they love me, but I also kind of feel like I'm on my own in a way I never have been before.

At some point, I fall back asleep. Deep sleep. No dreams, no surreal or scary images in the night. My body and mind must be so wrung out they can't summon anything from my subconscious.

Thumps wake me up. And more thumps. Hammering. *My head*. Is Dad having something fixed? I roll over and gently put the pillow over my head, muffling the sound. What could have broken so early in the morning?

Or is someone throwing eggs at the house?

The thumping continues. And it seems close. So close it feels like it's in my room.

Then someone calls my name.

*"Hunter? Hunter, open up."*

*Dad?*

I pull the pillow away. The room feels chilly. My bladder is full, my mouth dry. I feel a little nauseated. I'm frustrated that the concussion symptoms are still around. Dad says my name again.

He even turns the knob a few times. As usual, I had locked it before I went to sleep.

"What?" I ask as I'm walking across the room. I really need to pee, and the floor is cold against my bare feet. The temperature must have dropped to something more fall-like.

Why am I thinking about the weather when my dad is pounding on my door at...

6:11. The alarm doesn't go off until 6:30. What's his problem?

I undo the lock and open the door. "What?"

Dad isn't dressed, either. He's wearing a robe and slippers. Livvy opens her bedroom door and sticks her head out. Her hair looks like a purple bird's nest.

"What?" I ask again, my voice lower.

"Get dressed," Dad says. "The police are here. They want to talk to you."

"What?"

It seems to be the only word I can say. The only word that makes sense.

"The police are here," Dad says again, speaking slowly like I might not understand English. He glances back at Livvy, who is wide-eyed and looking even younger than her fifteen years. More like a kid than I've seen in a long time. Dad looks at me, up and down. I'm wearing boxers and an old soccer T-shirt. "Put some clothes on before you come down."

"I will," I say. "I have to pee, too."

"Then do that." He backs away. "Livvy, get ready for school."

I expect her to argue because she argues about everything, but she just nods and goes back into her room, closing the door.

"What do they want, Dad?" I ask. "Why are they here?"

Dad shrugs. "Chloe, I guess," he says. "Just tell the truth, and you'll be all right."

Before he goes, he reaches out and squeezes my shoulder, and then gives me a little nod.

But the gesture feels forced, and as he goes back down the stairs, I feel more nervous than if he hadn't touched me at all.

# TWENTY-FOUR

I EMPTY MY BLADDER IN THE BATHROOM. SWEET RELIEF for a moment.

*But the cops are waiting downstairs.*

In a daze, I go back to my room and pull on jeans and a sweatshirt. My body shakes more.

My body must be ahead of my mind, because I don't know why I'm shaking. Then the thought crystallizes. *Why would the police be here at this hour?*

*They found her. They found Chloe.*

It can't be good news. If it was good news, the phone would be ringing. A million texts and calls. A celebration.

At least ten times a day, I've thought about what I'll do when I see Chloe again. Would just hugging her and kissing her be enough? Would I ever let her out of my sight? Would we be able to talk about everything she'd been through?

But it's the cops who are here. Early. Earlier than most people are awake. My body slumps onto the bed, letting the mattress take my weight.

I struggle to put on my shoes and socks. So I just sit here, barefoot, shivering and getting colder. Is this how things end? On a random cold morning?

Mom died in the afternoon. But we knew she was going to die. For weeks, we'd been prepared as much as we could be. Still the moment seemed so random. We were in the hospital, and I looked out the window. A school bus went by. Kids were on their way home. To their families. Screaming and laughing. Happy.

Then my mother took her last breath. After it was over, Grandpa Phil, Mom's dad, said something about how he had a craving for steak and insisted we all go to a chain restaurant where we watched him put away a giant ribeye. Odd. Random. The weird shit we remember. Is that what I'll remember about Chloe—that the day they came to tell me she was dead, I had to pee? And then shook so much I couldn't put on my socks?

Someone knocks on the bedroom door. Loud. Like thunder.

That's the way Olivia knocks, like a drill instructor waking fresh recruits.

She comes in. She isn't dressed, and her hair looks like something out of a Tim Burton movie. Dark and wild and tangled.

She sits next to me on the bed. "Are you okay?"

"I'm scared," I say. "If I go down there, I'm going to find out something. And it might all be over."

She rubs my back. "I'll come down with you."

"It's okay. Dad told you to get ready. I'm okay."

My hands still shake, but I force myself to put on my shoes and socks. When I'm finished, I stand up and take a deep breath.

Livvy stands, too.

"Okay," I say. "I'm ready to go down."

"If you need me, just call me and I'll come down."

"I know you have my back," I say. "Thanks, brat."

She looks genuinely moved. "Aww. You haven't called me that in years. Hunter, seriously. Call me if you need anything."

At the top of the stairs, I hear voices. One is unfamiliar and the other is Dad's.

The voices get clearer as I descend. "You'd better believe I'm going to stay right here the whole time you talk to my son," Dad says. His voice sounds louder and sharper than I've heard in a long time. "And if I have to call our lawyer, I'll do it. In fact, I might just make that call right now."

"That's your right, sir," the voice says. "Actually, it's your son's right."

"You haven't even told me what this is about," Dad says. "I don't like this cloak-and-dagger stuff. And at this hour. You're disturbing my family."

The detective I'd talked to a few times last week about Chloe is in the kitchen. Detective Haley. He's younger than Dad, maybe early thirties, with close-cropped hair. He wears tight shirts that accentuate his thick muscles. In the hospital and even after I came home, he spoke to me in a low-key way about the events of the night of the dance. And about Chloe. He never said he thought I was guilty, but he never gave me any reason to believe he thought I was innocent. I couldn't tell *what* he thought of me, and that made me more nervous than anything else.

I'd watched enough true crime documentaries—the kind Daniel was making—to know that the police are always working some angle, that they have ways to make people trust them in order to get more information.

I reminded myself of that every time I talked to him.

But it's been a few days, and even though everyone else in town seems to think I'm the prime suspect, maybe Haley doesn't. He seemed to be on to other things, investigating other people. He'd probed every part of my life, so maybe he's ruled me out. A lot of theories are swirling online, and not all of them involve me. Some say Chloe ran away. Some say she's the victim of a serial killer. Some say a gang of boys from our school—or maybe from another school—kidnapped her or worse. Some say members of a Satanic cult use the woods where we crashed to sacrifice animals. Maybe, people theorized, they'd started sacrificing humans.

"Hunter," Detective Haley says, "why don't we take a seat and talk?" He reaches for a chair at the kitchen table. He's wearing a tan suit and a white shirt with no tie. When he moves, I see the black pistol and holster attached to his belt. "I have some questions for you, and your father is welcome to stay."

Dad nods his approval, and we all sit down. Dad's face looks like it's been chiseled out of granite. He sits with his arms crossed.

Haley gets out a little notebook and flips it open. He studies what's inside for a moment as though he's alone. An obvious stall meant to unnerve us…and it works.

I'm ready to jump out of my own skin. "What's going on?" I ask. "Is there news about Chloe? Will you just tell me what happened?"

Haley looks up from the notebook. He seems to be moving in slow motion.

I want to pound the table and demand more. But that's exactly what he wants to do—put me on edge.

He clears his throat. "Hunter, do you think something happened to Chloe?" he asks. "Do you have something you want to share?"

"No. I just want to know why you're here. I've told you everything three or four times. Did something else happen?"

And then Haley does something he's never done before, not in all the times he and I have talked.

He starts to read me my rights.

# TWENTY-FIVE

DAD'S UP SO FAST HE KNOCKS OVER HIS CHAIR. HE WAVES his arms like an umpire signaling safe.

"No, no, no, no," he's saying. Over and over. *No, no, no, no.*

But Haley keeps reading me my rights while my heart races like a runaway boulder. This means there's been a crime. This means something happened to Chloe, right?

What Haley said just moments before comes back to me: *Do you have something you want to share?*

No, I don't. I really, truly don't. But I'd desperately like to know what he knows.

"I'm ending this now," Dad says, slamming his hand on the table. "And I'm calling our lawyer."

Haley keeps on going like Dad's not making a racket, like he's an actor in a play who has to keep saying his lines even if there's some guy in the front row talking on his cell phone. When Haley finishes reading me my rights, Dad pulls out his phone and scrolls through, looking for the lawyer's number.

Haley has turned in his chair and is looking up at Dad. His face is still patient, his skin as smooth as glass. He looks completely untroubled.

"Mr. Gifford?" he says to Dad. "If you heard the rights I just enumerated to your son, then you know you are allowed to have an attorney. I have no problem with that."

"You shouldn't. I have to protect my son from the police."

Haley smiles without much warmth. "I'm a Black man, Mr. Gifford. I understand better than you about sons being protected from the police."

Dad doesn't say anything, but he keeps a watchful eye on us both.

Haley goes on. "I just want to ask Hunter something. If he answers that one simple question, there may be no need for this conversation to continue."

Dad looks like he has the number and is ready to call.

"What's the question?" Dad asks, his finger poised above the screen.

"You're okay with me asking your son a question?"

"Ask the question, and I'll decide."

"Dad," I say.

They both turn to me.

"I want to know what the hell's going on." I turn to Haley. "Is Chloe okay? Do you know something about where she is? Can't you just tell me that?"

One corner of Haley's mouth twitches a little, almost the start of a smile. But he puts it off, not wanting to reveal too much. He places his hands flat on the table and looks at me, his face smooth as glass again. "Okay, Hunter. Can you tell me where you were last night?"

Dad says, "He was home. We went to that clown show of a vigil, and then we came home. He was here, in his room doing homework all night."

Haley doesn't even glance at Dad. He keeps his eyes boring in on me. Dad turns from Haley and looks at me, too, because I haven't spoken. Everything is quiet. The only sound is the water running upstairs where Olivia is taking a shower.

"No, Dad, that's not right. Remember? I went to Daniel's house. He wanted to show me something, and you told me to drive instead of walk."

"Oh. Right."

But Haley jumps right in. "So you *were* at Daniel's house last night? This is Daniel Nevin, right?"

"Right."

"What time were you there?" Haley asks.

"I don't know. About nine or so, I guess."

"And what time did you leave?" he asks.

"Around ten."

"And what happened while you were at his house?" Haley asks.

Why is Haley asking me about Daniel? Doesn't he want to talk about Chloe? Isn't that why he's here?

Is there some weird connection between Daniel and Chloe?

But how could there be? Did they know each other outside of talking in trig?

"He showed me something, a stupid movie he's working on. And then I left."

"You just left?" Haley asks. "Just said goodbye and left?"

"Hold on a second—" Dad says.

I cut him off. "We had a fight."

"A fight? With fists?"

"No, an argument," I say. "About his movie. He's making a movie about Chloe. It made me look guilty, so we argued about it. And then I left."

"You didn't like that the movie made you look guilty?" Haley asks.

"No, of course not. Would you like to be under a cloud of suspicion?"

"I know the feeling," Haley says. "When I drive into certain neighborhoods in Bentley."

"Hunter," Dad says with an edge in his voice, "stop talking."

"And you got mad at Daniel because of that?" Haley asks.

"Yes."

"You hit him?"

"No, I didn't."

"Hunter," Dad says, his voice louder. He's moving toward me, his hand out. "Stop. Talking."

"Why?" I ask. "Why can't I defend myself?"

"Were you defending yourself with Daniel?" Haley asks. "Did he try to hit you and you hit him back?"

"I didn't—"

He's not asking about *Chloe*. He's asking about *Daniel*. He's asking if I hit him. "Why are you asking me about Daniel?"

Haley's eyes narrow. He watches me like a cat. Then he seems to decide something. He looks at Dad and then back at me. "Daniel Nevin was murdered last night."

# TWENTY-SIX

MY EYES ZOOM IN ON THE WOOD GRAIN OF THE TABLE. It's way more detailed than I had ever realized, even though I've been sitting at this table several times a day my entire life. There's even a knot that's shaped like Kentucky. How have I never noticed that before?

All of a sudden, there's a rushing sound in my ears like a train going through my head.

The table is covered with spots. And I blink over and over trying to clear them away.

It's the concussion again. Pounding. Taking over my brain...

Dad is next to me, holding a glass of water, which I gulp down like an animal. I didn't even know I was thirsty.

From far away, light years away, Haley's voice comes again.

"Did you hear what I said, Hunter? Daniel Nevin was murdered last night. His mother found him when she came home from work. Are you sure there isn't anything you want to tell me? The sooner you tell me, the better. Maybe he tried to hit you—"

Dad's voice booms through everything. "Stop this. Right now."

I've heard Dad angry before. I've even heard him yell on a couple of occasions. But those four words fly through the room like Japanese throwing stars. Haley stops talking and looks at Dad who goes on. "Can't you see that Hunter's had a shock? If you want to talk to him again, bring a warrant. And be sure his lawyer and I are both there before you do. Right now, I don't want another word or another question."

Haley pushes himself up from the chair. The spots are clearing from my eyes. Once he's standing, Haley looks even bigger. He places his hands on his hips and puffs out his chest like a strutting bird.

"Hunter needs to come to the station," Haley says. "He needs to answer questions and sign an official statement. I can take him now—in handcuffs, if need be—or you can drive him. And you're correct. He has the right to an attorney but pushing me out the front door isn't the answer. You have problems, and they're not going away."

The spots are almost gone. *Daniel*. Standing on the front lawn, both of us saying awful things to each other. That was about eight hours ago.

It doesn't make sense. Murdered? Daniel?

"I'll talk to our lawyer," Dad says. "And she will be there when *anyone* talks to my son. I'll bring Hunter to the station myself. I'll have him there as soon as the lawyer is able to meet us."

"Ten minutes," Haley says. "I'll wait outside, and you better have him outside and be driving him to the station in ten minutes. And I'm going to follow you. If it's more than ten minutes, I'm coming back in here with the handcuffs. And backup." He moves toward the front door but keeps his eyes on us. "Think about what I said, Hunter," he says. "The sooner you tell the truth, the—"

"Out," Dad says, pointing the way.

Haley opens the door and leaves without another word.

Dad has his phone out as soon as the door shuts. He walks down the hall toward his study, leaving me alone at the table. I gulp more water.

"Hunter?"

It's Olivia. She's in her bathrobe, and her hair is wet. "What the hell is going on?" she asks. "What's that cop talking about? Did they find Chloe?"

I tell her about Daniel, and her mouth falls open like someone unhinged it.

She leans down and puts her arms around me, and I feel her cold, wet hair against my cheeks and face. "First Chloe," she says. "Now Daniel. What the fuck is going on around here, Hunter? What's happening?"

I hang on to her longer than I have since Mom died. Even then, I don't know if I held her as tight as I do now.

"I don't know. I really don't. But I'm scared, Livvy. I'm really, really scared."

# VIDEO #2

IT'S LATE. EVERYONE'S ASLEEP.

I take Olivia's advice and sit in front of my bookshelf. It feels phony, like I'm auditioning to be the host of a show Dad would watch on PBS. But I stay there. I adjust the angle of the phone, up and then down. I looked pasty in the last video. I wonder if shooting myself from above will make a difference—if it will magically add color to my cheeks.

"Hi, again," I say as I start recording. "This is Hunter Gifford. And I'm back in my house. For now. By the time you see this—and I know a pretty decent number of you watched my last video—you'll already know that someone has died here in Bentley. Daniel Nevin. Daniel was my best friend when we were growing up. We played football together. And video games. And we made movies that were a lot better than these videos I've been making. If Daniel were still here, I'd ask him to help."

Something catches in my throat. A memory floods my brain—Daniel in his backyard. We're ten or eleven, spreading plastic knights and horses in an elaborate formation in preparation for a scene in one of our movies. Daniel was always so diligent, so careful. He acted like every little thing mattered, like no detail could be overlooked.

I push away the memory.

"I already told you about my girlfriend, Chloe. Everyone in Bentley knows, but if you live somewhere else, you need to be reminded that she's missing. Even though she's been missing for more than a week, it doesn't seem like anyone knows anything more about where she is than they did the night of the accident. All the people I expect to know things—the police, the teachers, the principal, the parents—none of them seem to know anything about what's going on. It seems like they know less than I do because they think I know what happened to Chloe, and they think I'm the person who killed Daniel."

I spent most of that day in the police station, barely speaking. The lawyer Dad called showed up right when we did, and she told me to keep my mouth shut unless she said it was okay for me to speak. She spent her time arguing with Detective Haley, while I looked on like a spectator at a tennis match. I kept wanting to jump in and say, "You know as long as we're in here arguing, there's no one out there looking for Chloe or for the person who killed Daniel."

But I didn't say that.

But I'm going to now.

"I don't know what happened to Daniel. We had an argument

the night he died. But I didn't touch him. He and I never fought like that. Not in all the years we were friends. Daniel was really one of the nicest people I've ever known."

There's a noise downstairs. Could it be Dad? If he knew I was making another video, he'd flip his shit. He keeps telling me to keep my mouth shut and put my head down. He keeps telling me to let the police do their work, even though he also spends his time bitching about every little thing the cops do.

He can't make up his mind, either.

The house is silent again.

Was I hearing things? Either way, I need to finish.

"If you know anything about what happened to Daniel or Chloe, please call the Bentley police. Tell them anything you know, even if it seems unimportant. Chloe and Daniel…they're two of the best people I've ever known. And they don't deserve to be hurt. So please make that call. Okay?"

I turn off the camera.

Do I share on the Ex Libris channel again?

Everyone's already seen the last one on Ex Libris…

Besides, it's fitting that a video about Chloe would be there on the channel we created.

So I share this one as well.

# TWENTY-SEVEN

DAD KNOCKS ON MY DOOR EARLY THE NEXT MORNING.

He's already showered and dressed for work. His freshly shaven skin glows red, and he smells like the lotion he smears on his face to prevent razor burn.

"What's wrong?" I ask.

I think the worst—the police are back, and this time they have a warrant to arrest me. Even though I'm wearing an old, loose T-shirt, I feel a tightening around my neck.

Dad looks surprised by my greeting. He stands there for a moment not knowing what to say, before clearing his throat. He comes into my room and looks around, as if he's not sure where to go or what to do. Eventually, he picks up one of my soccer trophies and examines it before putting it back. Then he grabs a book he gave me by Ursula K. Le Guin.

"Have you read this one?" he asks.

"Not yet."

"Hmph. Your mom always loved it. We read it for a class in

college. The whole time the professor was discussing it, I was staring at your mom."

He puts down the book and sits on the edge of the bed. "Everything's okay," he says. His thinning hair looks a little grayer, and the skin under his chin sags more. Dad once said a parent is only as happy as their least happy child. "I made a decision."

"Okay," I say.

"I called the school and talked to Dr. Whitley. He's the assistant principal, right? We agreed you should stop going to school for now—"

"Dad—"

"Hold it," he says, raising his hand. "It's for the best. I've been thinking about this ever since we left the police station yesterday. You should lay low until the cops know what happened to Daniel. There's someone out there who's hurting people. Young people. I don't want you to be next. Besides, going to school isn't going to help anything. Not with the mood people are in. They're sending assignments to you today. You can keep up without distractions."

A million excuses spring to mind—my friends, the search for Chloe, clearing my name, college—but he won't be swayed. He's right.

What would school be like with everyone knowing Daniel was murdered and the police questioned me? It's been all over Twitter that I was the last person to see Daniel alive. Would things escalate beyond throwing things and nasty notes?

"Do you want me to stay home?" Dad asks.

"That's not necessary."

"Are you sure? I have two exams to give, but I can get someone to cover for me."

A lot of parents would insist on staying home. They'd take a day off and cancel their meetings just to be around their kid. But Dad isn't like that. He never takes a sick day, never stays home. His offer to do that is as rare as a unicorn.

"You're already dressed."

He looks down as though he's forgotten what he's wearing. "I know. But I'm second-guessing myself. I hate the thought of you alone here all day. I worry…the things people say and do. You can come with me and work in the campus library. You used to do that."

"Yeah. When I was ten."

"Well…all right…"

"It's okay, Dad. I'll get caught up and I've got essays to work on for my applications. But who's going to drive Olivia to school?"

"I'll drop her on my way." He smiles. "Maybe I'll even let her pick the radio station."

"That might keep her quiet for a few minutes."

Dad reaches out and pats my leg. He touches me like I'm a hot stove. "I'm skipping afternoon office hours and coming home immediately after the exams. Call me if you need anything while I'm at work. And if the cops come around, don't answer. They can't talk to you without the lawyer."

"Okay."

"Just keep the doors locked. Okay? All of them."

"I will."

But he doesn't get up. He remains on the end of the bed, his hands resting on his knees. The neighbor's German shepherd starts barking, which means people are stirring on the street. He always barks when people and kids start leaving for work and school. Then he's silent again until late afternoon when everyone comes home.

"What's wrong, Dad?"

"I'm just thinking of Danny's mom. I know she's been raising him alone, working nights, and then she comes home and finds him dead in his room. Strangled. His room ransacked. There must have been a pretty good struggle. I can't imagine what she's going through. It's ugly."

"Kind of like when we lost Mom," I say.

"Kind of. But losing a child…that's the toughest of all."

"Like Chloe's parents," I say.

"Yes. Except they still have hope. Right?"

"Right."

Dad looks like he doesn't know what else to say. He stares straight ahead, lost in his own thoughts.

"The two things don't have to be related," I say. "Chloe and Daniel. Just because someone broke into Daniel's house and killed him doesn't mean it's connected to Chloe."

"I know," he says. "Two very different things. But Bentley hasn't had a murder in two years, and now…all at once a student is killed and one is missing. And both from the same high school."

"And both connected to me," I say.

Dad pats my leg again, and this time it looks and feels more natural. He stands up. "Look, I'm going to call that therapist, the one you talked to when you were in the hospital. You liked her, right? You can't go through all this without professional help."

"Dad, that's not—"

"No argument," he says. "I'll only be gone a few hours. Call if you need anything. And I mean anything."

"I will."

And then he's out the door.

# TWENTY-EIGHT

WITH DAD AND OLIVIA GONE, THE HOUSE FEELS QUIET. Too quiet. Who ever thought I'd miss Livvy's chattering, swirling energy so much?

My mind starts to race the way it did when I was a kid and saw something scary in a movie or on TV. I go through every inch of the house, making sure all the doors are locked. I check the windows, too, thinking how close it was the other night at Daniel's house. Someone killed him right after I left.

If I'd still been there...

Is that what Dad was thinking about this morning?

Maybe I should have gone to work with him. But I don't want to act like a scared little kid.

Just because it's part of the morning routine and a distraction, I fill a bowl with cereal. I'm tempted to check my phone to see what's been said about the latest video, but it's the last thing I need. Nothing online could possibly be helpful.

So why did I even post the video?

I pour milk, dig in with my spoon.

Maybe because I want to be heard. Maybe because I want people to know there's a real person on the other end of this story, someone who loved Chloe and Daniel. Someone who wants to know what happened just as much as everybody else.

Someone whose own mind is working against him. *Why the fuck can't I remember?*

Did I black out at Daniel's house, too…? The thought makes me shiver.

The cereal is mushy and bland. Before I can dump it down the sink, someone knocks on the back door.

I jump what feels like three feet in the air. The spoon goes tumbling off the edge of the bowl, sending up a spray of milk.

My heart thumps inside my chest like a crazed bird trying to escape. My phone is upstairs. The landline is here, the one that's tormented me with nasty messages. What would they think if I dialed 911? The kid at the heart of two major crimes calling the police because someone is at the door?

The knocking again.

I grab a knife from the block. It's a giant one my parents received as a wedding present. Dad never cooks. He's probably never touched it. Could I actually use it? Drive this steel blade into someone's body? Could I?

Everyone already thinks I did something to Chloe. And Daniel.

And I'm not even sure myself.

I start for the back door, moving slowly. Maybe it's the cops. Maybe it's someone selling magazines.

Maybe Dad forgot something. But that's ridiculous. The next time he forgets something will be the first. Besides, he wouldn't knock—he'd use his key.

I move cautiously, still in my T-shirt and boxers, and try to catch a glimpse of the door from the hallway without revealing myself. I peek around the corner just as they knock again.

And say my name.

"Hunter? Open up."

I lower the knife, and then unlock and open the door for Chad and Hannah. The cool morning air rushes in and prickles the skin on my legs. When Chad sees the knife, he takes a step back.

"Whoa, chill," he says. "Remember us?"

"Yeah," I say. "And I'm really glad it's just you."

# TWENTY-NINE

THE KNIFE GOES BACK INTO THE BLOCK, AND THE THREE of us settle around the kitchen table.

The three of us. We've hung out before, plenty of times. But, like I said, it's always a little weird. Or maybe it's just me. Maybe I think about it, and no one else does anymore. Chad never cares what anyone thinks.

Looking back, it all seems so silly that I cared about a three-month relationship with Hannah ending.

The summer after we broke up, Hannah and Chad started dating and have been together ever since. It bothered me at first—why did I have to keep spending time with her after we broke up? Chad, as always, acted like it was nothing unusual and never mentioned it. Not to me, not to anyone. Hector asked him about it once, and Chad just shrugged as if to say, *What's the big deal?*

Maybe Hannah likes soccer players.

When I started dating Chloe, I mostly forgot about it. But

Chloe occasionally made a snarky comment about Hannah and me. Chloe never really liked Hannah. I always assumed it was because we'd once dated, although Chloe had a couple of other boyfriends before me, including Basher, and I never talked shit about them. But Chloe told me once that she didn't like Hannah because she couldn't be trusted—and cheating on me when we were fifteen was Exhibit A.

"I'm glad to see you," I say again. "But aren't you going to be late?"

Chad shrugs. "It's fine. That new secretary, Elisa, she likes me. She's a soccer fan. She always writes me late slips. No questions asked."

"You know what's going on, right?" I ask, looking from Chad to Hannah and back again.

They both nod. "Everybody's talking about it. A lot," Chad says. "You know how it is—one person hears, and then the whole school knows." He leans forward and puts his hand on my forearm. I don't know any of my other friends who would make a gesture like that, but Chad makes it seem natural. "I'm sorry about Daniel. Seriously. I know you guys used to be buds. It's pretty messed up that somebody killed him. And right after you were at his house."

"Thanks."

"I sent you a million messages yesterday, but I guess you couldn't respond."

"The cops had my phone. Again. They already searched it when Chloe...."

I don't finish the thought. I don't have to.

"That's a fucked-up invasion of your privacy," Chad says.

"I'm kind of getting used to it," I say. "That's what's really wrong about it. Are you two just here to check on me?" I force a laugh. "As you can see by the way I answered the door, I'm a little anxious."

Chad looks over at Hannah, who has her arms on the table, her hoodie sleeves pulled over her hands. She nods when Chad looks at her.

"We wanted to tell you some stuff we found out," she says.

I sit up a little straighter. "Okay."

"My dad obviously knows every lawyer in town," she says.

"Yeah," I say, waiting for the other shoe to drop.

Hannah's dad is one of the best-known personal injury lawyers in Bentley. His ads run on television what seems like twenty-four hours a day. It's not clear why anyone gave him any business since he has a comb-over that looks he's wearing bacon strips on his head. But he apparently makes a lot of money, because Hannah's family lives in a huge house on a lake outside town.

"Well, he was talking on the phone last night to one of his lawyer friends," she says. "And they were talking about Daniel." She squirms a little. "About him getting killed."

Chad jumps in. "I was there, and I heard it, too. Her dad is louder than fuck. You know that, right? We didn't even have to eavesdrop. We could just hear him, like he had a megaphone."

I sit up even straighter, my spine rigid. "So what did you hear?"

Hannah nods again. She touches her hair, pats a strand into place. "My dad was saying that whoever broke into the house and killed Daniel—well, it wasn't your typical robbery where the person just takes everything. They only took certain things from the house."

"Yeah," Chad says. "It's like they were looking for something specific."

"Like what?" I ask. "They aren't rich."

"You're right," Hannah says. "But from what we heard Dad say, Daniel's mom had some jewelry in her bedroom. A couple of antique rings she got from her mother. And a bottle of pain pills from when she had knee surgery. And..." She scrunches up her face as she tries to remember. "Oh, and a laptop. She had a laptop in her room that they didn't touch. It was right out in the open, too."

"And there was a gun and a bunch of papers in the closet," Chad says. "Apparently, people love to break in and steal guns."

"Exactly," Hannah says. "All that stuff is just what some random burglar would want to steal. A gun. Pills. Jewelry and computers. Those are the kinds of things they can sell easily."

"So what did they take?" I ask. "What was missing if all this stuff wasn't?"

They exchange a look, as if deciding which one of them is going to deliver the news. They look at each other that way for what feels like an hour, so I jump in.

"Well?" I ask.

Chad looks away from Hannah and directly at me. "Whoever did it only took *Daniel's* things. His computer and all his film equipment. It's like that's what they were looking for. Daniel's movie stuff."

It feels like something pushes me, knocks me back against the wooden slats of the chair. *His movie stuff?*

"Do you know what he was doing, Hunter?" Hannah asks. "On Twitter, people are saying you went over there to look at a movie or something."

"Yeah. He was making a movie about Chloe's disappearance, and he wanted to show me. He thought it was his big break."

"You saw it?" Chad asks.

"Part of it. And it made me look guilty."

"How?" Hannah asks.

"It just rehashes all the same shit," I say. "How I was the last one to see Chloe. How I can't remember the accident. Everything everybody is saying about me."

"That's messed up," Hannah says.

Chad lets out a long sigh. "Damn."

"Yeah, damn," Hannah says. She squirms in her chair. "My dad said that the person who movie stuff must not have wanted what was on there to ever see the light of day."

# THIRTY

THEIR WORDS SINK IN AND MAKE ME FEEL COLDER.

"So they took his film equipment?" I ask. "He probably has it all backed up. It's probably on the cloud."

"Not everyone keeps things backed up," Chad says. "I don't."

"Shit," I say, feeling a mixture of hope and fear. "If they find out who killed him, maybe they can find out who took Chloe. Maybe the two things are related after all."

They exchange another look before Chad clears his throat and says, "But you just said the movie made you look guilty. So…"

I shiver again. "Do you two have to leave soon? I was going to put some clothes on."

"Get dressed, Hunter," Hannah says. "We'll wait."

I go upstairs with a hurricane of thoughts swirling through my head. Whoever killed Daniel didn't want anyone to see the movie. And I don't want anyone to see it. Also, I can't remember what happened the night Chloe disappeared. Can I remember everything that happened the night Daniel died?

I pull on a sweatshirt, jeans, and shoes. I look at the rumpled sheets on the bed where I barely sleep anymore.

Am I sure of anything? Has my mind broken down entirely?

I hustle downstairs, moving with greater purpose, remembering what Chad told me at school the other day.

Hannah's tapping away at her phone, while Chad stares out the back window where leaves fall at an accelerated rate in the wind.

"Hannah, you need to tell me something," I say. "Chad said you told him Chloe was upset the night of the accident. And she said *I* was mad about something. What's that all about?"

"Oh, yeah." Hannah stops tapping on her phone and looks up.

"So, what happened the night of the dance?" I ask. "Chloe told you I was angry about something and she wanted to get out of there before I…" I turn to Chad. "What did you say? Before I 'acted on it'?"

Chad nods. "Tell him, Hannah. Go ahead."

"I thought you already told him," she says.

"He wants to hear it from you."

I sit down across from her. "Actually, what I want to know is…" My eyes move back and forth between them, and I'm hoping Chad will step in and help.

Chad knows what's coming. Something dark moves across his face and dims the wattage by about 20 percent. I've seen his face do this before, subtly change when he doesn't like what someone is saying. It happened at the vigil when the guy in the Titans hat pointed me out and Chad tried to shut him up.

But Chad is silent—he's going to make me put it in words.

Hannah watches me, uncertainty on her face.

"Okay, Hannah," I say. "You saw Chloe do and say all of this, and Chad says you only told the police the part about Chloe being upset. Not the part about her being afraid I'd act on it or whatever. But here's the thing—how do I know it really happened? How do I know you're telling the truth?"

For a frozen moment Hannah just stares at me, phone in one nearly sleeve-covered hand, her lower lip out a little farther than the upper. Then a flush passes over her cheeks, one deeper than the red that's almost always there.

"Are you shitting me, Hunter?" she says. "Are you really going to accuse me of lying?"

"I'm saying this is important, Hannah. No exaggeration. Okay? It's life and death. And you didn't tell the police all of this...so I can't help but wonder."

"I didn't tell the police to help you," she says. "Because you and Chloe are my friends. But now you want to throw something that happened when we were fifteen back in my face. Because I made out with some guy on vacation."

"It's not about that," I say. "You're just making it sound like Chloe was afraid of me and...look, Chloe had no reason to be afraid of me. I love her. You both know that."

My voice cracks a little, and their eyes widen.

"Besides," I say, "why would Chloe tell you all of this? I mean...Hannah, Chloe doesn't even like you that much."

"Oh, okay," Hannah says. "You're going to go there."

"It's true," I say.

Hannah is undeterred.

She stands up and pushes her chair toward the table. "I'm not doubting that you love her, Hunter. I know you do. Okay? I see the way you look at each other. But whatever happened that night had Chloe freaked out. And scared. She said you didn't understand, that you felt betrayed. And it wasn't good. That's literally what she said. 'This isn't good.' Okay? Are you happy? And maybe she talked to me because she couldn't talk to you. Because she was so nervous about what you were going to think. And I was there for her when she needed someone." She looks at Chad and waves her hand toward the door, shaking her head. "Come on, Chad. We're going to be late. Elisa likes you more than she likes me."

Chad gets to his feet. He nods my way but doesn't say anything as he follows Hannah out the door.

# THIRTY-ONE

BACK IN MY ROOM, I TRY TO MAKE SENSE OF WHAT CHAD and Hannah have told me. Someone not only killed Daniel, but they took all his movie stuff. His movie equipment—and the movie he was making—implicates me.

Daniel sent me the file, the very thing someone tried to cover up.

I grab my phone and start to scroll through my messages to find it. I'm almost there when Dad calls.

He doesn't even say hello. He just starts talking. He sounds sort of out of breath like he just ran up a flight of stairs before he made the call.

"Did you make another video and post it on YouTube?"

Before I can answer, he keeps going.

"Damn it, Hunter. I just got a call from the lawyer, and she's furious about this. And so am I. Do you know how bad it is when you go off and talk without a lawyer around? The cops can use anything you say against you. Do you understand how serious all of this is?"

"Dad—"

"She's threatening to drop your case. And I already paid her a retainer."

"Dad—"

"I know you're upset. And I know you're grieving. I get it. And I know all you kids put everything online all the time. You always have your phones—"

"Dad!"

He finally stops. His breathing comes through the phone. "What?"

"Did you see the video?"

"No, I haven't."

"But you're jumping my shit about it?"

"Hunter, the point is you have to keep quiet and listen to your lawyer. You're in way deep here."

"Dad, the video is just me asking for help," I say. "It's telling people what happened to Daniel, just like the other one is about Chloe. I'm asking if anybody knows anything. How else are we supposed to get the word out?"

"Let the cops handle it," he says.

"How are they going to do it? On the evening news? The newspaper? This is how young people communicate. Don't you think kids are more likely to know what happened to Chloe? And Daniel? Maybe it's Mike Basher, Chloe's ex-boyfriend. He kept hanging around Chloe's house long after they broke up. Maybe they need to talk to him. Or maybe it's—"

I stop myself. I can't say it.

"Maybe it's what?" Dad asks.

*Hannah?*

"Forget it," I say.

"Hunter, just…look, I'm coming home in a little bit. After this exam. We can talk more about it then. But for now, just stay in the house and stay off the internet."

He hangs up on me.

"Shit," I say.

I hold the phone in my hand like it might bite me.

*The lawyer thinks. The police think. The school thinks.*

*Dad thinks.*

Second period starts in twenty minutes. I forget about Daniel's movie for a minute and send an email to the one person I still haven't talked to, the one person who might be able to make sense of everything. He's free next period, and despite his aversion to social media, he does check his email.

He's in class and can't answer right away, but I'm hoping to hear from him by the time I get there.

I park at the far edge of the school lot, away from any prying eyes.

It takes a few minutes to get a response.

Hunter—See you in five. Ron H.

# THIRTY-TWO

RON COMES OUT THE BACK OF THE BUILDING AND, AFTER looking around for a moment, sees my car and heads my way.

Ron's a thin guy, a few years older than my dad, which puts him in his early fifties. His clothes are always rumpled, and his hair always looks like he was just out in a storm. But he's not a slob. In fact, Ron speaks in a very precise, educated way, even more so than any of the other teachers in the school. He was born in Maryland, but he seems like a guy who came from another country, maybe even another time. He's that well-mannered.

He pulls open the passenger door, letting in a cool gust of air, and slides into the seat. Once he's in, he runs his hand through his hair. It makes no difference.

He slaps me on the knee. "Good to see you, Hunter. I've been reflecting on your situation a great deal. And it's terrible. Just terrible."

"Yes, it's been kind of wild. Obviously. It's scary just to leave the house."

I've found it odd that Ron hasn't reached out to me more often. He sent one get-well message after the accident, but other than that, nothing. He has to know he's my favorite teacher. He knows he's the guy I go out of my way to talk to every day.

It's as if he reads my mind.

"I'm sorry I haven't been in better touch," he says. "I went by the hospital the morning after the accident, but you were in no condition to have visitors. I imagine you were consumed with talking to the police. And I know how fraught that can be."

"Yeah. I heard you came by."

"I was also informed that you stopped by the office, but I'd come down with something wicked, and it kept me laid up for a few days. I've thought of you often—and Chloe, too, of course."

"It's been pretty terrible. I'm not sure... I guess I don't know what to make of any of it. I don't know who to trust. I can't even trust my own mind."

Ron nods as though he understands. "You've become the unreliable narrator of your own life."

"I guess so."

"And you really can't remember *anything* from that night?" he asks.

"Nothing important."

"I see." He taps his fingers against his thigh. "I suppose it's possible that if memories do come back, they may not be reliable, either. They might be some kind of false memories. Almost worthless."

"Are you serious?" I ask.

"I'm afraid so."

"Everything is a mess. And I'm sorry I used the Ex Libris YouTube channel to share those videos. I wanted to reach people in the school."

"Oh, someone mentioned that to me. I don't know what any of that stuff means. Besides, it's free speech." Ron cocks his head, studies me from under his shaggy brows. "Do you want to tell me about some of the important things that have been going on? I presume that's why you reached out. For my words of wisdom?"

It feels good to have someone listening. Really listening.

I give him a rundown of the past week or so, especially the past couple of days. The words just pour out of me. Ron is the first person I've told all this to—besides the police—since the accident. Everyone else was either right there as things were happening or they knew more about them than I did.

Ron listens, nodding along. His attentiveness encourages me to keep talking.

When I pause, he rubs his chin. There's ink on his fingertips. "It has been quite a whirlwind around here," he says. "And it sounds like you're in the eye of it."

"Right. But I can't remember what happened to Chloe. And even though I was with Daniel that night, I left before it all went down. At least I think I did. Maybe I'm losing my mind. Maybe the accident did more harm than anyone realized, and I can't remember any of the things I've been doing."

"You really think that?"

"I'm starting to wonder," I say. "I don't know."

Ron taps against the window, indicating the school. "This whole community is in distress. There was talk about canceling classes when Daniel's body was found, but it was decided we'd be better off letting students come in and use the resources here. The administration has brought in extra counselors. Everybody's raw. You are wise to stay away."

"That's what the school wanted," I say. "And so did my dad."

"An intelligent man, your father."

"Did you know Daniel? Did he ever take your class?"

"I don't believe so. There've been so many students over the years. I'm sorry to say I'm starting to forget more and more." He rubs his chin again. "So, you really can't remember anything of that night? Not a thing?"

"Bits and pieces, mostly from earlier at the dance. Nothing about the accident."

"And, yet, you said your friends, Chad and…what's the young lady's name?"

"Hannah."

"Right. Her father's the lawyer, isn't he? You just told me your two friends say Chloe was upset about something that night. And she was worried about you losing control in some way. She never mentioned anything to you about why she was so upset? I thought the two of you seemed quite close."

"Yes. But I don't know what was bothering her. I mean…"

"You mean…what?" he asks.

I've thought about telling Dad, but it just seems too weird. I could talk to Chad or even Olivia, but I'm not sure they have the perspective I need. I want to hear from someone with life experience, someone with some wisdom.

"Something did happen between Chloe and me. And maybe that's what caused all the problems."

# THIRTY-THREE

CHLOE'S PARENTS WERE GOING OUT, AND WE KNEW WE'D have the house to ourselves.

Scott had some kind of work banquet in Leesburg, about thirty minutes away from Bentley. They went every year on the same weekend, and they never once missed it.

So we knew they'd be out. We'd been talking about having sex for weeks. The longer we dated, the closer we got. This happened in the back seats of our cars, in spare rooms at parties, on a blanket in the park. We'd explored every inch of each other's bodies—and had an amazing time doing it—but we'd always stopped just short of having sex.

Things never progressed very far with Hannah or with any of the other girls I'd dated. So most of the things I did with Chloe were new to me, and they all blew my mind.

Fooling around with Chloe was different from anything I'd ever experienced.

Maybe it was because of how beautiful she is. Maybe because of how much we trusted each other.

Or maybe because of how into each other we are, how much we love each other. Whatever the reason, when we were together, it was unlike anything else.

Even though I'd heard that the first time having sex can be more than a little awkward, I didn't believe that conventional wisdom. Chloe and I wouldn't be like everybody else.

At first, we weren't.

We were in her room. The lighting was perfect, and a couple of candles burned on her dresser. She played a mix we both loved.

Everything was full-steam ahead until it was time to put on the condom.

They never show that part in the movies. I'd awkwardly practiced at home a few times, and it seemed pretty easy, but having to do it in the moment, in Chloe's bed, with the music playing and the candles burning and her waiting there, watching me...

It was a struggle.

The first one broke. By the time the next one was on, the moment had passed.

We scrambled to get it back, and we started to get there. But it also felt a little like work. I was in my head, feeling self-conscious. And Chloe tried to direct me, which made me *more* self-conscious.

Then it finally happened. Something gave, and Chloe yelped a little. I asked if I'd hurt her, and she shook her head, but it just didn't seem like all the other times we'd been together. It just didn't seem like us.

We held each other afterward and talked. I'd never been

happier to be with Chloe, to know my first time was with her. But I also silently cursed myself for not being in the moment and looked forward to the next time, hoping we would finally get it right. That it would feel as good as it was supposed to.

But the next time never came.

It was tough to find a place to be alone. Dad never went out at night or on weekends. Olivia came and went with the unpredictability of an earthquake. Chloe's mom worked at home, so she was always at their house.

And trying again—after how unsatisfying the first time had been—in a car or on a blanket in the woods in the dark seemed to be setting us up for failure.

I told myself not to push, not to be the guy who insisted. I wanted it—I really did—but I didn't want it more than I wanted Chloe to be happy.

And then about ten days after we tried the first time, Chloe started acting distant. Distracted. And by the time homecoming rolled around, our sex life—even without the actual sex—had cooled considerably. Which is why I looked forward to the dance, thinking we could try again. Or just be with each other the way we had before.

But clearly that didn't happen.

Not even close.

When I finish talking, Ron is staring straight ahead. He steeples his fingers and rests them against his chin. "There's nothing unusual about your experience, Hunter," he says.

"Really?"

"Really. You're right to say the first time is never quite the fireworks-filled extravaganza we hope it will be. The movies do get that wrong. Over and over."

"Maybe I'll write a book someday that shows the reality," I say.

"Maybe people don't want to see that." He laughs a little. "And, sadly, because of the society we live in, it is different for a young woman than a young man. Maybe Chloe was contemplating what it all meant. Maybe she was reconsidering. Maybe she was speaking to a friend or her mother about it."

"I don't think she'd talk to her mom that way."

"I don't know her mother." He gets an impish look in his eye. "But she gave a lovely speech at the vigil."

I appreciate his attempt to make a joke.

"Yeah," I say. "She practically handed me a cigarette and a blindfold."

"You say Chloe hadn't been acting like herself in the days leading up to her disappearance. I have to admit, I hadn't noticed anything unusual about her. She seemed like her typical capable and confident self."

"Really?"

"I don't know her the way you do, of course," he says. "She's a student, not a friend."

His words sting a little. Does he think of me as just a student? I've always thought we were more than that, that he saw me and

Chloe as not just typical kids, not simply two of the thousands who will pass through his classes during his career in Bentley.

"I really want to get an answer to her disappearance soon. I want someone to admit to something. Or come forward with a key piece of information."

"And it might be me," he says.

"What do you mean?"

"I might be the one to reveal something to you." He taps on the window again. "Right over there, outside the gymnasium. I saw you and Chloe leaving the dance that night. And I have to say neither of you looked very pleased."

# THIRTY-FOUR

"WHAT DO YOU MEAN?" I ASK.

The air in the car starts to feel close and confining despite the cool temperatures outside. I crack the window a little.

"You really don't recall?" Ron asks, cocking his head.

"Apparently not."

"Well, I'm afraid for how it makes you look. To the police."

"I'm afraid, too. What if something happened that I don't remember? What if I did something? What if my brain is hurt, and I'm never normal?"

"Yes," he says, rubbing his chin again.

The outside air from the cracked window brings no relief. It's like I've slipped underwater. "What did you see?"

Ron seems to be choosing his words carefully. He opens his mouth and then closes it before finally speaking. "You approached me during the dance. You'll recall I had the supreme honor of being one of the chaperones. You know I hate doing that job—having to monitor the restrooms and make sure no has snuck in a bottle or a flask or a joint. Who cares? You're kids. But, sadly, it's part of my duties. Anyway, I was on patrol that night, when you approached me in the hallway and told me you needed to talk to me."

"Was I upset? Scared?"

"Angry I would say. Very angry. Not like I've ever seen you before. I explained that I had to make one additional circuit of the dance, and then we could meet in the parking lot to talk if you wanted. You agreed. In fact, you said that would be perfect. So I executed my rounds and then made my way outside, expecting to find you. Instead…"

"What?"

"Well, the fact is you weren't there. I waited for you, only too happy to have a reprieve from chaperoning. It was a lovely evening, lots of stars. I enjoyed the break immensely."

"But what did you see?"

"Eventually I heard two voices raised in what sounded like anger. It was you and Chloe. You were arguing with each other loudly. Or so it appeared. I took a step toward you both—you were a good hundred feet away and hadn't yet seen me—but then you moved to a nearby vehicle and got in together. Not a minute later, the car tore out of the parking lot, and I went back to my chaperoning duties. It couldn't have been long after you left that you had your accident. But I knew none of that then. None of us did. I only heard about the accident the next morning, and as I told you, I went to the hospital, but wasn't allowed to see you."

I close my eyes and try—very hard—to bring back memories of that night. But there's nothing but blackness. A complete blind spot—no memory of talking to Ron, being mad at Chloe, or arguing with her.

I certainly don't remember getting in the car and speeding off.

But two very different people—first Hannah and now Ron—have told me I was angry that night. Ron confirms Hannah's story. *Shit*.

That has to mean Hannah is telling the truth.

I try and try to remember but see nothing except starburst patterns swirling against my closed eyelids.

"Nothing comes back?" he asks.

"No. Nothing."

"Sadly, I have to be getting inside," Ron says. "Duty calls. And you shouldn't worry so much about your memories. You'll make many more in this life."

My eyes open. The sky is turning gray and starting to spit rain against the windshield. "Yeah, I guess you have class to teach," I say. "Thanks for coming out."

"It's my pleasure," he says. "We can talk again. Anytime. Just keep working with the doctors. And, well, trust that the police will figure out all this sordidness."

"Did they talk to you?" I ask.

"They did. They talked to everyone in the school. Everyone who had any contact with you or with Chloe. And now they're starting all over again about Daniel."

"So you told them what you just told me?" I ask.

"I did indeed. I had to. But I also told them you possess a sterling character. I told them I have never seen any hint of a problem from you. In short, I told them the truth."

"Thanks," I say. "Hey? When you were outside and saw Chloe and me, did you also happen to see Mike Basher? Do you know him?"

"Basher? The world's worst quarterback? Why do you ask?"

"He and Chloe used to date. Remember, he wrote that freaky poem about Chloe early in the year?"

"Oh, yes, that's right. I do recall that incident. A dreadful poem. So trite. Describing a beautiful girl as a queen on her throne? Blech. It's poems like those that make me feel my entire life has been a waste. Like I'm not teaching anybody anything." Ron's head shakes back and forth.

"Did you see him? Basher?"

"Basher? No, I didn't."

Ron holds out his hand, and we shake. We've never done that before. It seems so formal, so adult.

"Keep up with your schoolwork as much as you can, Hunter," he says. "I know I have a college letter to write for you. Make sure you remind me of that."

"I will." Then I think of something else. "Do you know why Chloe isn't having you write her a letter? She was, but then she changed her mind. I thought maybe she was embarrassed by the Basher stuff. She thought I pushed her into mentioning that creepy poem to you."

"Did she?" He looks thoughtful. "I didn't know I wasn't writing her a letter. That's news to me."

"She didn't tell you?"

"Well, perhaps she forgot. And maybe she wanted someone from the sciences to write for her. That's what she's going to major in, after all. I would have written a glowing letter, but it's her choice."

When he opens the door, a stronger gust of air blows in. Ron walks right across the spot where he said he saw Chloe and I argue the night she disappeared. Moments before everything changed.

# THIRTY-FIVE

BEFORE I EXIT THE PARKING LOT, THE PHONE RINGS.

It's Dad.

I don't want to answer, but…

"Where are you?" he asks. "I came home, and you weren't here."

"I'm out."

"Out where?"

"I went to talk to Mr. Hartman."

"You went to school?"

"Not exactly. We talked in the parking lot. Now I'm going for a drive."

"Hunter, are you okay? Maybe you should come home. We can…talk…or whatever."

"I'm okay," I say. "As okay as I can be. I'll be home soon, but I don't want to drive and talk."

"Be careful."

"I will."

I pull out of the school lot, heading east. I don't mean to take anything out on Dad. He cares. And now I know I fought with Chloe the night she disappeared, and I argued with Daniel the night he died.

Doubt creeps in like it never has before.

The houses around school quickly give way to a stretch of cornfields. They've already been harvested, the stalks cut down to the ground like dead soldiers. It starts to rain harder, and I turn on the wipers, which smear the windshield even more.

My destination is a place that's been calling ever since I came home from the hospital.

We're coming up on two weeks since the accident, two weeks since Chloe disappeared. I've tried not to let my mind go there, tried not to imagine where she might be or what might be happening to her. But I've seen enough TV shows to know if a missing person isn't found within the first forty-eight hours, it becomes more of a long shot that the person will be found alive.

*Is Chloe locked up somewhere?*

*Is she suffering?*

*Is she dead?*

I push away the thoughts with as much mental force as I can summon. I remember the girl in Utah who was gone for almost a year before they found her. Alive. There are other cases like that, too. In America and in Europe. All over the world.

But the young women in those cases—and it's almost always young women—suffered horribly while they were gone.

I can't think of that happening to Chloe.

Dad should forget about me—he needs to worry about Olivia and Gabby. We should never let them out of our sight. The world is not a safe place.

The cornfields turn into trees so thick I can't see through them. I make a right onto County Road 250 that runs from Bentley to the next little town of Flatwater. There's nothing there, maybe five hundred people, and nothing but trees and corn in between.

It's not unusual for Chloe and me to come out this way. We used to take long drives out in the middle of nowhere all the time, just exploring. Being out here on homecoming night supports the idea that we might have been fighting. When we went on those drives, we always talked and talked about whatever was happening in our lives. If we had something serious to discuss, we might have done it on County Road 250 heading toward Flatwater.

I slow, reduce my speed to 35 miles per hour in a zone where everyone is allowed to go 45. If I slow down and take my time, will the memories start to come back? Will being here shake something loose?

But as I try to force my mind back to that night, nothing comes.

The present explodes with the vibrant colors of fall. Orange and red leaves litter the road and are piling up along the berm. Three deer at the tree line hear me approaching and jump back into the brush. I crest a small rise and come down the other side into a dip in the road. That's when I see first the skid marks and then the tree.

And something else.

A car. Parked along the side of the road.

A car I don't recognize.

# THIRTY-SIX

IT'S A DARK SEDAN—NEW, SO MAYBE A COP CAME TO collect evidence. Could be a reporter working on yet another story. Could be one of those technicians reconstructing the accident in order to figure out what happened.

The person is entitled to have their time at the memorial.

But it really looks like the car is empty. No one's in sight, either inside or outside.

So where are they? Back in the woods?

And why?

I work up saliva in my dry mouth and push the door open. My shoes hit the damp blacktop.

I feel warm, despite the cool rain falling. Except for the chirps of a few birds, it's dead quiet. No other cars come by.

I move forward.

Just like they did at Chloe's locker, people have come out and left notes and candles and stuffed animals. It's a nice thought, at first. But they probably never come back to see what those things look like after they've been out in the elements for almost two weeks. Rain, wind, and passing cars have conspired to beat the shit out of this stuff. The ink on the notes has run. The stuffed animals are wet and droopy, looking abandoned and forlorn. Maybe there should be a rule about roadside memorials—they can stay for a day or two or until the weather turns bad. Then everybody has to come and collect their stuff.

My shoes crunch over the gravel. Tiny pieces of broken headlights and plastic, ones the cops left behind, litter the ground. There's also other trash thrown away by inconsiderate drivers: plastic soda bottles, cigarette butts, a red sock. People throw out just about anything and never worry about the consequences.

The tree is huge and old and has a big gash in it. Hard to believe a car could hit this massive thing with any kind of force and still have survivors inside.

I stop a few feet from the tree. The rain continues to drizzle, pinging against my face and head. The wind blows a little, stirring up the fallen leaves, ruffling the notes and making a tiny stuffed bear shimmy on the ground.

I stand there on the edge of the road, close my eyes, and put my mind to work. I remember getting ready. I remember Dad helping me with my tie. I remember going to eat at Hannah's house by the lake. It was a fancy meal—some kind of Italian chicken—prepared by their housekeeper.

I remember the early part of the dance, walking into the gym and hearing the music. I remember dancing with Chloe at least once. Maybe twice.

And then…

Nothing.

My head starts to ache again.

I try to imagine what it must have been like when we walked out to the parking lot and headed for the car. Ron says we argued, but that doesn't fit what I know about us. And I have no idea what we could have been arguing about…unless it was about having sex again that night.

But I can imagine driving the route I just took—away from the school and through the cornfields. Then through the trees and out to where I stand.

It was a warm night. No rain. No wind.

Me driving. Chloe looking beautiful in the passenger seat.

At some point we came to this stretch of 250. The headlights would have illuminated the side of the road, the ditches and the weeds, the debris and the leaves.

Did an animal jump out? Was it a deer like the ones I just saw?

Or did something come rushing at us?

That's when something in my mind clicks over. Like a flash…

The pain disappears…

I'm no longer imaging. *I'm remembering.*

The tree illuminated by the headlights.

The tree growing larger and larger.

We can't stop.

We're out of control.

It's too late—

"Hunter!"

She calls my name.

Screams my name.

I put my hand out to brace her.

"Hunter!"

I yell something, a primal cry of fear.

My eyes spring open.

Chloe's dad, Scott Summers, is standing in front of me, and he's looking at me, face distressed like I'm completely out of my mind.

# THIRTY-SEVEN

IT'S LIKE EMERGING FROM A DARK CAVE.

I take in giant gulps of air. It came back. Something from that night came back. I saw it. I *remembered* it. The moment before we hit the tree.

"Hunter? Are you okay?"

Scott moves closer, eyeing me the way someone would watch a strange dog that might bite. Scott's body is turned sideways a little, crouched like he's ready to spring into action. Either to protect himself or to run away.

My heart pounds faster than ever. It takes a moment for my breath to return to normal.

"Hunter?"

"I'm okay," I say. "I was just…" I look into his eyes. "I saw it. I saw a part of the crash I've never seen before. I mean that I've never remembered before."

"Really?" Scott looks skeptical. And still looks cautious, although he straightens up some. "Just now, you remembered something?" He looks intensely curious, and his voice sounds urgent. "What did you see?"

"The last moment before the car hit the tree. It came in a flash. And...something... I don't know, it came at us before we hit. From the left side."

"Another car?" he asks.

"I don't know. When I was coming here, three deer were on the side of the road. I scared them. I wonder if a deer jumped in front of us that night. Is that why we swerved?"

Scott takes a couple of steps closer. "That certainly could be. The cops put that forward as one theory."

"I know. I wish I'd seen more."

"Didn't the doctors say you might have memories coming back?"

"Yes. But that's the first time one did. So maybe there are more."

"You think this could open the floodgates?" he asks.

"I hope so."

"Yes," he says, sounding distracted. "I hope so, too."

My eyes pass over every detail of the scene. If one moment came back, maybe more will if I just look hard enough. Maybe I can jump-start my memories, shock them back into my brain.

But nothing else comes to me. Just the same blackness, except for that small flash.

My fists are clenched in frustration. My fingernails dig into my palms, almost breaking the skin.

"Are you okay, Hunter?" Scott asks. "Seriously. Should you be in school? Or…"

His question brings me back to the moment. "I'm home today," I say. "Maybe for a long time. Going to the school…with everything going on."

"Yeah, right." Scott sounds understanding. "Are you wondering why I'm out here?"

"No. I guess maybe you're out here for the same reason I am."

"I think you're right," Scott says. "I'm remembering Chloe. Not that night, since I can't know what she went through, but it is a way for me to feel closer to her. This is the last place…"

He doesn't cry or wipe at his eyes. But he does turn away from me and toward the trees. I've never known what to say to the man, and I really don't now. The last time I was in his presence, his wife called me out over Chloe's disappearance. Maybe Scott shares her opinion, but that and his grief make it difficult to think of something to say.

And I don't want to make small talk.

"Have the police come up with anything new?" I ask.

Scott doesn't look back at me. "Nothing. There's never anything new. It's all just a nightmare that doesn't end. Like one of those dreams about falling, except this is real life and I never hit the ground."

"I'm sorry," I say. And I mean it.

He glances back at me. "I know you've been dealing with a lot, too. What Laura said the other night at that vigil…she's…Laura is struggling with everything. It's my job to help her through this, to *protect* her. To protect my family. It's not easy. Her sister's with her now, so I decided to take a drive. Just to have a moment."

"Me, too."

Scott looks at his car. "I need to get back."

"I guess you heard about my friend Daniel."

Now Scott turns back. "Yes, I did. I heard the two of you were close. I'm sorry."

"Thanks."

"I also heard he was making some kind of stupid movie about Chloe, about—" He gestures to the gashed tree and the memorial and then to everything surrounding us. "About all of this. I think that sounds really ignorant. The police don't need some high school kid getting in the middle of everything and stirring up the pot. He should just…should have just let the cops handle it."

"I think he was trying to help."

"It doesn't help," he says, his voice getting louder. "It's like you and those videos you've made. I've seen them. Everybody's seen them. Laura's watched them and is getting madder and madder. They don't help. They just get people stirred up and angry. I never understood why you kids feel the need to share so much. Every damn thought you have goes online. I just don't get it."

"I'm trying to find out if anybody knows anything. I want to find Chloe."

"Well, I'm not sure videos help." He shakes his head. "We're all just at the mercy of what happens. You can try to grab hold and steer as much as possible. You can try to take control, but sometimes it just slips away, spiraling fast, like water down a drain."

He stops talking abruptly. I'm not really sure what he's talking about.

Something crosses his face, a look of recognition. "I'm sorry. I...wait. I want to ask you something." He points at me. "The police keep asking us about Chloe's journal. We didn't know she even had one. Did you tell them about it?"

"I did."

"Did you tell them where she kept it?" he asks.

"I don't know where she kept it. It must be in her room somewhere, right?"

He shakes his head. "It's not. The cops have been all through our house. They've been through everything. Our bank records. Our computers and phones."

"She never told me where she kept it," I say. "And I don't have it, if that's what you're wondering. The police have been all through our house, too. They went through my drawers and my closet, lifted up my mattress and looked underneath. I can't think of where it might be."

He watches me, his eyes like a hawk's. And I'm the mouse on the ground being tracked. "And you never read it?"

"Never."

"Damn it all," Scott says.

"I thought the cops would have found it by now. And I thought it would tell us something. That's why I told them about it in the first place. I wouldn't want anyone going through Chloe's private things unless I thought it would help us find her."

"Yeah, I know." He turns to the trees again, as if I'm not there.

"Scott," I say. "Can you tell Laura, can you…I mean, you know I wouldn't hurt Chloe. I would never."

He keeps staring, and I'm not sure if he's heard me. But then he says, "I know that. But…Laura's in a different place." He turns to me. "Speaking of her, I have to go. Hunter, just take care of yourself. Okay?"

I should stay quiet, but I can't waste the chance to talk to someone who knows Chloe so well. "Maybe she ran off," I say. My voice sounds hopeful, like a little kid wishing for a new bike at Christmas, something they're starting to fear they'll never get. "Maybe that's what happened."

"In a homecoming dress? With no shoes? And no purse?"

"Maybe somebody met her," I say.

"Who?" Scott asks. "You're her boyfriend."

"What about Mike Basher? He's always hanging around your house."

"Mike?" Scott's eyes narrow, and his cheeks flush. "Are you suggesting something?"

"I'm just saying, he wasn't over her. Maybe he wanted her back."

"Michael is a fine young man. I know all about the drama around that stupid poem he wrote. Chloe was upset, and I told Mike he used poor judgment. But he was sorry, and he apologized. Leave him out of this."

"Maybe…" I can't think of any more maybes. I lift my arms and then let them fall to my sides, where they smack against my thighs. "If she'd just come back, I wouldn't care who she was with or what she was doing."

Scott shuts his eyes and keeps them closed. He looks like a knife has been slipped between his ribs and he's riding out a wave of intense pain.

I wish I'd kept my mouth shut.

His eyes open, and he nods like he's reached some agreement with himself.

"I guess we all wish we could rewind and go back to that night," he says. "We could just stop Chloe from leaving the house that night. We could make her come straight home after the dance. We could have driven her." He sighs. "Like I said, I have to go."

As he walks away, I say, "I didn't recognize your car."

He goes to the driver's side, tugs the door open. "It's a rental." He points to the tree. "Obviously. The Charger is…"

I feel stupid for saying anything.

But then Scott says, "If any other memories come back, let me know. Okay?"

"I will."

"Seriously, let me know the minute you remember something. Anything."

Then he's in the car with the door closed. I stand beside a waterlogged stuffed bear and watch him drive off.

# THIRTY-EIGHT

DAD'S TRUE TO HIS WORD. HIS CAR IS IN THE DRIVEWAY by the time I get home.

He's skipped afternoon office hours and anything else he might have needed to do on campus. This is a rare thing—like seeing a comet streak across the sky. Dad never skips work, never comes home early unless one of us is sick or needs something we can't get from anyone else. I guess I'm that something now.

Dad's at the kitchen table with his glasses pushed up on top of his head and a stack of exams spread out before him. He holds a red pen and is scribbling away, his tongue poking out the corner of his mouth. I worry he's too caught up in his work, but he stops writing and looks up.

He flips the glasses in place, magnifying the size of his eyes.

"Are you okay?" he asks. His voice is calm. As flat as a pond.

"Yes, I am. In fact, something good happened."

He touches the corner of his mouth with his index finger. The overhead light reflects off his glasses, making it tough to see his eyes.

"I want you to hear something." He's still using his calm voice.

"Okay. But I want to tell you something, too. Dad?"

He walks over to the kitchen counter. Some bills are stacked there, and a couple of history and news magazines Dad subscribes to. Everything is in neat piles.

He reaches for the landline. Dad has always said he likes to keep it in case the grid goes out. I always tell him that if all the cell phones stop working, we'll have problems so big the landline isn't going to help us. But Dad says it's ten bucks extra a month, so what do I care? Only telemarketers call, and most of the time, we just don't answer.

"What is it?" I ask.

"Listen," he says. He hands me the receiver and hits a button. "Go ahead."

I've never made a call on the landline in my life, and the phone feels odd in my hand. It's like I'm using a shoe or a rock and expecting to talk to other people. But I humor Dad and put the thing to my ear.

It beeps. A sound like something from a cheap sci-fi movie.

Then a husky voice speaks.

*You're a killer. Everybody knows you're a killer. Stop with the videos. Stop trying to—*

Dad hits the button. Another beep.

*I think those videos are a disgrace—*

Another beep.

*I'm praying you see your way to stop making videos so you*

*can confess to killing that poor girl so her family can give her a Christian burial—*

Dad takes the receiver and replaces it in the cradle.

"There are about ten more like that," he says when he turns back to me. "They'd finally tapered off after you posted the first video. Now that you made this one, it's open season again. And I didn't mention this before because I didn't want to add to your problems, but now the crazies have been emailing me at work and calling my office. I had to alert campus security."

"Why are you telling me all of this?"

"So you know you have to be careful, Hunter," he says. "There are a lot of nuts out there, and they certainly know where we live. Your sister still has to go to school. Hell, you're supposed to be in school. You should be doing your homework instead of going out. That's dangerous, too. It's a school day."

"Sorry," I say.

"I'm trying to protect you," he says. "And Livvy. But you're making it awfully tough."

"Just forget it," I say. "I'll be in my room."

"No more videos," he says, pointing at me. "You hear?"

"Do *you* hear?" I ask. "Did you even hear what I said when I came in?"

He pauses for a moment, considers me. "Okay, yes, I did hear you say you had something to tell me. What is it?"

"You really want to know? Are you sure it's not more important than the phone or the voicemail?"

"Hunter. What is it?"

I think about not telling him, but I want *him* to know.

"I remembered part of the accident today, Dad. I saw it. I saw what I hadn't been able to remember before."

Dad's face shifts. The lines go out of his forehead. He takes a step toward me. "Hunter, that's great. What did you—"

"Just forget it," I say. "It's not as important as the deranged phone calls."

"I didn't say that. Now just tell me—"

I brush past him, heading for the stairs.

"Hunter, don't be like that."

But I don't respond. And just to be a real dick, when I get upstairs, I slam my bedroom door.

# THIRTY-NINE

I FLOP ONTO THE BED, AVOIDING EYE CONTACT WITH THE stack of schoolbooks on my desk. It might as well be Mt. Everest. I *wish* I could lose myself in something as inconsequential as school, but I can't.

Instead, I pull out my phone.

I scroll to the message from Daniel. The one he sent me the night he died.

The one he must have sent me *right before* he died.

It makes me feel empty. Like I'm floating away.

I almost put down the phone and ignore the video, but I can't. This is what he so desperately wanted me to see. This is what meant so much to him. I owe him this.

I've seen the beginning already. But this time I'm not impatient or irritated. The poor quality and the clichés don't bother me. Instead, I think about the time it must have taken him to put the video together. The way he clearly selected the best photos of Chloe, of me, of the two of us together. The way his words—while occasionally predictable—also seem to be chosen with care and spoken in a thoughtful, sensitive manner.

Daniel's voice speaks to me from the past, summoning a million memories. Playing tag in our backyard until it grew dark. Eating frozen pizza on nights I slept at his house. The time we went trick-or-treating dressed as Harry Potter and Ron Weasley.

Tears fill my eyes. I wipe them away just as the voice-over stops.

I think that's the end, but when my vision clears, I see that the video is still going. The images look rough. Maybe this is the part Daniel hadn't worked on as much as the rest.

He promised something would blow my mind, but it isn't here. It's just random images of town, the road, the accident site, and the memorial.

But then the images end, and the screen goes dark.

This time, I really do think it's over. I'm about to put the phone down when the progress bar at the bottom tells me there are still five minutes to go.

Is it five minutes of black?

Curious, I keep watching. The screen flickers, and an image returns. It takes a minute. The image is dark and kind of grainy. It's a shot of the night sky. Blackness and stars. A light post.

Then the camera levels, showing rows and rows of cars. And then a building.

I straighten. It's the parking lot behind the school. At night.

There are lots of cars. Streamers and balloons cover the entrance to the gym, lifting and bobbing in the wind.

Homecoming. The night of the accident. The night Chloe disappeared.

My spine is rigid. My hand grips the phone so tight, my knuckles hurt.

The shot lingers on the gym doors for a few long seconds. The counter on the bottom continues to turn. Is this it? Is anything else going to happen?

But then the doors are thrown open and it's Chloe who emerges.

# FORTY

HER DRESS IS LIGHT BLUE. SLEEVELESS.

Exactly as I remember it.

Her hair is pulled back. Two intentionally loose strands frame her face. The blue corsage is still on her wrist. It's there when she brushes her hair out of her eyes. She walks briskly away from the door and stops after fifteen feet.

She crosses her arms. She looks unhappy. Beautiful, but unhappy.

The door flies open again, and there I am. Wearing a white shirt, a yellow tie that Dad helped me knot, navy pants, and brown shoes. I walk up to Chloe and spread my arms wide as if asking her *what's the matter?*

She looks at me for a long moment, but then she starts walking away.

There's no sound. We move across the little screen like actors in a silent movie.

Then Chloe stops. She turns and looks back at me. She's

upset. She's pointing at me as she says something. Or is she pointing at the gym? At something inside?

My arms go up again, and Chloe spins and starts to walk away. She's moving fast. Almost running.

I follow her, my arms still wide. Pleading. We go between the parked cars, the bottom halves of our bodies disappearing. But I can still see my arms. My mouth moving as I say something to Chloe. We don't look angry. We look…confused? Unhappy? She looks like she's trying to convince me to leave.

The camera pans and follows us. Whoever is filming—Daniel, I presume—moves so quickly. The camera shakes with his steps.

Eventually we stop on the driver's side of the car. Her face is a mask of hurt. It's so rare, I can't tell if she's crying.

I repeatedly point back at the school—like I want to go there.

Finally, Chloe throws up her hands and dashes around the back of the car. She opens the passenger door, her head disappearing from view as she gets in.

I get in behind the steering wheel.

A few long moments tick by.

Is that it? Are we just going to sit in the car?

But I know all too well what's to come. I know how the story has to end.

The car springs to life. We back out. Furiously. The brake lights are an angry red in the darkness. Then we shoot forward, barreling toward the exit and our collision course with that tree.

The car fades into the distance.

And the movie cuts, like the camera was turned off.

I figure *that's* the end. And I'm ready to put it aside.

I exhale. It's over.

Suddenly the movie starts again. The camera is back on, recording. It makes a quick pan to the right, picking up something else.

Another car zips across the parking lot, flying right up behind, like it's chasing us.

# FORTY-ONE

I REWIND THE VIDEO AND WATCH THE ENDING AGAIN. Again, and again, and again.

I study every part of the screen. But it's impossible to see any detail. It's a car. A dark car on a dark night. There's no way to see the driver, to even tell the make or model. Forget about getting the license plate number.

But maybe someone else can see more. Maybe the cops.

I spring off the bed and throw open my door. Dad's heading toward my room, as if he's read my mind.

But he looks surprised to see me.

"Dad? This…" I hold the phone between us. "This video. The one Daniel made. It shows Chloe and me on the night of the dance."

"What video Daniel made? What are you talking about?"

"The movie," I say. "Daniel's movie."

"I don't—never mind. You have to come downstairs."

"Dad, we have to tell the police. We have to make sure they're see this. They can enhance it or whatever. Let's call them."

"There's no need, Hunter," he says.

"What are you talking about? This is evidence. This shows what happened the night of the dance. Of course we have to call them."

Dad's shaking his head. "Something's going on, and they want to talk to you again. They're on their way right now. And I've got a call in to the lawyer."

"What happened?" I ask.

"I have no idea."

I can show them the video. If they can figure out who followed us that night, they might be able to figure out who ran us off the road. And whoever ran us off the road must be the person who took Chloe.

Instead, I feel deflated. If the cops are coming over, that means they have more questions. What could they possibly ask me that they haven't already?

Dad starts back down the stairs, but he hesitates when he sees I'm not following.

"What is it?" he asks.

I slump against the wall, the phone still in my hand. "I don't know."

He comes toward me. "What don't you know?"

"I don't know if I can do this anymore. I don't know if I can handle the cops asking me a bunch of questions that I don't know the answers to. Just thinking about it makes me feel worn out."

Dad nods his head. "I understand. You know, you don't have to answer any questions if you don't want."

"And then what?"

"You run the risk that it makes you look guilty."

"That's not how it's supposed to work," I say. "We just studied this in civics."

"I know." He stands with his hands in his pockets. For a moment, I think the awkwardness will descend over us. But when Dad speaks, his voice is clear and determined, and I imagine this is what he's like in class when he really gets going on some subject he feels passionately about. "When your mom was sick, we just kept going to all these different doctors. You probably remember some of it. And every time we went, I thought one of them was going to tell us something we hadn't heard before. I thought one of them was going to give us some piece of good news that was going to make her better. After a long time of only hearing bad news, I dreaded each trip. I just didn't want to hear any more bad news from people who were supposed to be helping us."

"But you kept going. Mom fought until the end."

"She did. She wanted to. She wanted to be here for you and Livvy. She really did." Because she wanted to try as hard as she could. Because I loved her. And I wanted her to stay with us as well." He looks at the floor and scuffs his foot over some minuscule piece of dust. "I guess we keep on going when we love somebody. As long as there's a chance…"

He starts back down the hall and says over his shoulder, "Just tell the truth, Hunter. And I'll be right there with you. And show them the video. You never know…"

# FORTY-TWO

DAD OFFERS DETECTIVE HALEY SOMETHING TO DRINK when he comes in, and Haley declines.

He's wearing dark pants and a white shirt with the sleeves rolled up to his elbows. No jacket or tie this time. There's some redness in the whites of his eyes, but his jaw is set firm like he means business. He holds a manila folder—the kind of thing people carry around in offices on old TV shows.

He speaks to Dad. "You understand Hunter can have his lawyer present. Those rights I read him the last time still apply."

"Our lawyer let me know she's in court," Dad says. "If I don't like your line of questioning, I'll stop it."

Haley lets out a sigh. "That's your right as well."

"I know."

The bickering and arguing tires me out. "Just ask your questions," I say. "And when you're done, I have something I want to show you."

"You do?" Haley asks.

"Yes."

Suddenly Haley looks curious, and his posture becomes straighter. "Okay, then. First things first. We've already discussed the fact that you and Chloe were sexually intimate."

My face burns. Dad is right there, and without even meaning to, my eyes cut to him. His face shows nothing, but he nods at me, indicating that I should answer the question.

"Once."

"One time about a month before the homecoming dance."

"That's right."

"And you said you used protection, right? A condom?"

"He's been over all of this with you," Dad says. "Chapter and verse."

Maybe Dad has my back. Or maybe he doesn't want to watch his teenage son squirm through another examination of his sex life. Either way, I'm glad he's here.

"I just need to make sure we agree on basic facts, Hunter," Haley says, an edge creeping into his voice.

"Yes, that's right," I say.

"And you said that, as far as you know, Chloe wasn't sexually involved with anyone else?"

I get a stinging pain in my chest. "Why are you asking me this? Of course not."

But do I know? Do I know anything for sure?

Why was Chloe acting distant? Why was she so upset the night of the dance?

Why was she afraid at the dance?

Was it Basher?

"But you don't know for sure," Haley says.

"I trusted her. *Trust* her. Completely. We're committed."

Haley reaches for the manila folder. He flips it open in a way that seems practiced. Something about it feels like a performance, like Sherlock Holmes lighting his pipe.

"It's taken us a while to go through Chloe's computer and phone records. It's a slow process, and a hardworking teenager uses her computer a lot. And makes a lot of calls. And sends a lot of texts. And we're kind of understaffed. The state has been helping us, of course, but we don't have an unlimited supply of computer technicians."

He picks up a stack of papers from the folder and tilts his head back as he refers to them.

"About two weeks after what you say is your first and only intimate encounter with Chloe, she did a number of Google searches about pregnancy. Specifically, she was looking into the likelihood of getting pregnant if a condom broke during sexual intercourse. Did the condom break when the two of you had sex, Hunter?"

Dad's staring at me. His cheeks are flushed. Mine are, too. I did not expect our conversation to head down this road.

Not at all.

"You need to answer me, Hunter," Haley says. "Or we can go back to the station and call the lawyers. You could be there for a lot longer this time. Days, maybe."

"No. I mean... I don't think it did. I guess I'm not sure."

"Chloe also placed a phone call to a pregnancy help line. A nonprofit geared toward young people who might find themselves in psychological trouble or have questions about their bodies. We found a call to that number on her phone. Twice. Around the same time as the Google searches."

"What did she say to this hotline?" I ask, my voice low, although I wasn't trying to be quiet.

"That's just it," Haley says. "These types of places are meant to be anonymous. You don't give your name. They don't record the calls. And they get thousands of calls every month, so to ask a volunteer to remember one specific call is impossible."

"What are you saying?" I ask. Although I know. I obviously know.

"Hunter." Haley scoots forward. His face is a mask of seriousness. "You're running out of chances to be honest with us. But I'm here giving you an opportunity to come clean. So, tell me. Was Chloe pregnant? Were you the father? Is that why you fought at the dance? And did that put so much pressure on you that you felt you had to do something about it?"

# FORTY-THREE

IT'S LIKE A DREAM WHERE I WANT TO SCREAM BUT CAN'T.

There's a big clock with a white face and black numbers above the stove, something Mom picked out a year before she died. It ticks and ticks while all of us sit there saying nothing. Words finally come. "Chloe wouldn't keep that from me. We didn't keep things like that from each other."

The words sound juvenile. Like something spoken by a fool.

Clearly Chloe was keeping things from me. She never mentioned her fears about being pregnant. About the condom breaking. She never told me what was bothering her in the weeks leading up to the dance.

She'd kept me in the dark about a lot.

Haley's face remains blank, even as a muscle twitches in his jaw. "So you're telling me, Hunter, that you don't know anything about this?"

My head shakes. Mind blown.

"Can I ask a question?" Dad says.

Haley ignores him, so Dad just goes on. "Hunter, I can remember when I was young, before Mom and I got married, and I was always worried about getting one of my girlfriends pregnant."

I sit as still as a statue. Dad has never spoken so casually about sex, never implied he had a sex life before Mom. My first instinct is to say, *Please, don't go there*, but Dad is talking to me like I'm an adult. We've crossed some invisible barrier, and it's good.

"What I mean is sometimes I talked about it with my partners," he says. "And, sometimes, we'd talk about what would happen if she became pregnant. What I'm asking is if you and Chloe ever had that kind of talk?"

It fits Dad that he wouldn't jump into sex without examining every possible consequence beforehand. He's not the most impulsive guy in the world.

Chloe and I talked about everything over hundreds and hundreds of conversations. And, yes, leading up to our first—and only—time, we did talk about pregnancy. Chloe was pretty clear. She told me she was *not* going to get pregnant. And if she did, she wasn't going to let it derail her life. She told me about her cousin in Virginia who was at the top of her class, but then got pregnant senior year. She finished high school and had the baby but never went to college. Chloe swore she would never let that happen to her.

"She has two kids now," Chloe said about her cousin. "And no degree. That won't be me."

I relay all this to Haley and Dad. Haley nods, still showing nothing.

"So it sounds like Chloe felt pretty strongly," Haley says. "If she found out she was pregnant, she intended to do something about it."

"Are you saying that's what she ran off to do after the accident?" I ask. "In her dress? And with no money? Or phone? Does that make sense?"

Haley looks thoughtful. He taps his chin with his index finger and studies me through his intense brown eyes. "If Chloe was pregnant, then it would be in both your best interests to keep that from everyone. Parents. Teachers. If Chloe thought a pregnancy would ruin her life, then she might be willing to do anything. Run away for a while. Stage an accident." He leans forward. "Hunter, maybe the two of you got in over your heads. You wanted to make this problem go away, but you got in too deep. And you're looking for a way out."

"That's not what happened," I say.

"Maybe Chloe pressured you," he says. "I bet she was a persuasive girl. Maybe she turned up the heat on you to help her. Maybe you got scared someone would find out. Maybe the two of you disagreed about what to do. Hunter, did you want to have the baby? Is that the problem?"

"I can prove that didn't happen," I say. "I can prove how nuts all of that is."

I pull out my phone, load the video—Daniel's video—and

slide it across the table toward Haley, who pushes his manila folder aside.

"What's this?" he asks. "Oh. Yes, I've seen it."

"You have?" I hit play anyway.

He frowns. "Daniel's mother gave us access to his cloud storage. The rough cut of the movie was there."

"You watched the whole thing?" I ask. "You actually saw the other car following us?"

Haley nods but without much enthusiasm. "Of course. The video is at the state crime lab being analyzed. Unfortunately, the initial results have been inconclusive. They can't identify the make or model of the car yet. And they haven't come close to the plate number. These things take time, but we're doing our best."

"But that's a big lead," I say. "Find that car, and you've got the person who ran us off the road."

Haley shakes his head. "We don't even know if that vehicle was at the scene of the accident."

He looks so certain. Almost smug.

That quick glimpse of the accident jumps back into my mind. The headlights. The tree.

"Let me tell you what I remembered," I say.

# FORTY-FOUR

"I WENT OUT THERE THIS MORNING. TO THE SCENE OF the accident," I say. "I hadn't been out there since that night."

"Why did you go to the crime scene?" Haley asks.

"To see it. I wanted to try to jar something loose in my mind. And it worked."

"Is this what you were telling me when you came home?" Dad asks.

"Yes."

Haley's brow is wrinkled. "How did you feel when you went there? Was it…exciting to you in some way? Did you get an adrenaline rush?"

"Detective," Dad says, "I don't think you—"

"Just hold it," I say to Haley. "Please. Just hold on and listen for once."

I detail the slow drive to the scene, the deer that scattered. Then parking and approaching the tree, that brief piece of memory that raced back into my brain like a flash flood.

"Something happened that night," I say. "Something came at the car from the left side." They're both focused on me, and I feel like a fortune-teller who suddenly starts speaking in tongues, communicating with the other world in order to solve a mystery. Except what I'm describing comes from my own memory. And I'm right here in this world. "It had to be another car. Why else would we go off the road and hit that tree?" I stare right into Haley's eyes. "You've thought all along it was possible there was another car, one that ran us off the road. Well, now you have the video showing the car following us *and* now you have what I remember."

Haley reaches into his pants pocket, brings out his little notebook and a pen that he clicks open with his thumb. He scribbles some things in the book but takes his time speaking.

I push him. "What do you think? Isn't this something?"

He presses his lips together and leans back in his chair. His eyes look wary, cautious. But also curious. He must see the possibilities here.

He has to.

"Okay," he says. "But you said you saw deer when you went driving out there today. Three of them. It's fall. Mating season. There are deer all over that road. Not a night goes by that we don't get a call about a vehicle hitting one. And people sometimes get hurt pretty bad. You may recall a few years ago a woman was killed when she hit a deer. Maybe you saw a deer out of your peripheral. Maybe that caused the accident, and there *wasn't* another car. Maybe Chloe was hurt in the accident. Maybe she was hurt bad. And you saw that, and you knew you were going to get blamed, so you panicked. And you moved her. Just tell us where she is, Hunter. We can work out something."

It sounds so calm and logical coming from Haley. Like nothing could be thrown at the guy that he couldn't bat away. Like he's a world-class Ping-Pong player when it comes to smacking down someone else's ideas.

"He's baiting you, Hunter," Dad says. "Don't say anything. Detective, next you're going to tell us Hunter conspired with a deer to cause the accident."

"We're talking about wild animals," Haley says. "They're unpredictable. Haven't you seen on the news when a deer goes crashing through a store window and then runs around inside, busting up everything? Or how about when someone's out in the woods and a deer goes nuts and attacks them? They're not all peaceful animals."

"This isn't making any sense," Dad says.

Haley leans farther forward. "Okay, so that's unfounded speculation. Let's stick to facts, Hunter. You and Chloe were arguing, witnesses have verified that."

"Okay, you say arguing. To me it looks like I'm trying to *convince* Chloe of something. To go back inside. You don't know it's an argument. I can't say for sure that we're angry."

"Hey, Daniel's movie shows it. Maybe Chloe was too upset to drive, and that's why you got behind the wheel. And maybe you continued to argue—or *convince*—as you drove out into the country. So you're arguing. You're saying heated things to each other." Haley shrugs, tries to look more casual. "Hey, I understand. We've all been there with a partner or a wife. Things get heated. It's *emotional*. Maybe she loses control of herself and makes a grab for you. Distracts you. And, boom, you go off the road."

"Don't say anything to that, Hunter," Dad says.

"I can't say anything to that because it isn't true. Chloe didn't do that."

"But you *don't remember*," Haley says, his words gaining a harsh rhythm as he speaks. "You don't remember anything from the ride except that last moment before impact. So you say. But you have the accident. Chloe's hurt. She's bleeding. Or she's crying. Or… maybe she's unconscious and you panic. This is on your record. An accident. How will that look to the college admissions office at your top choice school? Do they want someone with a record?"

"Okay, don't say anything else, Hunter," Dad says.

Haley leans back. He considers me from across the table like a poker player about to place a large bet. "You *don't* have to say anything, Hunter," he says. "Your dad's right. But let's imagine for a moment you're correct about what you've said. Let's say that car in the video, the one following you and Chloe out of the parking lot, followed you all the way out to the scene of the crash. Let's say that's true. Okay?"

Dad gives me a look that says, *Not a word.*

"But let's also say there's something going on with Chloe.

Something you don't know about. That seems obvious, doesn't it? After all, she was calling a pregnancy hotline. She was upset. Distant. Crying. She thought you'd be really mad about whatever was going on. You've mentioned her ex-boyfriend, the football player. Mike Basher. So maybe, just maybe, that car that followed you, the one that might have—I say *might* have—come alongside you out there... Maybe the person in that car knew Chloe's secret. Maybe the person in that car was *part* of Chloe's secret. They were in on it, and you weren't. Maybe Chloe arranged to meet them out there and that's why she went off with them after the accident."

Haley doesn't frame it as a question. He clicks his pen shut, letting his words hang in the air like a toxic balloon.

Then he stuffs the notebook back into his pocket and gets to his feet. He nods at Dad and me.

"Hunter," Haley says, "this has been a useful talk. I think you see more clearly now some of the possibilities concerning that night. And I hope you know it will always be better for you if you and I talk about these things. If we keep the line of communication open. You can call me any time if you want to talk more about these possibilities."

He turns and goes, leaving me more confused than ever.

# FORTY-FIVE

ONCE HALEY'S GONE, DAD SAYS, "HE'S JUST TRYING TO shake you up. That's a cop's job."

"Then Haley's a very good cop," I say. "Because he shook me."

"Hunter, why don't you—"

"Dad, can I just—I think I want to go to my room."

"Sure, okay. If you need me, I'll be down here. Grading."

My room feels off, a little strange. My thoughts rev like a NASCAR engine. Haley has taken up residence in my brain.

Did Chloe plan to meet someone out there? Was she just using me to drive her away from the school?

I text Hector and Cameron and Chad, seeking human contact. Just asking how they're doing. What's up at school.

Hector claims he misses me in physics because now he's the dumbest guy in the room. Cameron complains about having to buy his own french fries since I wasn't there to steal from. Our conversations linger for a few minutes then die out.

Chad doesn't answer. Soccer consumes them all.

Haley's bombshell—about Chloe possibly being pregnant—thumps in my head, making it ache again. It's such a private thing—if one person found out, then everyone would know. And when Chloe comes back, she's going to have to face all the people who know her most intimate business…

But what if telling the *right* person makes the difference?

But who is the right person?

The next text I send sounds super casual. Hey. How are you?

Natasha writes back immediately, as if she was waiting for me. She asks how I'm doing. She says lunch is boring without me, because Chad is off with Hannah and Cameron and Hector act juvenile.

The exchange seems to have run its course. We almost never talk one-on-one.

I know you talked to the police already, but can you think of anything going on with Chloe?

Then I add: You know, anything weird?

Those three little dots appear. And they sit on my screen forever.

They taunt me. Torment me.

She must have a lot to say.

No. Not really.

That's it?

Nothing about our sex life?

I mean she told me you were going to try to do it again.

Even though I'm alone, my face flushes. But Natasha keeps going.

She was worried about going on the pill. I told her to go for it. I've been on it for a year and don't have any problems. But Chloe was worried.

Chloe shared more with Natasha than I would have guessed. The conversation seems finished. A long time passes without Natasha texting back. My calculus book waits for me. Berning would say something like: *Do you think being a suspect in your girlfriend's murder means you don't have to do your homework?*

The phone dings again. Natasha.

Clo said she could tell you wanted to try again at HoCo. But she didn't think she wanted to. She felt weird about it.

Natasha has my attention.

Weird about what?

Trying again.

Why?

I don't know. She just said sex felt weird to her. She wasn't sure she wanted to do it again. I don't think you did anything. She legit loves you.

She loves me.

But she might have been keeping the biggest secret of her life.

# FORTY-SIX

MY ROOM FEELS LIKE A CELL.

Stale. Confined. The same books. The same walls. The same view out the window of the neighbor's tree, even though it's turning a thousand shades of orange and red. It all feels stale.

I keep thinking about what Natasha said. Sex felt weird to Chloe.

*Weird.*

Why?

*We* talked about it. *We* wanted to do it.

But maybe our wires got crossed and fucked up.

Had she written it all down?

Scott told me the cops had been all through their house. They'd been through her locker, the car, her room.

But what if someone *else* had the journal?

Ron might have it. He encouraged Chloe to keep it, so maybe she turned it in to him. My email to Ron asks him to call, says there's something I forgot to ask that morning when we spoke.

Ten minutes pass. Then fifteen. And twenty. The floorboards squeak as I pace back and forth. Back and forth.

"What the fuck?" I say.

The phone rings, and I jump like someone has shocked me with a defibrillator. The phone almost falls to the floor when I pick it up.

"Hunter," Ron says, "I have a message here to call you. I almost missed it. We have some kind of inane faculty meeting coming up soon."

"I just need to ask you something."

"You sound breathless," Ron says. "Were you running?"

"No. Just…anxious."

"An affliction we all suffer from. Ask away."

"I'm wondering if you have Chloe's journal," I say. "You encouraged her to keep one in Ex Libris, I know that."

"I encouraged you *all* to keep a journal," he says. "I believe Chloe's the only one who actually did it."

Again, it feels like he's jabbed me with a needle. Even though he's right. My attempt at keeping a journal lasted three days. Chloe is the only one who did it. That was Chloe—she didn't do anything halfway.

"Did she turn it in to you?" I ask. "Or show it to you? If we could find that, we might know what's going on."

"Ah, yes," Ron says. "You know, Hunter, those journals are private. A way to work through feelings and ideas."

"That's not the question," I say. "Did she give it to you?"

"That's a really good investigatory notion. And one the police have already explored. They questioned me and specifically asked about the journal, but I've never seen it. Nor do I know where it is."

"That's not what I wanted to hear," I say. Of course the cops have talked to Ron. Of course they asked about the journal. Do I think I'm smarter than they are?

"I know this is difficult, Hunter. I know this is tearing you up inside."

"It is," I say.

"There are a lot of people hurting in Bentley," he says. He sounds sad, as empty as I feel. "It's affecting us all. I have to say, it's gotten under my skin. Why, just last night, I thought I heard someone outside my house. It woke me up. I tromped all around with a tennis racket in hand, checking doors and windows. When I went out to the car this morning, I kept looking over my shoulder like a burglar. It's a sorry thing."

"Yeah, it is."

"You're sure Chloe didn't share these concerns with you? Has your memory made any improvement?"

"A little."

"Really? And did you remember what Chloe was so upset about at the dance?"

"No, just some details of the accident. But maybe it's a start."

There's a long pause on his end of the line. His breathing is deep and steady.

"Ron?"

"Hunter, there's something I've been meaning to tell you. I thought I'd tell you in person, but I'm about to share this with the faculty, so I better tell you here and now."

"Is something wrong?" I ask.

"No. But it's a change. I'm turning in my resignation," he says. "I've been contemplating this move for a while, and it just seems now the time is right. I have an opportunity to go back to my alma mater in Ohio, and, well, it's just hard to say no to a thing like that."

"Oh." It's unexpected. Totally. I flail a little but find a silver lining. "Okay. But that means you'll be here the rest of the year. I mean, until graduation and everything."

"Well, that's just it. This position starts at the semester break. I'll finish the term here, and then I'll be moving on. I know it's a surprise to you, but these transitions are normal in life. And, like I said, it's my chance to go home. My mother still lives there, and she's getting close to ninety. I'd like to be near her for whatever time she has left."

"Right. Of course."

"Hunter, I'm sorry, I must go. I have my meeting to attend. We can talk about this more another time. Please, keep in touch. Okay?"

"Yeah. Sure."

"Excellent. Chloe is smart and capable. Quite remarkable, really. Just have faith that this will be resolved."

# FORTY-SEVEN

AROUND DINNERTIME, SOMEONE KNOCKS ON MY DOOR. Thunderously. Like she wants to break the door down. For someone so small, her fist pounds with the force of a sledgehammer.

And she barges in before I can even answer.

Olivia closes the door behind her. She's wearing Mom's oversized black hoodie that says "New York City." We were supposed to take a family trip to New York the year Mom got diagnosed, but that news ended any chance of a vacation. Dad ordered the sweatshirt online, and we all signed our names on the card. Since Mom died, Livvy's been wearing it around the house, even though it's big enough for another small person to fit inside it with her.

"Time to eat?" I ask.

"No. Dad said he might order sandwiches from Ray's later, but right now he's busy grading. As usual." She rolls her eyes. "I'm thinking I might go vegan. Do you know the way they treat chickens?"

"I'm familiar with it."

"I'm sure Ray doesn't serve anything organic."

"He probably isn't humane enough to pay his employees minimum wage."

"No doubt."

She sits on the edge of my bed and twirls the hoodie's drawstring. She has something to say, but it's not like Olivia to be coy. Or cautious.

"Was today your last day of detention?" I ask.

"Yeah. Whitley told me if I hit anybody else, I'll get suspended. I told him I'd hit anybody who defamed my family. Maybe I shouldn't have said that."

"If you hadn't, then you wouldn't be you."

"True that." She continues playing with the string. "How's the homework going?"

"Is *that* what you came in here to ask? I can tell you want something. Why are you acting so…I don't know…reluctant to spill it?"

She sighs. It's beyond theatrical. "Okay, fine. I talked to Dad, and he told me what the police said. About Chloe maybe being pregnant. I guess he's worried about you."

"So he sent you to check up on me?"

"Pretty much. You know he can't talk about sex stuff."

Dad's trip down memory lane at the kitchen table comes back to me. Details of his adolescent sex life coming out with Detective Haley looking on. Maybe Dad is much more complex than any of us know.

"Chloe never mentioned anything like that to you, did she?" I ask.

Olivia scrunches her face. "Ewww. I never wanted to hear about you and her...you know." Her hands flutter in the air.

"I thought you were so liberated."

"Not about my brother's sex life," she says. "I mean, I figured you guys were doing it. After all, you were together over six months and totally in love. I also figured you two would be completely cautious about birth control and stuff, like you'd be all wrapped in condoms from head to toe. Ewww. Now I just pictured that."

"Thanks."

"Soooo...it's not possible?"

"I don't know, Livvy."

Briefly—and tactfully—I relate my struggles with the condom. Part of my brain feels relieved, and another is fully aware my little sister is hearing intimate details about my sex life. We've talked about a lot, and I mean a lot. We're close—especially since Mom died—but we've never talked about anything like this. But it actually feels kind of right to open up to her in this way. If I add it all up, who do I trust more than Olivia and Dad? Before today, Chloe would have been in that group, even above the two of them, but after everything that's happened, I'm just not sure.

"So you're wondering if Chloe was pregnant?" Olivia says. "Like, maybe it was possible?"

"Maybe."

"Hmmm."

"Did Chloe ever mention Mike Basher to you?" I ask.

"That idiot? No. He's so gross."

"We'd know so much more if we could just find her damn journal. But the cops have searched her locker, the car. They've been all through her house and her room. Why would she keep a journal and then just get rid of it? What's in there?"

Olivia continues to twirl the drawstring. She seems to be twirling with greater intensity, and there's a distant look on her face.

"What?" I ask. "What are you thinking?"

"The cops looked *everywhere* in her house?"

"Of course. They're cops. Why?"

"Did you tell them about her secret hiding place?"

She's joking, right? But the look on her face says something else.

"Olivia, what the hell are you talking about?"

# FORTY-EIGHT

OLIVIA'S MOUTH OPENS BUT NOTHING COMES OUT FOR one of the few times in her life. Then she says, "I–I just assumed you knew."

"How do *you* know?"

She drops the string and holds out her hands, asking me to calm down. "Okay. I'll tell you. But you have to promise not to get mad."

"Mad?"

"Not mad exactly. Just that overprotective big brother shit you do sometimes. You know, where you act like you know more than I do just because you're older, but you really don't, because we all know I'm the smart one."

"Livvy—"

"Okay, okay. So right when the school year started, Gabby's cousin came to visit. You know, the one who was here from San Antonio? Anyway, when she was leaving, she gave Gabby a joint. Just one. And she said we should try it sometime. Well, Gabby couldn't keep it in her house because her mom is so uptight and checks her room all the time, and I didn't want to ask you if it was okay to hide it in here because I knew you'd be all condescending and overprotective."

"I'm supposed to be that way."

"Yeah, I know. But…anyway. I was talking to Chloe about it one day at school, and she said she'd hold it for us. Well, *first* she gave me a lecture about being careful when we smoked it, but then she agreed to hold it. I thought being an only child her parents would be more up in her shit, but Chloe said she had a place in her room where she could stash stuff. A place her parents didn't know about. She called it her secret hiding place." Olivia shrugs as if it's just that simple. "I figured you knew, too. I mean, you smoke, don't you?"

"Sure. But I never kept any in the house. Not that I think Dad would ever look. But Cameron always has weed when it's not soccer season. His brother gets it for him."

"Okay, well, Chloe held our joint until we wanted it."

"So you did smoke it?"

"Ugh. I don't want you to ask that."

"Did you?" I ask.

"Yes. Of course," she says.

"What happened?"

"First, I giggled for thirty minutes straight. Then I just got really hungry. I mean, hungry like I've never been hungry. And, you know, I'm always hungry. Then I curled up in a ball and fell asleep on the floor. Gabby threw a blanket over me and went to bed."

"But you don't know where Chloe kept the weed?"

"No. She just said in her room."

"Damnit." The sun slips away outside the window, leaving the sky orange and red along the horizon. The streetlight out front is coming on, casting a blue glow across the front yard.

"You could just tell the police to search again," Olivia says. "They could really dig in and find the spot."

"Yeah." My breath steams against the window. I turn around, grabbing my chair and moving it closer to the bed so I'm within a foot of Olivia. "There's just one problem with that. If the cops find that journal, then it might tell us—tell everyone—what was going on with Chloe. And what if…"

"What if it makes you look bad? And by bad, I mean guilty. I mean, more guilty."

"Yeah."

Olivia shrugs. "I don't know, Hunter. Isn't that the risk you take?"

"Her mom and the whole school already think I'm guilty."

"Her mom seems pretty bizarre," Olivia says. "What a fake bitch."

"She's worried about her daughter. It's understandable."

"Sure. You're right. Well, she'll get the chance to trash you again tonight."

"What do you mean?"

"Oh, yeah. I forgot you weren't at school. The church Chloe's parents go to is having some kind of dinner tonight. It's a law enforcement appreciation thing, and I guess they're using it to make sure people don't forget about Chloe. The cops and volunteers are searching again this weekend. Massively. They want to get a ton of people out, and they're worried they can't get enough. Dad always says people have short attention spans and start to lose interest."

"I think he's right."

"If they let her mom have a microphone again, she'll probably start railing against you. Talk about people I'd like to punch…"

"What time is this thing?" I ask.

"I don't know. Seven, I guess. Why? Do you want to go and get roasted in person again?"

I can't believe I'm about to say what I'm thinking.

But I say it anyway.

"No, of course not. But it means their house is going to be empty."

# FORTY-NINE

WE RUN INTO DAD IN THE KITCHEN.

He comes out of his office, a red pen stuck behind his ear. He looks surprised to see the two of us leaving.

"Where are you going?" he asks.

Not only is Olivia the most honest person I've ever known, she's also the world's worst liar. On the rare occasions she tries to lie, she stutters and mumbles and ends up sounding exactly like someone who is lying.

If she tries to tell Dad a story, we're doomed.

"Over to Hector's," I say. The lie appears in my mouth like magic. "They invited us. His mom is making fajitas."

"Fajitas?" Dad says the word like he's never heard it before. "I was going to order Ray's."

"Oh, yeah," I say. "Sorry. We won't be gone long."

"How are you doing on that homework?" Dad asks.

"It's slow," I say, telling the truth. "But I made a little dent."

Dad nods. His eyes roam over the two of us, settling on Olivia. She shifts her feet and twirls a strand of hair.

"Why are you going together?" Dad asks.

"I figured you wouldn't want me out alone. Right?"

Dad nods at this. "And your sister can punch someone if there's trouble?"

"Dad, I—"

"Easy, Olivia," Dad says. "Dr. Whitley told me about your little dustup with the lacrosse player. He was actually pretty understanding given the circumstances. Just don't deck anybody else. Got it?"

"Sure, Dad, I was just going with Hunter because—"

"It's Hector's grandmother's birthday," I say, cutting Olivia off. "That's why they're having a little party."

"And Olivia is really close to Hector's grandmother, right?" Dad says.

"They want a lot of people there," I say. "She's turning eighty."

"Okay." Dad studies Olivia for a moment. She presses her lips into a tight line. "Drive safe. Stay together and keep an eye on each other, you hear? And don't stay out long. I don't want you falling so far behind on homework that you can't get out of the hole. I know you have a lot on your mind, but you also need to get back to those college applications."

"Of course, Dad."

And with that, we're out the door—in the car and free.

I drive slowly and carefully, taking my time. Olivia is texting in the passenger's seat.

"I'm going to drive by once we get there," I say. "The cops might be watching the house or something."

"Good idea." She puts her phone in her lap. "Have you ever lied to Dad before? That was pretty badass. Does Hector even have a grandmother?"

"I don't know. Have you ever not talked back to Dad before?"

"Never. It's so unnatural."

"I guess I did lie about stuff I did with Chloe sometimes. You know, where we were going and what we were doing."

"It's none of his business if you're having sex. That's private."

"I thought you hated that word."

"Don't argue with me, Hunter."

"I didn't know talking to you was the same thing as arguing."

"It's none of Dad's business. Okay?"

"It's certainly his business now," I say. "Everything about our sex life came out with the cops. And with Dad right there."

"For real? That's the most awkward thing I've ever heard."

"I think Dad gets it. We're not little kids. You have a girlfriend now."

"Still, it's so weird."

Chloe lives in a subdivision called Brighton Mews. It's about thirty years old and has a lot of winding streets. The houses are all brick ranches, the yards green and perfectly trimmed. Despite having a lot of trees lining the streets, stray leaves and branches never land in anybody's yard. It's like they all magically disappear before they hit the ground. Haley mentioned not feeling comfortable in certain neighborhoods. Brighton Mews would be one of those places. It's awfully, awfully white.

It's just turned dark, and most of the houses are lit up inside and out. Chandeliers over dinner tables, TVs in family rooms, computers in home offices. Everything glows. There are matching pumpkins and cornstalks on nearly every porch, the occasional bedsheet ghost hanging from a tree.

I turn down Chloe's street and take my time, expecting to see a cop car parked right out front. Maybe more than one. What if Chloe came home and no one was there to greet her? What if whoever took her came back?

We cruise by her home, but there's no one out front. A few lights burn inside, but there are no cars in the driveway or at the curb.

"Are you sure they're going out tonight?" I ask Olivia. "Her dad has a gun, you know. He keeps it in a safe, but still. I don't want to get shot."

"Her mom tweeted about it."

"Laura's on Twitter?"

"All the time." Olivia starts tapping her fingers against the door. "All. The. Time."

"Livvy? What is it?"

"Well…you know… she's just on there a lot. You know, saying things. About the case."

"About me?" I ask. "Is that what you're not saying?"

"Yeah. She's keeping your name alive. And, let me tell you, I want some credit. I've managed not to mix it up with her. I mean, I really want to go after her, but I don't. I just don't."

"That's good. We don't need any more gasoline on the fire."

"I know that's what you prefer, but sometimes you just need to light the match, you know? Kaboom."

We go around the block and check the Summerses' house from the back. No cops there, either. No one on foot or any cars. We go around two more times and still see nothing.

"You're sure her window will be open?" Olivia asks.

"It always is. The lock's been broken for years. That's how Chloe used to sneak out. Or how I would get in. Her parents even know about it."

"They might have fixed it after...you know, after she was gone."

"I guess so," I say. "But if your daughter disappeared without her keys, and you knew there was a way for her to get back in, would you get it fixed? Maybe you'd leave it broken just in case?"

# FIFTY

WE PARK TWO BLOCKS AWAY. WE SIT IN THE CAR AND GO over the plan one more time.

"If you see anybody coming," I say, "and I mean *anybody*, then you text me or call right away. I'll have the phone set to vibrate. Okay?"

"You already told me this," she says. "I get it."

"You're sure?"

"We're not landing at Normandy, Hunter."

"Okay, if you're sure…And if you want to back out…"

"Uhhh, you're my brother, so we're in this together. Okay? And the cops have to read you your rights and let you call a lawyer if there's trouble. No matter what. Do you understand?"

"Yes," I say. "I've seen *Law & Order*."

We walk back toward the Summerses' house. Someone is burning leaves, and there's a smoky scent floating on the light breeze. The stars are out, like crisp and clear pinpoints in the dark sky. We move slowly, side by side, and except for our lack of costumes, I could imagine we were back in time, back to some previous Halloween when Olivia and I went trick-or-treating together. But we're both in high school now, and we've been through too much for the illusion to last.

We're half a block from the Summerses' when something rustles in the bushes to my left. It sounds like a dog, maybe a giant one about to bite us. But then a person climbs out wearing dark clothes, and I jump back, not sure if I should run or prepare to fight.

"Easy," a familiar voice says.

The figure steps forward and gives Olivia a hug.

"Gabby?" I ask.

"It's me," she says.

"What are you doing here?" I ask.

"Liv texted me. She said you needed backup."

"Livvy…" The more people who know…

"She can watch the back while I watch the front," Olivia says. "I can't cover the whole place alone."

"Gabby, I don't want you getting in any trouble. You don't have to stay."

"Oh, I'm going to stay. Look, I'm dressed in black." She points to her leggings and sweatshirt. "And I brought my switchblade."

"Your what?"

"I'm kidding, Hunter. Chill. I don't have a switchblade. Don't you know immigrants commit crimes at a lower rate than natural-born citizens?"

"I don't care about that," I say. "But Olivia shouldn't be dragging you into this. It's not a game."

Gabriela places her hand on my arm. "Hey, I'm here for you, Hunter. Don't worry."

"Okay," I say. "Thanks. But if there's any trouble—if the cops come or whatever—then just run. Forget about me and get out of here. Both of you."

"You got it, boss," Olivia says. Then she leans in and kisses Gabriela. "I'll miss you, my love."

Gabriela rolls her eyes, and they head to their posts. I give them a few minutes to get positioned, and then I cut through the next-door neighbor's backyard, heading toward the window into Chloe's bedroom. The same window I've climbed through dozens of times when she was waiting on the other side.

# FIFTY-ONE

I CROSS THE YARD, CROUCHED DOWN, MOVING LIKE A
soldier in a war movie.

Except I'm no soldier. My way of ducking across Chloe's
property might make me hard to see, or it might make me stand
out like a firework in the night sky.

I reach the back of the house and the windows to Chloe's
bedroom. There are two of them. They're fairly large, side by side.
Chloe always said she was glad she didn't have any siblings to
fight her for the bedroom with the big windows. She also liked
that her parents' bedroom was on the other side of the house,
separated from Chloe's by the kitchen and the living room.
She—and we—always had a lot of privacy on her end of the
house, which was something I liked, too.

The left window is the one with the broken lock. I've opened
it dozens of times, so I don't even have to think. Using my fingers,
I push the screen up as high as I can. I place my hands on the
wooden frame and start to push it as well.

At that moment, a shout comes from next door.

I drop to the ground like someone has fired a gun. I lie there, frozen, the grass tickling my nose, the rich scent of damp earth filling my nostrils.

Was it Olivia? Gabriela? But why would they shout?

The person yells again.

"Trevor?"

"What, Mom?"

"Get in here right now."

My held breath escapes. Just a kid getting chased inside by his mom. Although I never knew his name, I've seen that kid, Trevor, playing in his yard many times.

I pick myself up, brush the grass and twigs off my clothes, and return to the window. I get a good grip on the frame again and push. As the window moves up it makes a squealing sound I never noticed before. It's a surprise because the window used to have the opposite problem. It was so loose it would just slide closed behind me without anyone touching it. Or is it possible I never noticed the squeak because the stakes were never this high? How would it look if I got caught inside Chloe's house now? What would everyone think?

I push the window farther up, even though it sounds like a chorus of banshees howling in the night.

Now the hard part.

The part I'm not really sure I can do alone.

Every other time I came over, Chloe was there, waiting for

me. And when I boosted myself up, she would grab me by the arms and help pull me in. Chloe is strong. She's almost as tall as I am. She's lean and fit. When she'd grab my arms as I pulled myself up, I could feel the strength in her grip.

Conversely, when Chloe snuck out of the house to see me, it was easy. She'd just jump out, and I'd steady her when she landed.

All of a sudden, I wonder—had she been sneaking out of the house to meet someone else?

Had she helped someone else in to see her?

It doesn't matter now. Tonight, I have to do it by myself. I have to jump up, pull myself in, and swing all my body weight over the sill without anyone helping me.

Olivia or Gabriela could give me a boost, but they can't be that close to the house. If something goes wrong and the police come, they can still avoid them. This is my mess and my plan.

I let out a deep breath, like a diver on the high board, and leap for the opening.

Both hands grip the sill. My forearms hit the frame. My feet push against the brick to try to propel my body up, digging for purchase, my sneakers scraping, gaining some traction. My body moves up slowly, and I arch my back like an inchworm and keep going. Once I'm over the sill, I take hold of the small end table just below the window inside Chloe's room with a lamp on it and use it to pull myself forward.

But just as make some headway, the table slides toward me across the hardwood floor, and my body weight goes backward.

The lamp tips over and crashes. Thank goodness it's not ceramic. My heart jumps, and I grab for anything. But I only get air, and I'm starting to go back out the window again like a falling piano.

# FIFTY-TWO

MY ARMS GO OUT AND CATCH THE SIDES OF THE WINDOW frame.

My biceps scream in protest as I hang there, suspended like a poor imitation of Spider-Man.

"Crap," I say. "Holy crap."

It's not far to fall, but I don't want to have to start all over again. I'm not sure I can get myself out of the position I'm in, either. *And* I've now made enough noise that if anyone is listening, they'll definitely know something is up.

Then the mom from next door starts again.

"Trevor?"

"Oh, shit," I say.

"Don't you dare, Trevor," the woman says.

"I'm going to the Summerses' house, Mom."

My legs pump, my shoes searching for some traction, but it's not enough.

"Trevor. Come back here this instant."

*Go away, Trevor,* I think. *Go the hell away.*

"Okay, Mom."

I dig with my feet and then pull harder against the edges of the window frame. I reach out far enough to grab the leg of Chloe's desk. It's solid oak, made by her grandfather, and there's no way it's going to move. It's like gripping an anchor.

I pull and pull until my body slides over the sill. When my waist hits the frame, I know I'm home free. I slide the rest of the way and tumble onto the floor of Chloe's bedroom with a loud thump.

If anyone is home, it's all over. I might as well prepare myself for handcuffs.

But I'm too tired to care.

I lie on the floor in the dark, my chest rising and falling. When my breathing finally slows, I get up.

And then it hits me. I'm standing in Chloe's room. I'm standing in Chloe's room, but no one knows where she is.

Everything is so familiar. The white comforter, the yellow striped pillows, the gray walls. The novels she's read and loved: *Eleanor and Park, Their Eyes Were Watching God, The Fault in Our Stars.* A photo of her parents on their wedding day. A photo of us at the lake, the one on my phone. A pair of black Converse sneakers by her closet door. The familiar scent that can't be found anywhere else in the house. Something soft, almost fruity. Something that let me know I was in Chloe's room with Chloe.

But nothing is the same. Not by a long shot.

I want to soak it all in. Get in the bed, pull the blankets and pillows around me, and pretend she's there with me like so many times before. The space holds so many memories. The word "shrine" jumps into my head, but I push it away. No shrines. No memorials. Those are for dead people.

And Chloe isn't dead.

I tell myself to focus and get to work. Time is short, and I can't just stand around in a house I've basically broken into.

Okay, I think. The secret hiding place.

It can't be in the closet, under the bed, or in one the drawers. Those places are all obvious, and the cops would have turned them inside out right away. It has to be someplace else, someplace more obscure.

I spin in a slow circle, searching. It's dark, but my eyes are beginning to adjust. I've spent enough time in this room to know nearly every inch of it. But that doesn't mean I can discover a hiding place that's meant to be hard to find.

Could it be hidden under the floorboards? The room is carpeted from wall to wall. I go to the corner to see if the carpet comes up, but it doesn't move. I try the other three corners with no luck.

I drop down on all fours and look under the bed, the flashlight on my phone shining at the underside of the mattress. Maybe Chloe tucked it under there. There's nothing besides dust balls and a lone yellow sock.

It all seems hopeless. A terrible idea I never should have tried. I curse myself for not remembering more about the accident, for not coming up with a better plan than to break into Chloe's house and try to find something that may not even be there.

But then it gets worse.

Much, much worse.

I'm still under the bed, cursing myself, when my phone vibrates.

A text from Olivia.

Chloe's parents. Pulling in now! GET THE F OUT!!

# FIFTY-THREE

WHEN I STAND UP, MY HEAD BANGS AGAINST THE EDGE OF the metal bedframe.

It's a sharp, jarring pain, one that causes starbursts to appear before my eyes.

*No. No. No more head pain…*

I wince. The pain eases, so I start around the bed for the open window. I grab the lamp and the end table I'd knocked over and stand them back up. My movements are frantic and urgent, the blood rushing in my ears like a roaring wave. When I let go of the lamp, my hand gets tangled in the cord, and it starts to fall again. I catch it before it hits the floor.

Once I'm sure it's steady, I turn back to the window.

But it's closed.

It slid shut like it always does.

"Damn it."

My phone buzzes, but I ignore it.

I try to work my fingers into the small space between the

bottom of the window and the sill. I can barely do it. A splinter pierces my index finger, and I pull my hand back.

"Shit."

My phone buzzes again. And again. I know it's Olivia. Or Gabriela. Do they think if they text me over and over it will make me move any faster? Do they think I don't recognize the urgency of the situation?

My heart does. The roaring wave is now a tsunami.

I work my fingers back into the narrow space.

That's when I hear it. A door slams in the house. Followed by voices. Two of them.

"Are you just going to sit in there again? Is that really for the best?"

It's Scott. His voice muffled by the closed bedroom door. But it's him.

And then Laura, her voice closer. "I'll do whatever I want. This is my daughter's room. I'll sit here all night."

"You're already sleeping in there," Scott says. "You spend all your time in this room."

"You spend all your time going out to your garage. You're out there now more than ever. Is that how you're staying sane? Do you have a problem with me staying relatively sane my own way?"

"No, honey. I don't. I just…that event tonight…"

"I don't give a damn about the event. What do I care about the police? What are they doing to bring Chloe home? Detective Haley couldn't find his ass with a funnel."

They're right outside the door.

I have a choice to make. And a split second to make it.

I push the window down gently, shutting the quarter-inch gap I've been trying to work open. Then I take two quick, long strides across the carpet to Chloe's closet, pulling it open and slipping inside. I ease the door shut just as Chloe's bedroom door opens, and I crouch on the bottom of the closet between the shoes and a basket of laundry.

The doors are slatted, so when Laura flips the overhead light on some of it leaks through. But the slats are at an angle, so no one can see in unless they open the door. I hold my breath, willing every muscle in my body to freeze.

The bedsprings squeak. And then two thumps as she kicks off her shoes.

"I'm sorry that was so hard," Scott says. "I shouldn't…if you want to sit in here, that's fine."

"Thank you."

"Can I get you something?"

"No. Thank you."

"Okay. I'm going to check the voicemail."

Scott leaves, and I try to make my body as small as a dust bunny. I want to be insignificant or, better yet, invisible.

The bedsprings squeak again. I hear Laura's soft footsteps against the carpet. They get louder. She's coming to the closet. Her silhouette rises through the slats.

My body tenses. Every muscle clenches like they're made of wires and bands stretched to their breaking point.

Laura is right outside.

"What are you doing?"

Scott again.

"I don't know," Laura says. "I just like to look at Chloe's things. Her clothes still smell like her."

"Detective Haley called. He said he's sorry he missed us at the church."

"Screw him," Laura says.

"He's doing his best."

"Did you fix the closet?" Laura asks.

"The closet? What about it?"

"The hole in the plaster. Remember? She threw her boot in there last winter and made that hole? You were so pissed when she did it. Remember?"

"Oh, yeah. That."

Scott sounds confused. But also like a guy who doesn't want to admit he knows what his wife is talking about.

"Did you fix it, Scott?" Laura asks.

"Not yet. It doesn't seem like the most important thing."

"I want you to fix it," Laura says. "I want everything perfect for when she comes home. Maybe we should get new carpeting, too. She wanted the room painted. But why wait until she goes to college? And you know what else? She needs a new winter coat."

Laura's hand reaches for the door and starts to pull it open.

# FIFTY-FOUR

I SQUEEZE MY EYES SHUT LIKE A LITTLE KID. AS THOUGH she won't see me if my eyes are closed.

Scott says, "No, no, honey. Stay out of the closet. Come on, don't worry about that. Don't go in there. Why don't you lie down?"

"I want to look at her coat and see what size it is. She needs a new one, something nice for college visits. We're going to be doing those when she gets back."

"We'll get her a new coat. I promise. But she can pick it out herself."

"Will we? *You* want to move. *You* keep talking about leaving town and starting over. We need to be here, Scott, in this house. For when she comes back."

"I know. You're right."

They move away from the closet. Just as they do, my phone vibrates again. Over and over like someone is calling.

I cup both my hands around it, hoping they can't hear it.

"What was that?" Laura asks.

"What was what?"

"Didn't you hear that?"

Scott doesn't speak. Then I hear the noise, too. Not my phone, but a distant chime.

"It's the front door," Scott says.

"Who could be bothering us now?"

"It might be the police. Or maybe the neighbors with more food. Someone brings a casserole or a cake every day, you know that."

Scott's heavy steps leave the room. And the bedsprings squeak again.

Everything is quiet. Dead quiet.

Then sniffling from Laura.

"Oh, Chloe. My little Chloe. Where are you, little girl? Where are you?"

This gets to me. Tears burn at my eyes, and I choke them back, trying to keep them from spilling over. Trying to keep from making a sound.

Laura continues to cry softly until Scott comes back.

"Honey?" he says.

"Yeah."

"You okay?"

"No."

"Well, there's someone at the door who wants to see you."

"Who?"

"A girl from the high school, someone who knows Chloe.

She wanted to go to the church tonight but couldn't, so she came here."

"Do you know her?" Laura asks.

"No. She says her name is Maria. She's a Latina girl with purple hair."

A Latina girl with purple hair?

*Gabriela!*

"I don't know if I'm up for it," Laura says.

"Come on," Scott says. "Just say hello. It will do you good to see how much these kids care about Chloe."

There's a long silence, one that feels like it stretches for days. Then Laura lets out a long, loud sigh. "Okay. I'll say hi. But, Scott, then I'm coming right back here. I might sleep in here again tonight. What if Chloe comes back, and I'm not in here?"

"That's fine," Scott says. "That's really a good idea, Laura."

Their footsteps slowly leave the room.

I wait—but not so long I miss my chance.

And when it's safe, I stand up, my muscles aching now from being squished down in the closet for so long. I slowly push open the door and peer around the edge.

The room is empty. Just the bed and the furniture. And the window I need to get through.

I start across the room but freeze in my tracks. I remember the hole in the closet wall—

I go back and look around the closet. I clearly see Chloe's shoes. Clothes on hangars, the sweaters neatly folded on the shelf above.

And down on the lower right-hand side there's a hole in the plaster. Like Laura said—smashed with a boot. I go right over, and the opening is just large enough for me to put my fist in. I half-expect to grab a dead mouse or a wire that will shock me into unconsciousness. It doesn't seem big enough to hold a journal.

But the space opens up, and it's larger than it looks. My hand scrambles through dust and grit, and then I feel something leather and smooth. I grip it and pull back, but the only way to get it through the opening is to roll it over like a tube. When it's out, I don't even bother to look but just dash back across the room.

I face the challenge of the window.

I put the journal in my armpit and slide my fingers under the window again. With the light on it's easier for me to see and get my fingers into the space right away. I push up and the window slides open, squeaking as it did before.

But I have to go. I have to get out.

I throw the journal out the window and follow it, landing on my feet in the grass, my knees buckling with the impact. I reach back and up and pull down the window, hoping Laura isn't in the room.

Then I turn, grab the journal, and run like hell across the yard in the direction of the car.

# FIFTY-FIVE

I DASH TOWARD THE CAR, MY LEGS PUMPING AND pumping.

But no one is there. There's no sign of Olivia or Gabriela.

I flop into the driver's seat and sit for a moment, unable to move. My breathing is heavy, and sweat runs down my forehead and into my eyes.

Did I leave some trace of myself behind? Did I shut the window? Is the closet door open? Did I drop my wallet or phone...

My wallet is there. The keys got me in to the car, so I know I have those. The bulk of my phone fills my other pocket. I closed the closet and the window, put the lamp and table back in place.

"Okay," I say out loud. "It's okay."

I'm clutching the journal in my left hand. I angle it to catch the light from the nearby streetlamps. It's a Moleskine, the cover dark brown. I don't open it. I hate the thought of looking at her most private thoughts, even if it might shed light on what happened to her. Will she be pissed when she finds out?

But I have no choice. I have to look. In the weak light, I squint to see Chloe's handwriting appears on page after page. Neat. Bold. Written in black pen. I don't focus on any specific words or phrases, don't stop to read anything. I just marvel at how much of herself is spilled here in black and white.

Are there things in here she never told me?

And what if there's nothing helpful? What if I risked everything for nothing?

At least I'd know and could stop obsessing over the journal.

The passenger door flies open, and I jump.

Olivia's face is flushed, her hair looks like she's been in a windstorm.

"Are you okay, Hunter? My God, I've been trying to get in touch. I thought for sure they caught you."

She leans over and hugs me, her thin arms much stronger than they look. She nearly crushes me.

"I'm fine," I say. "I got out."

When Olivia leans back, she sees what's in my hand. Her face lights up like a kid at their own birthday party. "You got it. Holy shit. Where was it?"

"A hole in the closet wall. It's a total fluke I found it. Where's Gabriela?"

"She's coming. Just wait. How did the cops miss it?"

"They must have overlooked it. I really had to stick my hand in there and work it around to find the journal."

"What's in there? What does it say?"

"I haven't read it yet, Livvy. I just got here."

"Okay, easy. I'm just dying to know."

"I feel weird, like *should* I read it? This is her private business. Maybe it's wrong…"

Olivia's face is hard to read. Then she says, "What are you thinking, Hunter? You *have* to read it. What if you were missing, and Chloe got ahold of your journal? Wouldn't you want her to read it to help you? Wouldn't you want that?"

"Of course."

"Even if there was embarrassing personal stuff in there like how many times you masturbated or whatever."

"Okay. I get your point."

"We didn't do all this for you not to read it," she says, scolding me with her index finger raised.

"Enough, Livvy. Where's Gabriela?"

Olivia looks out the window. "There she is. There's my baby."

Gabriela gets in the back seat, and as soon as she does, I put the car in gear, and we take off. As we drive away, Olivia leans over and takes hold of Gabriela's hand.

"Are you okay, Gabby? Are you?"

Gabriela is typically unruffled. She says in Zen-like voice, "I'm good, baby. No problems here."

"Thank you, Gabriela," I say. "I don't know how you thought of that or how you had the guts to do it, but you saved my ass. I never would have made it out of there if you hadn't gone to the door. I'd be in jail now."

"Probably. But I've been in high-pressure situations before," she says. "Those two are nothing compared to the Border Patrol."

Border Patrol? Gabriela's comment doesn't go by unnoticed. Gabriela's seen some shit in her young life.

"He got the book," Olivia says. "It worked."

"Sweet." And Olivia and Gabriela bump fists.

"So what did you say to them?" I ask.

"Well, the dad was kind of suspicious obviously. He looked at me like I was a nuisance. I knew I had to get both of them to the door, so I said the thing about praying. I know they're Catholic, so they'd believe a Mexican girl wanting to pray with them."

"And they did?" Olivia asks. "Baller move, baby."

"I didn't lie by the way," Gabriela says. "I just told them how sorry I was about Chloe. And that's the truth. They were pretty chill honestly. They must have had a million people reaching out to them. So we talked for a few minutes, and then we all three said an Our Father and a Hail Mary together. And then I left."

"That's it?" I ask. "They didn't say anything else?"

"Chloe's mom was pretty nice," Gabriela says. "I assumed she'd be a bitch because of the way she's been talking about you. But she seemed really sweet. Totally sad, of course."

"Yeah," I say. "I heard her crying in Chloe's room. It was awful."

We all grow silent as we drive. I'm heading for Gabriela's house, and we turn down her street. I figure that's the last word on Scott and Laura, but just before we stop, Gabriela says, "Her dad was kind of weird, though."

I pull over to the curb. A light burns on the porch just above the house number. Two jack-o'-lanterns sit on either side of the door.

"Weird how?" I ask.

I glance into the rearview mirror and catch a glimpse of Gabriela. She's looking thoughtful and taking her time answering.

"When I was leaving, I said I hoped they found Chloe soon. And I meant it. But when I said that, her dad was all like, 'Well, we have to prepare ourselves for the worst' or something like that. And when he said it, her mom looked shocked, like he'd just slapped her across the face. It seemed low-key rude, that's all."

# FIFTY-SIX

DAD SITS AT THE KITCHEN TABLE, SIPPING A BOWL OF canned bean soup, his glasses off to the side instead of on top of his head.

He puts his glasses on and studies us, his forehead scrunched in confusion.

"What happened to you two?" he asks.

"What do you mean?" Olivia asks.

"You said you were going to eat fajitas." He glances at the clock above the stove. "You've been gone less than an hour, and you both look like you ran a marathon. You're flushed and all twitchy."

Olivia and I look at each other. "Well, Hector's mom didn't have enough food," I say. "So we went to McDonald's, and we drove with the windows down. It isn't that cold."

Dad shrugs. "Hmmm. Okay. I'm glad you're home safe. That's all I care about."

"I need to get going on my homework," I say.

I grab Olivia's arm, and we start for the stairs, side by side.

Then Dad asks, "Was Chad over at Hector's?"

We freeze. "Chad?" I ask.

"Yeah. Chad. You know, tall guy. Kind of handsome. Goalie on the soccer team. Your best friend. Was he over there?"

I sense a trap. And that's not like Dad. He's pretty straightforward. If he has something to say, he says it. When there's nothing to say, he's quiet. And that's most of the time. But given how jacked up Olivia and I looked when we came in the door, probably like we just robbed a bank, it's no wonder he's suspicious.

Dad never asks who I've been with or who was there. Mom did that all the time, but Dad never does.

I have a fifty-fifty chance of being right if Dad knows something I don't, so I play both sides.

"Well, not when we were there. We didn't stay. Not enough fajitas."

Dad watches us. His eyes move from my face to Olivia's. She grins like a store mannequin. It's the most still I've ever seen her. That's when I think of all the things that could have gone wrong. Do Chloe's parents know I was in the house? Did they call the cops? Did they call Dad, and he was right now catching me in a lie?

Then he says, "Well, Chad came by while you were out. You might want to get in touch with him."

My lungs release all the air I've been holding.

"Great. Sure, Dad."

Olivia and I don't wait for more questions. We both run up

the stairs and remain quiet until we go into my room. Olivia flops onto the bed and puts a pillow over her face and starts laughing. And, despite everything going on, I laugh, too. It's not because we're happy. It's just because of all the tension of the past hour, and the strange feeling that comes when you get away with something you shouldn't be getting away with.

I cover my mouth, so Dad doesn't hear.

When we both calm down, Olivia takes the pillow away from her face. "I can't believe you lied so well. You're turning into quite the criminal, big brother."

"That's what I hear," I say.

"Oh, Hunter, I was just kidding. You know I don't really think that."

"You and Dad might be the only ones."

"And Chad. And Hector. Even obnoxious Cameron."

"I guess you're right."

Olivia points to my stomach, changing the subject. Before we came inside, I had tucked Chloe's journal into my pants and pulled my shirt over it in case Dad was waiting for us.

I pull out the journal, expecting it to glow like the Holy Grail. Instead, it's just a regular Moleskine journal. Nothing special. The kind of thing anyone could buy in a bookstore. It feels as light as a feather in my hands.

"Are you going to read it?" Olivia asks. "You'd better."

"Yeah," I say. But my voice is kind of low and distant. "I guess I'd better open it."

Again, I'm hyperaware of the problem. Digging into Chloe's personal thoughts without her knowing. Maybe I should just take it back. Or lock it up.

"You should do it alone," Olivia says, standing up and stretching. "I have homework anyway." She goes to the door. "But if you need anything, let me know."

"I will."

She pauses at the door. "You did ruin one thing for us tonight."

I look up. "What?"

"You told Dad we went to McDonald's. I haven't eaten, and now if I do, I'll blow our cover."

She laughs when she says it. I smile, too.

"Thanks, Livvy."

"See you, brother."

And then I'm alone with Chloe's journal. Her thoughts. Her secrets.

# FIFTY-SEVEN

MY HANDS SHAKE. A FAINT TREMBLE LIKE A LEAF IN A light wind.

I flip open the journal, starting at the beginning.

Chloe's familiar large script, the one that decorated silly notes and "just because" cards she's given me over the past seven months—ones that told me she loved me or wanted to kiss me—fills the pages. Just seeing her handwriting gives me a lift, a touch of her essence spilled across the pages.

The first entry is from July:

*I'm really going to keep this journal. I've tried before, and it never worked. I didn't stay with it and stopped writing after a few weeks. I'm hoping this time is different since this can be a way to practice my writing. And a way to put down all those things too weird to share with anyone else. But I know myself. Sometimes I'll write things and then just tear them out right away because it's so bad.*

Disappointment courses through me like cold water. Chloe and I were dating when she started this. We were close when she started this. We told each other "I love you" every day. As many times as we could. We shared everything.

What did she have to put in her journal that she wouldn't share with me?

A few days later:

*The most amazing night with Hunter last night. Under the stars and under a blanket in Ryan Park. I'll never forget it. I love him.*

That night. We went to a movie, alone. And then the park. It was late, so the park was closed, and we were in danger of being chased away by the cops. Unlike me, Chloe didn't worry about being caught. She grabbed the blanket and spread it on the ground. We stared at the stars for what felt like hours, identifying the constellations. My full attention shifted to her, and now I wish the moment had consumed me the whole time. That I'd never let one second slip by without appreciating being with Chloe.

The pages flip by. Chloe says she loves me. Chloe says she cares about me.

Nothing is wrong…

Then, an entry in which Chloe talks about the future:

*God, when I think about all the work ahead of me and trying to get into a good college—the kind of college Mom and Dad want me to get into—I just really don't know if I can do it. It's like a giant weight pressing down on my shoulders every day. Sometimes I just want to quit everything and go away.*

She felt a lot of pressure from her parents to get into a great college. Preferably Ivy League like Harvard or Penn. If not those, then the University of Chicago or Vanderbilt. But she seemed to handle it with ease. She made jokes and rolled her eyes. More than anything, she just kept doing the work. Everybody knew she'd get into a good school.

But is it possible it all became too much for her? Did she crack in a way no one would ever have thought? Not even me?

Did she use the accident to run away?

A fist pounds against my bedroom door, and the journal falls. It's an angry knock. Louder even than Olivia's.

They're *here*. Chloe's parents figured out what happened in the house and called the police.

Forget graduation. Forget college. Do not collect two hundred dollars. Do not pass Go. It's prison for me.

"Come on, Hunter. Open up."

More knocking, lighter this time.

It's Chad.

# FIFTY-EIGHT

I STUFF THE JOURNAL UNDER MY MATTRESS.

Olivia is out in the hallway, leaning against the wall, and she and Chad are staring each other down and exchanging insults. As usual.

"I need to tell my dad to call the exterminator," Olivia says.

"That's so sweet, little Livvy."

"Don't call me that."

"I remember what a fun little kid you used to be."

Chad and I haven't really talked since the day he and Hannah came over. And Hannah stormed out because I raised the question of her lying about Chloe at the dance.

He failed to answer my text earlier.

"Come on," I say to Chad. "Are you here to see me or her?"

"I barely noticed her," Chad says, as he enters my room. "She's so tiny, she's almost invisible." He looks back once. "Bye, little Livvy."

Olivia flips him off and turns for her room.

Chad takes my desk chair, and I sit on the edge of the bed right over the journal.

"What are you doing knocking like that?" I ask. "You sounded like a cop."

"I figured I had to make a lot of noise. I came by earlier, and you weren't here. Your dad said you were at Hector's house." He looks perplexed. "Really? Hector's studying at the library. His grade in physics is in the shitter, and Coach is on his case about it. What were you doing?"

"I texted you earlier, and you didn't answer."

"I was at practice. Some coach from a small college in Indiana came by and wanted to talk to me."

"Really?"

"I don't want to play soccer in college. You know that."

"Okay, okay," I say. "Look, I'm sorry things got weird when you came over with Hannah. It feels like I'm apologizing a lot."

"It doesn't make my life any easier when you get Hannah pissed," he says. "But don't worry about it. Life goes on."

"I guess it does."

"So where were you earlier?" he asks.

"It's a long story."

Chad studies me, waiting for more.

"Okay," Chad says, stretching. "If you don't want to tell me…"

It's good to see him. I feel like one of those kids who live in a bubble because they have a disease that keeps them from real contact with other human beings.

Except my disease is suspicion. Everyone thinks I'm guilty.

"So, what are you hearing?" I ask. "About the case?"

"Oh." Chad looks a little disappointed. "Well, I guess the gossip at school is the same. Just wild rumors."

"Like what?"

"Some people are saying Chloe and Daniel were secretly dating, and she killed him and then ran off to California to become a Scientologist. They sat next to each other in trig last year, and people think they conspired to do it. Maybe since Daniel wants to make movies." He shrugs. "I don't know, man. People don't say as much about it because they know we're friends. When I walk into a classroom, I can tell they're talking about it, but they shut it down when they see me."

"That makes sense."

"Anyway, I wanted to—"

"What about Hannah's dad?"

"Her dad?"

"What's he hearing? Did she manage to get any more information from his phone calls?"

"Oh, that." Chad nods. "No, she didn't hear anything else. Hannah kind of just caught that other stuff by accident. She's not really that plugged in. You know how she is."

"Yeah." I know I'm not hiding my frustration.

"What?" Chad says in a slightly irritated voice.

"What, what?"

"You seem pissed."

"I guess so. It's not fair, but I really want someone to tell me something useful. Something that clears things up. When you said you came by, I figured you'd heard something important."

"That's not why I came by," Chad says, his voice mellow again. "I'm here to see how you're doing. You know, everybody's worried about you."

"I'm worried about me, too," I say. "Every time someone knocks on the door, I think it's the cops coming to take me away. And that's preferable to the alternative."

"What's the alternative?"

"That they're coming to tell me Chloe's dead. That they found her body in a ditch somewhere."

"Shit, I'm sorry, man. I know that's a black cloud to live under. That's why I came by. You should get out of the house and do something. Nobody's seen you. Nobody's hung out with you. Why don't we all do something? Or just you and I can do something. I don't care what."

It feels really good to hear him say that. A weekend with nothing to look forward to but time with friends. Even if there aren't big plans, sometimes it feels good just to hang out.

But the black cloud passes over my mind like an eclipse.

No Chloe. No answers.

People will recognize me. The kid who murdered his girlfriend and his former best friend. How would it look if I went out while all of this is going on?

"I don't think I can," I say.

"Are you sure? We can be really low-key."

I can't bring myself to say the word "yes." I just can't. "Maybe once all this is over…if it's ever over."

Chad face shows his disappointment and that only makes me feel worse. Like I've slammed the door on him.

My mind is already racing back to the journal, which is right below me. It screams to me to pick it up.

"Well," he says, "if you change your mind."

"Yeah. Sure."

Should he see the journal? Get his help making sense of it all?

But what would Chloe think if I let him see it?

"I've got a lot of homework to catch up on," I say.

Chad's his usual smooth self. "Yeah, sure, man. I get it." At the door, he looks back one more time. "And, seriously, think about this weekend."

"I will," I say.

Both of us know I'm just saying it.

# FIFTY-NINE

AS SOON AS CHAD IS GONE, THE JOURNAL COMES OUT.

*Hunter is wonderful—*
*Hunter and I went to—*
*I talked to Hunter about—*
*What's it going to be like when Hunter and I go away to college*
*next year?*

She wrote that at the end of the summer. Chloe and I never talked about the future very much. We knew it was coming, that the chances we'd go to the same school were slim. And once or twice, we made vague promises about visiting each other.

But we knew the odds.

We'd seen plenty of other couples try to make a relationship last past high school, and they almost always failed. Is that why Chloe had been pulling away? Is that what was wrong?

If it were that simple, why didn't she just tell me?

My hands shake as I flip to the date when we had sex. September 15.

*Well, Hunter and I finally had sex for the first time last night. All those people who told me the first time might suck weren't wrong. Mom told me that on her honeymoon with Dad, it was like the blind leading the blind. That's what Hunter and I were like. Ordinarily we maul each other like two cats in heat, but trying to have sex was like trying to launch a space shuttle.*

Everything she says is true. In Chloe's voice. Reading what she wrote is like hearing her whispering in my ear. Chloe's spirit is all over those pages like her fingerprints. I'm so happy to hear her again.

*But we made it work. Eventually. So…it's official! We're no longer virgins. Yay!*

*Seriously, Hunter was so great. Patient. Gentle. Loving. I'm so lucky to have done it with him when so many other girls have to do it with douchy guys the first time. And then you have to remember losing your virginity to a douche for the rest of your life.*

Thank God she remembered it that way.

Maybe there's nothing in the journal. Maybe Chloe doesn't have any secrets.

But ten days later, there's an entry that leaves me cold.

*What happened today… There are no words. I feel like I must have dreamed it. Or it's more like a nightmare. Did it really happen? Will things ever be the same?*

*Will they?*

I want to scream at the pages: *What happened?*

The next page has been torn out. Jagged edges of paper peek out of the binding like broken teeth. Why was *this* page torn out?

Maybe she started writing, made a mistake, and ripped it out. She was writing by hand. She said at the beginning she knew she'd rip some pages out if she didn't like the writing.

It's the middle of an entry. The page after the one torn out doesn't follow from the page before. Which means it was probably taken out for a reason.

But was it taken out by Chloe?

There's then a gap of about a week when nothing is written. The pages aren't torn out—Chloe just wasn't writing.

Then the entries resume, but they're shorter. All of them.

*I don't think I enjoy writing anymore.*
*I'm tired of thinking about all of this.*

And then she wrote:

*I need to tell Hunter what's happening. But not sure how he will respond.*

*Not sure at all.*

# SIXTY

RESPOND TO *WHAT?*

The entries aren't coming every day. Sometimes she skips a day or two or three.

But a feeling of doom has settled inside my gut like a rock. Heavy. Dense.

Uncomfortable.

And then:

*I'm just not sure who I can tell. A counselor. Should I tell my mom and dad?*

*Would they even understand? Would anyone?*

"Fuck," I say out loud. "Fuck, fuck, fuck."

Haley told us about the broken condom. The pregnancy hotline.

"Fuck."

It has to be true:

*Chloe was pregnant.*

# SIXTY-ONE

THE ROCK IN MY GUT FEELS LIKE IT'S GROWING. LIKE IT'S going to push its way out of my throat.

I stand, hands on knees. Breathing.

The first wave of nausea passes. Slowly, but it passes.

Everything is shaking when I sit on the bed again and flip ahead like a madman. Some of the entries are totally mundane, as though her crisis was the furthest thing from her mind.

*Went to lunch with Mom. Such a great time. It felt more like we were friends than mother and daughter.*

*This physics lab is wiping me out.*

*Found a dress today!*

But then:

*I can't sleep thinking about it.*

*I feel sick.*

*I need to talk to someone.*

The Tuesday before homecoming, Chloe wrote:

*I'm going to tell Hunter after HoCo. I can't wait. He has to know. And I don't care what the consequences are—I can't keep this from him. I know he's going to be hurt. Confused. Maybe very angry. I hate this.*

The next day:

*I can't believe Basher came over. And I can't believe I wanted to talk to him.*

Basher?

Did she really want to talk to *Basher*? Why?

When I turn the page, there's nothing there.

The next two pages are ripped out.

And the rest of the journal is blank.

# SIXTY-TWO

BASHER?

There's nothing else in the book.

An idea grows in my mind like a poisonous weed. Basher was always hanging around Chloe's house. Basher never got over Chloe. Basher is tight with Scott.

He wanted her back. After Chloe and I had sex the first time, she pulled back. She didn't want to do it again. She pulled back in every way and told Natasha it felt weird.

The sex felt weird?

Or sex with *me* felt weird?

Does that mean she had sex with someone else? Did she have sex with Basher after me?

Did she cheat on me—with Basher—and become pregnant? Is that what she wanted to tell me at homecoming?

Is that why we were both so unhappy that night?

Is that why Basher was there when we left the dance? Was he waiting for us? For her?

Is that who ran us off the road?

And then he killed Daniel because Daniel caught it all on film.

Only one way to find out.

# SIXTY-THREE

OLIVIA IS IN THE KITCHEN EATING A GIANT BOWL OF vanilla ice cream smothered in chocolate syrup. She sees the journal in my hand and drops her spoon onto the table.

"Hunter, what are you doing?"

"I've got to go somewhere."

She jumps up and puts her tiny body between me and the back door. "Did you find something? Something we need to talk about?"

"I think I know what's going on," I say. "But I just want to make sure."

"Then I'm coming with you," she says.

"No. Don't. I'm fine."

"I'm not letting you do this alone. Whatever it is. You look... not right."

"I have to do this alone, Livvy." I look down at her bare feet. "And you don't even have shoes on. And I have to go. Now. Just tell Dad I'll be right back."

She tries to put her hands on me, but I easily brush past her. "Hunter…"

Basher's house isn't far. Back in January, right before Chloe and I started dating, he had a party when his parents went on a cruise. It was one of those epic parties that starts with a small group of people, but then everybody texts their friends, and pretty soon the whole school is there. I went with Chad and Hector. We couldn't get close to the beer, but we hung out in the basement, shooting pool. Basher's parents had a whole shrine devoted to his lousy football career. You'd have thought he'd won the Heisman Trophy instead of mostly being a backup quarterback on a mediocre high school team.

On the drive to Basher's, I make a call.

It takes a few rings, but Detective Haley eventually answers, his voice clipped and efficient.

I say, "I need you to meet me at Mike Basher's house right now. I have to show you something that could be the most important thing in the whole case."

"You want me to go to Mike Basher's house?" Haley asks. "Right now?"

"Yes, I do. You'll see when—"

"Whoa," Haley says, sounding surprised. "Are you on your way there?"

"Yes."

"Okay," Haley says. "I'll meet you outside. I'm already at the Basher residence, but I don't want you coming in until we talk."

I want to ask why he's there, but he hangs up.

I let myself believe I'm right.

Why else would Haley be there unless he's reached the same conclusion I did?

At the Basher residence, there's Haley, standing on the lawn, hands on hips, looking like a statue.

# SIXTY-FOUR

THE BASHER'S HOUSE GLOWS LIKE A GIANT SPACESHIP. Every window shines with light that spills across the lawn.

The journal is in my hand, and Haley watches me with his hands on hips, his sleeves rolled up to his elbows like always.

"Look at this, Detective."

Haley eyes me the way someone watches an unfamiliar dog—one they think might bite. But Haley extends his hand and takes the journal. He examines it in the light that spills from the house, turning it first one way and then the other as though it just fell out of the sky, an artifact from another world.

"What is this?" he asks.

"It's Chloe's journal. Remember, you couldn't find it?"

Haley looks up at me, his brown eyes tough to read. "Oh, I remember. But how did you come up with it? Did you have this in your possession the whole time, Hunter? That's obstruct—"

"Can we just hold off on that for a moment?" I ask. "What matters is what's inside. Or maybe what matters even more is what's *not* inside. See, this journal tells us what was going on right before she disappeared. Something was on her mind, something she didn't think she could share with anybody. Not even me. Maybe she *was* pregnant."

"Does the journal *say* she was pregnant?"

"It doesn't. But it does say there was a problem. And she felt like she couldn't say anything to anyone." I point at the journal, which is still in Haley's hands. "And then, right before homecoming, Chloe says she talked to Basher. He came to their house. You know he used to hang around there and work on cars with Scott."

"I know that."

"Why did she talk to him? Why not me? Or her parents? Maybe he was the cause of the problem. Maybe *he* got her pregnant. That's why he followed us on the night of the dance. He was outside the school when we were leaving."

Haley flips through the pages, the paper making a rustling sound. He stops where a page has been torn out.

"Did you do this?" he asks.

"No. No way."

He keeps flipping, and I know nothing I've done has been very well thought out. And that Haley may not see things the way I want him to.

"But the journal doesn't say any of that?" he asks. "And you don't know that. Chloe didn't say Mike Basher did anything to her. And no one else did, either. Right?"

"But something was wrong at the dance. Something made her upset."

"You had a fight."

"Stop saying that. You don't know for sure."

"Do you know why I'm at this house tonight?"

It starts to dawn on me that Haley knows something. This has happened to me in class before. I think I know more than one of my teachers only to find out they possess knowledge I hadn't even anticipated. I feel that way now, standing face-to-face with Haley. He seems to know more than I do. And he's just waiting for the right moment to prove it to me.

That moment is now.

"I'm here, Hunter, because we've been investigating—"

The front door opens, and Basher steps into the rectangle of yellow light on the porch. He wears a smirk on his face, the kind guys like him always wear. It's a look that says, *You can't touch me. No matter what I do, you can't touch me.*

"Hunter, stay here—"

*No. Someone's going to touch you.*

I run past Haley and across the lawn, heading for the front door. Basher struts out into the yard, still wearing the stupid smirk. He's almost a head taller than me and twice as broad. He may be a terrible football player, but he lifts weights and runs and stretches and does all the athletic things I don't.

But I don't care.

"What did you do to her?" I ask. "What did you do?"

Basher crouches, ready for battle, shaking his head as if I'm the strangest thing he's ever seen.

When we come together, I swing both my fists like windmills, hoping to connect. Mostly I miss.

My fists harmlessly connect with his shoulder, his back, his sides. I'm not really sure what's happening, but Basher lowers his head and torso, his gorilla-like arms wrapping around me. They clasp me tight, and all of a sudden, I'm seeing the ink-black sky, the pinpricks of stars. I'm upside down.

Then the grass slams against me so hard that all the air leaves my body.

More hands are all over me. And voices reach me.

"Break it up, guys."

"Knock it off."

"Did you see that? The kid's violent.."

My breath is gone. No words come.

Basher has been pulled off me after executing a perfect tackle. And there are more people in the yard than just Basher and Haley.

Dew seeps into my shirt. My wind comes back. Painfully.

And my head…it hurts again…a dull thump…

*Will the concussion symptoms roar back?*

*Please, no. No.*

"Just go inside, Mike," Haley says. "I've got this."

"I want to press charges for the way he went after my son."

"Forget it, Dad. I've got this." And then Basher is close to me, leaning over my body. "You shouldn't be mad at me, dude. You think her family is all into me. Let me tell you, they haven't even talked to me. I went over there to try to work with Scott, to take his mind off things, and he told me he isn't even going into the garage anymore. He acted offended—pissed really—at the idea that he or anyone else would go in the garage and work on a stupid car. So quit thinking about me."

The door slams. A satellite blinks overhead next to the half-moon.

Haley's face enters the sky above me. "When you can get up, you and I are going to have a little talk."

# SIXTY-FIVE

WE'RE IN THE FRONT SEAT OF HALEY'S CAR, AND MY
breathing returns to normal. Haley is holding the journal again,
riffling the pages with his thumb.

He says, "You never let me finish. I was going to explain why
I was here when you ran off like Usain Bolt and got dumped on
your ass."

"I don't know why *I'm* the one in the car," I say. "I know I
shouldn't have gone after him that way, Detective. I should've let
you handle it. But why aren't you questioning him?" I point to the
journal. "It's all in there."

"In here?" Haley asks. "In this book you gave me? Which you
still haven't told me how you got."

"If I tell you, will you arrest Basher?"

"No. And do you know why? Because I came over here
tonight to tell the Bashers that we looked into Mike's alibi, and
it's rock solid. You know how someone saw Mike and his friends
outside the dance that night?"

"Yeah. What were they doing?"

"They were getting a ride from Mike's mother. She picked up those guys because they'd had a little to drink, and she drove them back to this house. All four of them. And they met up here with some other friends."

"So she's lying for them."

Haley shakes his head. "She's not. There are texts. And the other three guys, Mike's friends, they all tell the same story. So do all the parents. They came back here when they left the dance. They weren't anywhere near where Chloe disappeared."

I slump back against the seat. "But in the journal…he was still hung up on Chloe… He was at their house a lot…"

Haley tosses the journal onto the dashboard. "Where did you get it, Hunter?"

A car pulls up behind us. The headlights blind us for a moment, and then both doors open and close, one on each side. Haley rolls down his window, and Dad's face appears, leaning down to see inside the car.

*What is he doing here?*

"Mr. Gifford," Haley says. "Your son put on quite a display tonight."

Someone taps on my window, and I lower it. Olivia. She looks a little worried and a lot embarrassed.

"Are you okay, Hunter? This detective guy called the house and said you were coming over here. So Dad was worried you were going to do something dumb, like get in a fight."

"It wasn't much of a fight," Haley says.

Dad looks concerned. *Really* concerned. And I'm the cause of it. Again.

"Can I take him home?" he asks.

Haley shakes his head. "Not a chance. You see, Hunter here was just about to explain to me how he ended up with a journal the police haven't been able to find since Chloe disappeared. So if you'd like to stick around for that revelation…"

"*I* did it."

My head whips back to the window. "Livvy. No."

"I did it," Olivia says again. "I knew about Chloe's hiding place. So I went into her house and found the journal. I gave it to Hunter. It was me the whole time."

"Livvy," I say. "Just stop. Don't say anything else."

"Well, it kind of was my idea."

Haley pretends Olivia isn't here and says to me, "Are you saying you went into the Summerses' house without their permission and stole this journal?"

"It sounds a lot worse when you say it that way. But, yes, I did go into their house and find the journal. And I always intended to bring it to you, Detective."

Dad's face still fills the driver's side window. His mouth hangs open, and his forehead is more wrinkled than I've ever seen it. But he doesn't say anything. He just looks at me like he doesn't know me.

"You'd better tell me the whole story," Haley says.

# VIDEO #3

THE RED LIGHT GLOWS.

It burns like an angry eye. One that sees me. And judges me.

Unlike the other times, I have no idea what I'm going to say. I'm not even sure I want to make the video. But something compels me to do it. Something makes me want to say... something. Anything.

To tell my side of the story.

Dad and the lawyer will be pissed again. Really pissed.

"By now, you know what I've done. And it's true. I did go into Chloe's house and take her journal. I didn't break in, which is what everyone else is saying. I knew her bedroom window would be unlocked, because Chloe and I had used it before. Maybe I'm splitting hairs. Or maybe I'm admitting I could get into their house anytime I wanted. Some people say that proves I'm the one who kidnapped Chloe, even though that doesn't make any sense. Everybody knows Chloe was with me at homecoming and that we left together. But I guess I'm done trying to make sense of everything."

I shift in the chair. The red eye still examines me, making me feel awkward.

"I turned the journal over to the police because I want them to find Chloe. That was my goal all along. That's why I went right to Detective Haley once I read it. And I know I made a wrong assumption about what I read in the journal. I know I was wrong about Mike Basher."

I nod my head, certain of something. More certain of this than anything else.

"I do want to say something clearly. I'm sorry, Mike. I'm sorry to you and your family and your friends. I was wrong, and the police know that. And I know everybody makes fun of the way you play quarterback, but if you decide to change positions, you should think of linebacker. You tackle very well."

I don't smile. But maybe somebody will think it's funny since everybody knows I went after Basher, and he slammed me to the ground.

"Anyway, I'm still a person of interest. That's what the police say. And I'm being charged with trespassing for going into Chloe's house without permission. They're threatening to charge me for tampering with evidence, too, but I don't know if that's for real or just a threat. But I know they really want to charge me with kidnapping and murder. They really want to get me for the big stuff, and they're just hoping something comes up that allows them to do that. Then everyone in town will be happy."

My throat feels dry. I swallow and decide to go on, even with a mouth that feels like I chewed on cotton balls.

"From reading Chloe's journal, I know something was wrong in her life, something she felt she couldn't tell me. She says she wanted to tell me on the night of homecoming, and maybe she did. I can't remember. But even if she did tell me, I'm guilty. I'm guilty of not doing enough to get her to tell me what was wrong before that night. Whatever was happening, she didn't feel right telling me. And that's a failure on my part. If not being able to hear what she had to say meant causing something awful to happen to her, then I'm guilty of that as well. I should have been there for her, and she should have felt safe telling me."

I clear my throat.

"If she'd done that, then maybe none of this would have happened."

I feel like I'm finished and reach to turn off the camera, but then something else occurs to me.

"Tomorrow morning is Daniel's funeral. I can't go. The police told me it wouldn't be right, and my dad agrees. I guess I do, too, even though we were once very good friends. But I think all of you should go, especially if you live in town and especially if you go to Garrett Morgan. Daniel's mother is a single mom, raising him on her own. She doesn't have a lot of family here and she needs all the support she can get. So please go. For her. And for Daniel."

I take a deep breath.

"I guess that's all. So. Yeah, that's it for now. Maybe for always."

I turn off the camera.

I really, really want to share the video. I know all the reasons not to: Dad, the police, the school, the town.

But I want to be heard as well. I want my side of the story to get out.

Everyone else is talking about me, and I want to have my say.

But is it worth it? Does anything I'm doing make a difference? Is any of it getting us any closer to finding Chloe?

Depression lands on my shoulders like a shroud.

My finger hovers above the phone, ready to share. But I can't summon the energy now.

I drop my hand and leave the video unposted.

# SIXTY-SIX

DAD ORDERS PIZZA, AND THE THREE OF US EAT OUR HALF-pepperoni, half-mushroom mostly in silence.

Olivia does her best to cheer us up. She tells a long story about Gabriela's cousin's Halloween costume. Gabriela's cousin is four years old and obsessed with *Frozen*, so she wants to dress up like Elsa. Her mother had the kid try on the costume just to see if it fit, but then she refused to take it off. She's been sleeping in it ever since.

Olivia laughs like it's the funniest thing she's ever heard, and even Dad, who usually refuses to act like little kids are funny, manages a small smile. The story strikes me as pointless.

"I'm going to do my homework," I say.

"There's ice cream," Dad says. "Vanilla and pistachio."

"Oh," Olivia says, "I kind of demolished the vanilla yesterday."

"I bought more on my way home," Dad says. "Besides, we all know Hunter's favorite is pistachio."

"I'm okay," I say. "Maybe later."

"Are you feeling sick?" he asks. "Your head? Haley said you hit the ground pretty hard at Basher's house."

"That really isn't bothering me much. Hardly at all."

Dad's worried about me. He's held off on a lecture about the trespassing charge. He knows every dead end means we're further away from finding Chloe. And every dead end means I look guiltier and guiltier.

So he tolerates my moodiness and lets me go to my room.

But what do I do there? I'm sick of homework. Sick of studying and never getting to talk about any of the things I've read. Sick of emailing my work in and then getting emails back from my teachers. I don't feel very motivated to write college essays, either.

I sit in front of my computer and open Daniel's movie, skipping ahead to where the homecoming footage starts.

Chloe.

Even though I've seen it so many times—backward and forward—her image fascinates me. We talk. *Argue?* We get into the car and drive off, knowing that only minutes remain before the mystery begins. There's a break in the filming like the camera was turned off. And then it comes right back on.

Again and again, I watch.

My brain feels locked and unable to look away.

Again and again. The same thing. After that break, I always stop before that second car comes up behind us. Maybe that car means nothing. Maybe it was just some kids who grew bored with the dance and wanted to get high or drunk or just get the fuck away from the smothering crowds in the gym. Maybe it was someone not connected to us at all. An Uber driver turning around. An old guy out for an evening drive. A teacher leaving his or her office.

The chair squeaks as I lean back. Thinking. The movie continues to play. The other car pulls out and then... Daniel cut the film poorly here. It's a rough cut, but everywhere else his cuts were precise and smooth. He seems to have the tech side of things down, but he still needs help with his storytelling. But this is the only weird cut.

After the car drives off, the camera drops quickly, as though Daniel is lowering it. It's like he put the camera down but didn't stop recording. The sudden movement causes a swirling like on an amusement park ride. Everything on the screen blurs, the landscape sweeping by. It passes over a row of parked cars and then drops to the ground before it cuts away.

Just a rushing blur of images.

But why is that blur there when the rest of the movie was edited so precisely?

Was that an accident? A mistake?

Five times. Ten times. I watch that blurring sweep of the camera so many times I feel motion sick. But at the end of the cut, which I freeze over and over, I see nothing.

Nothing.

I turn off the movie and close my laptop, with no choice but to go back to reading for class. At least I saved the best for last. A novel for my AP English class. One I've always wanted to read.

*Kindred* by Octavia Butler.

The words refuse to make any sense. They don't register because my head is somewhere else.

That movie. The weird, blurry cut.

Like Daniel wanted to show something on the ground but didn't.

Still, if it was so important, he'd show it to the viewer? Wouldn't he?

"No," I say out loud.

If it's important, and I mean *really* important, he'd put it at the end of the movie where it would have the most impact.

Maybe Daniel knew more about storytelling than I realized.

Maybe.

I'm off the bed, grabbing my keys.

# SIXTY-SEVEN

LIGHTS BURN INSIDE THE HOUSE, AND TWO CARS SIT IN the driveway.

As I wait after knocking, under the glowing porch light, I look back out to the yard. Where I last saw Daniel. We argued right there on the lawn when I told him we weren't friends anymore.

My face flushes with shame.

The knob rattles and turns, and all of a sudden, I'm face-to-face with Daniel's mom, Elizabeth. It's been a few years.

She looks the same. She's a tall woman, taller than me. She always seemed strong and capable, which makes sense since she's an ER nurse. Her reddish hair is a little grayer, and she looks tired. Her eyes are red, her skin pale. She buried her only child just this morning, and if she's mad at the world and wants someone to take it out on, that person is probably going to be me.

She stares at me for a long time, sadness on her face.

And then she says, "Oh, Hunter," in the saddest voice ever, and she's squeezing me tight. I start to cry. She's crying, too.

Then we're next to each other on the couch. Her arm is around me, and we both wipe our faces with tissues that appeared out of nowhere. Another woman is in the room, lingering in the doorway to the kitchen. She smiles at me.

"This is my friend, Kelcey," Elizabeth says. "She's been my rock through all of this. We've grown really close over the past year. I was so scared to be here after what happened to Daniel, but she stayed with me. And I wanted to be with all the good memories. Kelcey, this is Daniel's friend, Hunter. They grew up together."

The woman nods and asks if I want anything. Elizabeth tells her to bring me a glass of water.

I say, "I'm sorry, Elizabeth. And I want you to know I would never hurt Daniel. *Never.* We had an argument, but that's all."

"I know, Hunter," she says, pulling me closer. "Shhh. I don't pay attention to all the things people say on social media or anywhere else. None of that matters. This has been a struggle for me, a lot of complicated feelings. But I decided I know who you are. I've known you a long time."

"Well, I'm still sorry."

"I know you are. And I'm glad you're here."

"They told me not to go to the funeral."

"Someone told me that. I knew I'd see you sometime. I just knew. When someone knocked on the door, I thought to myself, 'Maybe that's our Hunter.'"

"I came over in case you wanted to talk about Daniel. In case you needed something."

"Thank you, Hunter. I've been talking a lot about Daniel. With friends and family…" She looks away and nods her head at a private thought. "Yes, I have."

Kelcey hands me a glass of water, which immediately makes me feel better. I ask Elizabeth if the police know anything more.

"They don't," she says. "Oh, they talk a big game about working every lead, but they don't know. This life is a mystery to all of us. And it's a mystery to them, too. I think they're hoping they find out what happened to Chloe and that will tell them what happened to Daniel. It's their best strategy so far, but it's not much." She rubs my arm. "More importantly, how are you doing, kiddo? You've been having a rough ride."

"I'm okay."

"Are you?"

"Not really."

"I didn't think so. None of us are."

"No, we're not."

"How's your head? You have a hellacious bump there. Concussions can be brutal."

"It's getting better."

It feels good to be held the way she holds me. It's the safest I've felt since homecoming. And it's something only a mother can do.

"Are you sure there's nothing I can do for you?" I ask.

"This visit is nice," she says. "But I get the feeling you're looking for something."

"I was. But let's just forget it. You have enough going on."

"Let me decide how much I have going on. What if I want the distraction? Maybe it would make me feel better to help someone."

"Are you sure?" I ask.

"I am."

"Okay, I did come over to ask for something," I say.

"What's that?"

"I was hoping I could look at some of Daniel's files," I say. "Detective Haley told me that everything was backed up."

"You can look at whatever you want," she says. "What're you looking for?"

"It's kind of a long shot," I say.

"Most good things are."

"I'm just wondering if there's something Daniel filmed that I might understand. And if I could just look at it…well, maybe we could all know what the hell is going on around here."

Elizabeth appears to think this over, nodding her head. "Well, I'd love for someone to find out what's going on around here. But my mind can't really imagine what that might be."

# SIXTY-EIGHT

"DO YOU HAVE A LAPTOP WITH YOU?" SHE ASKS.

"No," I say.

Whoever killed Daniel took his. They took every piece of computer and film equipment he had.

So Elizabeth gets out her laptop and logs onto the cloud. She explains that she and Daniel shared a storage account. "And," Elizabeth says, "I was the one paying for all of it. So here are his files."

Elizabeth sets me up at the dining room table. There are a lot of files on the screen. A lot. It hits me like my physics homework. Overwhelming.

I take a deep breath and start looking.

Daniel's folders are all labeled, and it looks like he was working on a ton of different projects. There are folders labeled "Cop Show," "Sci-Fi," "Epic," "War," "Pilots," and on and on.

One is labeled "True Crime." Within that folder there are hundreds of files: videos, word documents, images, designs.

Unfortunately, those files aren't labeled individually. They just say "scene" over and over. I have to click on each file to see what it holds.

When my neck feels stiff like an old man's, my phone buzzes. It's Dad asking me where I am. I tell him the truth. Dad writes back a simple: Okay.

Then a moment later: Please tell her how sorry I am.

Elizabeth appears at my side. "Tired?"

"He shot a lot of stuff," I say.

"You know Daniel. He always had his camera going." Elizabeth yawns and stretches. "Maybe you need a break."

"I should go. I'm keeping you up."

"It's okay," she says.

But I'm not sure.

"Can I show you one thing I found?" I ask, clicking a file on her desktop.

A handwritten sign appears: "Monster Wars"

Years evaporate. I know exactly where I am—a hot summer day. The smell of dirt and grass. Daniel and I are nine, and we're making a movie in his backyard. Plastic dinosaurs fighting it out for supremacy on a distant planet.

It all comes back when I open my eyes and watch. A T.Rex is the king of one group of plastic dinosaurs. A brontosaurus is the king of the other. The dinosaurs pile on top of one another, and you can totally see the strings we used to move them around. Even worse, you can see our hands moving into the frame from time to time when the strings didn't work.

It's the stupidest little movie ever. Also, the most amazing. Because Daniel is alive, right there on the screen. Alive the way I remember him: a smart, creative, energetic kid. And my best friend.

When those four minutes are up, tears blur my vision. Elizabeth sniffles next to me.

"I'm sorry, Elizabeth. I didn't mean to upset you."

"No, you didn't. I'm so glad you showed me."

I play it again. And again. I feel guilty over the way we drifted apart. And the way we fought that last night.

And I also want to roar along with it, because it feels so good to see Daniel again.

# SIXTY-NINE

ANOTHER HOUR PASSES, AND MY EYES ARE EVEN blearier.

My neck is killing me, and now my back hurts, too.

A thought starts to take root—maybe there is nothing to find. If the cops haven't found anything, why would Daniel?

Elizabeth comes back into the room. She and Kelcey have been in the kitchen talking and making plans for a trip to Florida. She places her hand on my shoulder. "Do you think I can help you figure out what you're looking for?"

"I wish you could. But I don't know what it is." I tell Elizabeth about the shot in the parking lot, the way the camera drops as though it's going to show the viewer something on the ground. "I just don't know what could be on the ground that's so important. And there's so much footage to get through."

"He wasn't the most organized kid," she says.

"Did he talk about the movie? Did he talk about…anything? Who he wanted to interview or what he still wanted to add?"

Elizabeth sits next to me. She has reading glasses pushed up on top of her head, resting in an unruly pile of her red hair. "He didn't say much. One of my big regrets, Hunter, is that I had to work so much. Daniel spent a lot of time on his own, and when I came home from work, I was tired. That's just the way it is as a single parent. Your dad is getting a taste of that."

"Yeah. He works all the time." I remember Dad's text. "Oh, my dad says to tell you he's sorry. He always really liked Daniel. They talked at the vigil."

Elizabeth smiles. "That's good to hear. But as far as your question, all I really know is that Daniel told me he was excited about this new project he was working on. And he said it was about Chloe. He mentioned that he wanted to interview a lot of people. Cops. Chloe's parents, if they were willing. Teachers and students from the school. I told him that might be a hard sell."

"I'm sorry. I should leave and let you get back to your life."

"You know, Daniel was lucky to have found people to fill the gap after his father left. Mentors. Friends. Teachers." She points at the screen. "Daniel was getting a lot of advice from Mr. Hartman. The creative writing teacher? I think Daniel said you were close to him."

"I am." I search back through all the conversations I've had over the past few days. "But Ron, I mean, Mr. Hartman, said he didn't know Daniel."

"I think it was Mr. Hartman. Is there another creative writing teacher at the high school?"

"No. Just him. Maybe I misunderstood."

Elizabeth scratches her head, almost knocking her glasses loose. "No, I'm sure. In fact, I think Daniel said Chloe put him in touch with Mr. Hartman. He and Chloe took a class together, didn't they?"

"Trig. Last year."

"Right. And I guess Daniel mentioned to Chloe that he wanted to be a filmmaker, and she suggested he talk to Mr. Hartman. I think Mr. Hartman has a friend who was a screenwriter."

"I guess I really didn't talk to Daniel about it."

Elizabeth reaches over and pats my arm. "I hope you don't feel guilty about that. About you and Danny not being as close as you used to be."

"I kind of do," I say. "That night I was here, the night…you know. I said things to him I shouldn't have said. And that's the last time we talked."

"A few words you say to someone in a heated moment doesn't cancel everything else you've ever shared."

"I hope not."

"It doesn't."

"I should go. It's late, and I'm not finding anything."

"You can come back any time. Kelcey and I would be happy to see you."

"Do you mind if I keep looking at those files at home?"

"Of course."

"And I will come back," I say. "I promise."

Elizabeth walks me to the door, and when we're there, she hugs me again and holds on tight.

"A parent never gets over losing a child," she says. "That's just a fact. But you're young enough to move on from all of this. I hope you remember that."

"I'll try," I say.

"Be careful out there," she says.

# SEVENTY

MY EYES SNAP OPEN.

Dreams. The images come back to me.

Chloe.

Right before my eyes. We were walking down one of the hallways at school, except it wasn't really our school. It was some school I'd never been in before, with giant ceilings and palm trees growing out of the lockers.

Chloe walked ahead of me. She kept looking back at me over her shoulder. And smiling.

And when I rushed to catch up to her, to reach out and touch her, she kept slipping away. Farther and farther away...

My T-shirt sticks to my back. My surroundings come back to me. My laptop sits at the foot of my bed. The lamp burns on my desk. I fell asleep looking through Daniel's additional files, using the password Elizabeth gave me. I searched and searched and still didn't find anything.

It's 6:17. Dad is always up by six, brewing coffee in the

kitchen, showering and shaving, and then preparing for class. Olivia will still be asleep. A cannon could be fired through her bedroom, and she'd snooze right through it.

Something sticks in my head, something about the movie. I've already seen the rough cut dozens of times, so I reach for my phone and pull it up once again.

While it starts, and I see the same familiar footage, I think about Ron. It's weird to me that he said he didn't know Daniel. Could Ron just have forgotten? Maybe. Ron's been teaching for thirty years and had a lot of students. Maybe he saw Daniel as a budding artist, a filmmaker instead of someone goofing around on social media. But it's still weird to me. And weird that Chloe is the one who introduced them.

Is that just a coincidence?

I know exactly the section of the movie I want to see. It's the end. Where the camera does that weird, blurry drop.

Once again, Chloe and I get into the car. The car drives off, red taillights glowing.

The other car right behind us out of the parking lot.

And then the camera drops, and I hit pause.

Too far. I rewind, then hit play again.

The camera drops, and I hit pause.

Daniel stood behind a row of cars while he filmed. The cars parked closest to the gym. In other words, where the faculty parks in their assigned spots.

The grainy image remains frozen on the screen. There's a

car on the left—Mr. Feltz's ancient Volvo. On the right, Mr. Haggerty's minivan. Gray and with a Berea College sticker in the back window.

In between those two vehicles—nothing.

That space is empty. The space where Daniel focused the camera.

I know whose car is supposed to be there.

# SEVENTY-ONE

I'M PACING BEHIND THE SCHOOL AT SEVEN THIRTY.

A few teachers have already gone into the building, including Dr. Whitley, the assistant principal. But he didn't notice me, or else he noticed me and didn't feel comfortable talking to me because of all the suspicion.

A few students trickle in: kids working early in one of the science labs or kids on the swim team slogging across the parking lot from the natatorium. Otherwise, it's quiet.

Ron's sedan comes my way. The car moves slowly, like a shark through deep ocean water, and pulls into spot number fifty-seven. He climbs out, wearing the clothes he always wears to teach—houndstooth jacket, white shirt, bow tie. He looks like someone's idea of an English teacher.

When he sees me, he smiles. But it looks forced, like my smile in the videos I've posted on YouTube. "Well, this is a surprise."

"For me, too."

He opens the back door of his car and pulls out a battered

leather briefcase. When he straightens, he looks me up and down. My heart is pounding. It's thumping so fast, I think I might have something wrong with me. My hands are shaking as well, so I stuff them into my jeans pockets.

"Is something the matter, Hunter?" he asks.

"You tell me. I'm confused."

"Aren't we all?"

"You said you were out here on the night of homecoming." I sound accusatory, like one of the lawyers from *Law & Order*. "You said you saw Chloe and me argue and then drive off, right? Isn't that what you said?"

"Hunter, I'll answer your questions if it helps you, but you need to speak to me in a more respectful tone. I know I've allowed things to be informal between us, but we are on school grounds."

I count to five, trying to slow my heart by taking deep breaths. I'm not sure I have any control over what my heart does. If I did, I wouldn't care so much about what happened to Chloe. Or Daniel.

When I finish counting, I use a warmer, calmer tone. "Okay. Can you just answer my question? If there's a simple answer that clears up everything, I'll leave and let you get on with your day."

"Fair enough," he says. "What I told you is true. I was out here in the parking lot. I saw you and Chloe having a rather intense discussion and then leaving. I told you that. I told the police that. Is there something else you want to know? I have a stack of poems to grade before first period."

"Did you drive this car to campus that night?"

"What?"

My voice rises a little again. "Did you drive this car that night?" I nod toward his sedan.

"Of course."

"And you parked here?"

"Hunter, where else would I have parked? This is my assigned spot. And you know I always follow the rules."

I always thought he was funny. I always laughed at his jokes and admired his irreverence, the part of him that enjoyed poking fun at the administrators who made all the rules that governed everything we did. But right now, he doesn't seem so funny.

"You were out here with Daniel Nevin, weren't you?"

"I told you I didn't know the unfortunate young man. I only learned who he was when he died."

"That's bullshit. And you know it."

"Hunter, don't forget where you are and who I am. You can't talk to me that way."

"You were out here with him on the night of homecoming. Right?"

"You wouldn't be asking me this question if you didn't know. A good lawyer never asks a question they don't know the answer to. I feel like you're cross-examining me."

"So you were with Daniel? While he was filming? Even though you said you really didn't know him."

Ron lets out a theatrical sigh, lifting his shoulders and then letting them fall. His jacket moves with him. "You caught me. I am guilty of the crime of standing in a large school parking lot generally in the vicinity of a student who was filming the scene. And I'm guilty of not precisely remembering how well I knew a boy who later ended up dead. You got me. Now, if you'll allow me, I really have to grade these, no doubt, risible poems."

He starts to walk off. I want to reach out and grab him by the arm. But everywhere I turn, the ice is as thin as tissue paper. School. The police. Chloe's parents. No more screwups.

So I stop him with my voice.

"The movie he made," I say. "It tells us all we need to know. It's rock-solid proof."

He looks back. I have his attention. "Excuse me?"

"Your car wasn't here," I say. "In Daniel's movie, your car wasn't here. After Chloe and I drove off, Daniel turned off his camera. But then he turned it back on and filmed your car leaving. After that, he showed *this* parking spot. And it was empty. You told me you went back into the dance and finished chaperoning after Chloe and I left. But your car was gone. Why?"

Ron stands about fifteen feet away from me. He looks at the school building, almost longingly, as though some reward awaited him inside. But then he turns back to me. "Hunter, some things are just too complex to easily understand. And this is one of them. Why don't we talk about it another time? You will be calmer, and I'll be able to speak more freely."

"No," I say. I take my left hand out of my jeans pocket and point to Ron's parking space. "Why wasn't your car here that night? Did you follow us? Did you run us off the road? Did you kill Daniel because he caught it on film? You knew him. You can't deny that." I take a step forward, feeling my calmness slipping away. "You and Chloe. Did she..." I can't say the words. I can't even find them. "Did she tell you she was pregnant? Did she tell you she cheated on me? Did everyone know but me? Is that why you're quitting? Because you want to get out of town before it all comes to light?"

Ron looks to the sky, as if seeking an answer there.

"Hunter, what went on between Chloe and me was much more complicated than that. Very complicated indeed."

# SEVENTY-TWO

RON WALKS TOWARD ME AND POINTS TO HIS CAR. MORE teachers are pulling in, more people straggling by. Some of them glance at us but say nothing.

Ron goes around and gets in on the driver's side. Once we're in, Ron starts talking, using the same voice he uses in the classroom—deep and lofty.

"You know very well that Chloe is a special young woman, Hunter. She's not like any other young woman in this entire school." He gestures with both hands just like he does when he's teaching. "She's unlike ninety-nine percent of the students I've ever taught."

"What do you know about her?" I ask.

He sighs and rubs his forehead, as if I'm the slowest student he's ever taught. "There's something that happens when a student and a teacher connect in a deeper way, an intellectual way. Dare I say, a spiritual way."

"You mean the way you and I do?" I ask.

"Chloe is an extraordinary person. And has extraordinary talent as a writer."

His words sting me for a number of reasons. Is he trying to be intentionally hurtful?

"Did you read her journal?"

"Like I said, we connected. I work very hard at my job. I've devoted my life to teaching. So much so that I don't get to write my own poems anymore. When I form a bond with a student in this way, the way I did with Chloe, it's a rare gift. But you're all so very young, and you all may not understand how precious it is to feel that way. You all have so much time ahead of you, so many opportunities to meet and connect. You and Chloe have had that to some extent these past months. When you both go on to college, you'll find it with others. But someone my age... with my life..."

My train of thought screeches to a halt. I'd come to campus assuming that Ron knew something about what was going on with Chloe. He said he'd stood outside on the night of homecoming. He'd mentored Daniel and was there while Daniel filmed, even though he initially claimed not to know Daniel. And Daniel, for some reason, pointed his camera at Ron's empty parking spot. Daniel sent a message with his movie—he let us know Ron drove off when he said he was—and was supposed to be at—the dance.

Ron and Daniel must have known Chloe's secret, and Daniel was going to put it in the movie. And it was going to be that Chloe was pregnant. Cheating on me...

But Ron is talking about something else. Something I really don't want to hear. Something I couldn't have imagined.

"What are trying to tell me?" I ask. "You're saying that you and Chloe…"

"We *connected*," he says. "Didn't you hear me? Are you too naive to understand what I'm saying?"

"Stop it. Just stop it."

The air in the car starts to feel stifling. I smell the odor of coffee and cigarettes coming off Ron, and there's a trickle of sweat on his forehead. He's never looked older to me. Much older than my dad.

"You're the one who followed us and ran us off the road," I say, no longer trying to control my voice. It nearly cracks like I'm back in junior high going through puberty. "Chloe was upset that night at the dance. She'd been distant from me…emotionally. Physically. She thought she was pregnant. Were you…"

Ron's eyes widen, the most unplanned gesture he's made since I got into his car.

"Did you touch her?" I ask, my voice ringing in my ears louder than a bomb in the enclosed space. "Are you the father of her baby?"

"Don't be absurd, Hunter. I didn't lay a hand on the girl. And I'm not the father of anyone's baby."

"It's going to come out one way or the other. The whole town is going to know. You can't keep these things secret forever."

Ron lifts his hands, but this time he's not lecturing. His

shoulders slump, and his hands look like they're surrendering more than anything else.

"I'm so tired of this," he says. "Everywhere I go, this narrow, conventional morality derails things. No one understands."

"What happened?"

He runs his hand through his hair. "Why is it that people don't understand what I've been trying to explain to you? They don't understand it at universities or in high schools. I may have to go back to Europe again when all of this is over."

"You said you were going to Ohio. Is that a lie, too?"

He looks almost sad. "Hunter, I don't want to see you in trouble with the police. Or in personal turmoil. That was never my goal here. And you may not believe me, but it's been tearing me up inside that you didn't know. And that you've been suffering as result of this. I am very fond of you, Hunter. The truth is, your…friendship has meant a great deal to me as well." He clears his throat. "But you deserve to know. I guess everybody deserves to know, given how dire things have become. The walls are closing in, and everyone is going to know the truth anyway. You might as well hear it from me."

# SEVENTY-THREE

"BUT," RON SAYS, "I DIDN'T DO *ANYTHING* WRONG."

"That can't be true. Unless you're saying you just accidentally followed us when we left the dance, which I don't believe. Did you do it because you were worried she was going to tell me about your relationship, and you wanted to stop it? Is that why you ran us off the road?"

"I've got to give you credit, Hunter. You're a smart young man. You've got about half of it right. Unfortunately, it's the most important parts you've got wrong."

Mr. Feltz pulls in next to us. He gets out of his car, and as he's locking the door, he glances over at us. Feltz studies us for a moment with concern on his face, but then he shrugs and walks off.

Here I'd always thought Feltz was the odd duck, the guy who didn't quite fit in. But had he ever done anything to a student like Ron has?

"I behaved inappropriately with Chloe," Ron says. "I see that now. And my behavior may have contributed to what happened on that road. But I didn't touch her. We didn't have any romantic or physical involvement. And I didn't kidnap her or anything else. Quite the opposite. Chloe repeatedly made it clear she wanted *nothing* to do with me beyond my mentorship." He swallows. Hard. "And I tried. I tried to do more. I pursued her, knowing she'd be graduating this year. I thought about her all the time, and I wanted more. But I want to assure you, she never reciprocated. She didn't want what I wanted. To be honest, the girl was hopelessly in love with you."

I don't know if I feel better or worse.

"You were harassing her?" I ask.

"That's such an ugly way to put it. Like I said, we had a connection. An *intellectual* connection that I wanted to explore further."

"What happened at homecoming? Why was she so upset? Was she going to tell me about what you were doing to her?"

Ron nods. "She was. She insisted. She'd warned me more than once to stop pursuing her. She told me if I didn't stop, she'd have to go to the administration. At the same time, she assured me no one knew, not even her parents. Not even you. She knew how much you admired me, and she wanted to keep you out of it for that reason. But she wanted me to leave her alone. She was under too much pressure. She didn't want to have to deal with me, too. That night at the dance, I made one more attempt to convince her. I...was heavy-handed in my approach. I tried to kiss her. I came very close, but she pushed me away. That's all that happened. And that's when she told me she couldn't keep it from you any longer. She felt it was hurting your relationship, that she hadn't been honest with you, and she couldn't go on that way. She was going to report me to everyone. To you, to the school. Report all of it."

"And you told her not to tell."

"Of course. I didn't think you could handle it. You'd be angry. Not at her, but at me. And hurt as well." He waves his hand as though dismissing those emotions. "But Chloe had a mind of her own. That's why she was so upset that night. She knew it would devastate you because she knew you hold me in such high regard."

"Held. I *held* you in such high regard."

A smirk spreads across Ron's face. "You haven't heard a thing I've said. No matter. She must have told you that night after my failed attempt at a kiss, and so you must have grown upset at the news. I can only assume the two of you had a difference of opinion on how to proceed with her news. Maybe *you* wanted to confront me right then and there. And maybe Chloe didn't. I'm not sure. But you debated it in the parking lot and then left."

"How did you know I wouldn't remember what she told me?" I ask.

"I didn't know. Not at all. I gambled like you wouldn't believe. I got lucky that you couldn't remember what Chloe had told you, and that she hadn't told anyone else. Except perhaps in the journal you so skillfully pilfered. I was prepared to lose everything then—and then again when you came back to school after the accident. That's why I was out that day, the day you came by the office. I was avoiding what I believed was about to land on me. And looking for another job. A safe harbor to jump to. But the call never came. Your memory remained a black hole. And no one knew what I had done to drive Chloe to that point."

"That's why you kept asking me whether my memory was coming back," I say. "You were worried I'd remember what Chloe told me and then the whole world would know."

He doesn't deny it.

"How could you do that to her?" I ask. "Treat her that way. Put that pressure on her. Try to... She was so unhappy that last month. She must have felt so alone. And hurt and scared."

"That wasn't my intent."

"And me? You did that when you knew I loved her so much. You didn't care about either one of us."

"That's not true." Ron raises his index finger in the air. He sounds more passionate, more emotional than at any time during our conversation. "You can't say that. I did care."

"You used us all. Especially Chloe. Like she was a toy."

"I cared. I still do." He shifts in his seat, turning to face me. "You say I don't care, but you've never figured out who took you to the hospital that night, have you? It was me. I brought you there and made sure you were looked after." He turns away and stares out the windshield at the slowly filling lot. "I found you, and I brought you there. Don't forget that. Don't ever forget it."

# SEVENTY-FOUR

THE SMALL SPACE OF THE CAR IS CONFINING. I WANT TO smash my fist through the window.

Instead, I slam it against the dashboard, which feels totally unsatisfying. And stingingly painful.

"*You* took me to the hospital? After you ran us off the road? What did you do to Chloe? Where is she, and why did you only help me if you wanted her so much?"

"I didn't run you off the road. And I don't know where Chloe is. But I did follow you that night. That's true. I believe that *is* my car behind you in Daniel's movie."

"Did you kill him? Daniel?"

"What? God, no."

"Why did you lie to me about knowing him? His mom said you were helping him."

"I was. He must have told the police we saw each other out there that night. When I was questioned, the police showed a great deal of interest in my movements in the parking lot and where my car was. I lied and told them I wasn't parked in my usual spot."

"But only someone who didn't want the movie to come out would kill Daniel."

"I don't give a damn about the movie, and I didn't kill him. I wouldn't kill *anyone*. Look, I kept expecting the police to show up at my door. Either because they found the journal or because Chloe had told someone. Or because some security footage showed my car following you out of the lot. Hunter, if I really had something to be afraid of, some deadly legal jeopardy, would I still be here? Living and teaching in Bentley? No, I'd be long gone already. I planned to leave at the semester break because I feared all of this would come out eventually. But I didn't break the law."

"I'm going to call the police and let them decide. But I can't even sit in this car anymore." I fumble for the door handle. "I can't believe you did this. You let us down."

Ron reaches out and places his hand on my left arm. "Wait."

"Fuck off."

"Just wait, Hunter." He uses his authoritarian voice, the one he breaks out in class when everyone is acting up. I have to admit, it's effective. It freezes me in my seat even now. "You can call the police if you want. I'll tell them everything. But I want you to hear this from me first, so it's not misrepresented. Just take a few minutes and listen."

I find the door handle and grip it. But I don't pull.

I wait.

"It's true. I started out after you. The two of you got into a car and left. And I jumped in my car and followed you. I thought Daniel was gone. He'd turned around and left after you drove off, but he must have come back and started filming again. That's why there is a car pursuing you out of this lot. I followed you down the road a couple of miles, heading toward Flatwater. I thought that if I could get to both of you and talk to you, I could contain the fallout. I could explain myself to both of you. But I never got the chance."

"Why? What happened?"

He grimaces as he tells me, the lines on his face etched more deeply than I ever realized. "We hit that spot where the road goes into the woods. It's dark out there. The road is narrow. And another car came up behind me. The headlights filled my rearview mirror. I thought they were going to hit me or run me off the road. I was white-knuckling it. Frankly, it shook me how fast that car was going. I don't know what that car intended to do to you, but when it came along and then passed me, I pulled over and stopped. I realized that it was very foolish of me to chase you and Chloe. The chips would fall where they may. I've faced this same music before, and I was due to face it again. I turned back to go home. I had no idea that car intended to do you any harm. And I don't know if it did."

"You said you returned to school, to the homecoming dance."

He raises a hand to silence me. "I *intended* to just go home. But then I worried about the car that passed me and how upset you and Chloe were. I turned around and went back in the direction you were driving, and eventually, there in my headlights, I saw you. Dazed. Wandering along the road. I pulled over, got out, and went to you. It was obvious you had no idea who I was. You were incoherent. But I couldn't just leave you out there. Once you were in the car, I asked you about Chloe and where she was, but you couldn't answer. I thought you were in shock, maybe hurt internally, so I rushed you to the hospital. I admit, I lost my nerve when we arrived there. I was afraid to go in. So I left you and went back to the dance to finish my duties. When we learned about the accident and Chloe's disappearance, I kept my mouth shut. I actually drove out there the next day just to look around, in case I might see Chloe. But the area was crawling with police, and there was nothing I could do that they couldn't."

"Except tell the truth," I say.

"Like I said, I expected to have the police come down on me. And when they didn't, I decided I didn't have anything to offer them. I didn't get a good look at that car that came speeding up behind me. For all I know it didn't even cause your accident. But even if it did, I couldn't describe it. Or the driver. That's what happened, Hunter." He points to my phone. "If you want to call the police or the principal, or both, I understand."

His eyebrows are ragged, his teeth yellow. He looks so small.

I shake my head and shove open the door, dialing Haley.

# SEVENTY-FIVE

OVER SUBS FROM RAY'S THAT NIGHT, OLIVIA TELLS US what it was like to be inside the school when the police pulled up to talk to Ron. Olivia is eating her usual vegetarian on multi-grain bread while she shares the details.

"Oh my God, it was like a movie or something," she says. "We were *all* watching out the window during first period. We saw the police cars fly up and then Detective Haley was questioning Mr. Hartman like he was a criminal. Of course, the teachers kept telling us to ignore it, but we couldn't—and the teachers were all watching, too. I mean, seeing a faculty member get arrested right in the parking lot."

"He didn't get arrested," Dad says, ever the voice of reason. "They're just questioning him. And he's told the police everything he told Hunter. At least that's what Detective Haley relayed to me. I don't think they know yet if they have enough evidence to arrest him."

"What about the other stuff?" Olivia asks. "The really shitty stuff?"

"I doubt he'll be arrested for that," Dad says, calmly eating his tuna sub.

Olivia's face contorts with outrage. "Why not? I don't care if he didn't touch Chloe. Are you saying he can just come on to a student like a gigantic, sweating creep and then totally skate?"

"He's not skating," Dad says. He looks at me, gauging how I'm responding to the conversation about Ron. I shrug, so Dad goes on. "He didn't break the law by sexually harassing Chloe. And the police are still going to investigate him regarding Chloe's disappearance. Of course they're going to look into him for that."

Olivia starts to argue, but Dad holds up his hand and she stops.

"He's in a lot of trouble at school, Livvy. They sent an email to all the parents this afternoon. He's been suspended and will probably be fired. Apparently, he's been fired for this kind of thing before."

"Oh, gross," Olivia says. "That's just..." She puts her sandwich down. "I might vom."

"And the school hired him anyway?" I ask, even though it's clear they did.

"Sadly, it happens. It happens at colleges and universities all the time. But he won't be teaching in Bentley anymore. Since he wasn't entirely forthcoming with the police about his actions on the night of the accident, they might be able to charge him with obstruction. Who knows? Haley acted like the school board was going to throw the book at him. He won't be able to leave town as long as he's a person of interest. They'll keep close tabs on him if they don't charge him." Dad looks over at me again, his face full of sympathy. "It's hard when you find out your heroes are flawed."

"They're not all flawed like this," I say. I remember his words. I can't stop picturing him coming on to Chloe. Harassing her. Trying to kiss her at the dance so she had to fight him off. My stomach curdles. "A flaw is…not answering your emails on time or returning papers late. This is…repulsive."

"I can't believe you ever liked the guy," Olivia says. "He always seemed like a creep to me."

"Livvy," Dad says, warning her.

"Seriously, remember when he read that poem at opening assembly?" Olivia says. "He was so full of himself. Just totally flexing in front of the entire school." Then Olivia changes her voice to a very credible impersonation of Ron at the assembly. "'This is a poem I wrote about the beginning of a new academic year while sojourning in Paris.'" She mimes sticking her finger down her throat. "Blech."

I get what she's saying. But in my heart, I still haven't reconciled the person I knew with what he did to Chloe. And I'm horrified that it was all happening right in front of me, and I didn't see it. Maybe I could have done something.

But I didn't.

We all missed it. Everyone. Me. My friends. Chloe's friends. Teachers.

Chloe's parents.

"I just wish she'd told me," I say.

Dad looks me right in the eye. "She was going to. She wrote that in her journal. She probably wanted to protect you. Chloe's a strong young woman. She probably thought she could handle it on her own, until it just grew to be too much. It's tough for some people to ask for help. That's probably why she called that hotline. It offered psychological help. And you were probably right about something. You and Chloe *were* arguing that night. But I bet you wanted to tell someone about Ron. Or confront him. I think you were trying to protect Chloe, not fight with her. And you weren't angry with *her*. You were angry with Hartman."

"Yeah, I guess so."

"I know why she didn't tell you," Olivia says, her voice much more serious than it normally is.

"You do?"

"Yeah. Because she was embarrassed."

"It wasn't her fault," I say.

"Not because it was her fault. But a creep like that harasses a woman to make them feel small. It's a power trip. And then she wants to handle it on her own to prove she isn't small, and then it gets to be too much for her, and she nearly cracks. That's why she waited so long to tell you. That's probably why sex felt weird, right?"

"Yeah," I say, staring hard at my sister. "That would make sense if she was being harassed."

Dad looks concerned. *Really* concerned. "Is someone harassing *you*, Livvy?"

"I've told you that people have said shit about me and Gabby. That's them trying to make *us* feel small. I haven't told Gabby about every comment. And she's probably kept stuff from me. We don't want to bring the other person down." Livvy takes a big, deep breath. "I hope Chloe knows she's not small. She's a fucking giant."

I squeeze Livvy's hand. "Thanks."

Then Dad reaches out and puts his hand near mine without actually touching me. "Ron Hartman has done one thing that is very helpful for you. The story he's telling confirms your version of events and the piece of your memory that came back. There *was* another car. And it's pretty likely *that* car caused the accident, not you."

"Yeah, but you heard what Haley said. How do we know Ron didn't read what I said about the other car in the media and just repeat it? Wouldn't that be the perfect way to get yourself off the hook?"

Dad is trying to be optimistic, trying to act like a big part of the mystery has been resolved.

It's just a wish.

It feels to me like we're right back at the beginning:

Who was driving that other car?

Why did they run us off the road?

*Where's Chloe?*

# SEVENTY-SIX

AN HOUR LATER, DAD SHOWS UP AT MY BEDROOM DOOR.

He always acts like he's invading my space and needs special permission to be here.

He sits down at my desk.

"Is something wrong?" I ask.

"Yes, it is."

My body tenses. "What is it?"

"I'm disappointed in myself," he says. "Here you're faced with this big problem, and everybody in town is thinking about it and trying to figure it out. I'm your father, and I'm supposed to be smart, but I don't have any answers for you. I feel like I've let you down."

"I don't expect you to solve everything," I say. "You're not a cop. And you're working…"

"I know all that. Still…my most important job is taking care of you. And Liv—Olivia. And my other job, the one I get paid for in actual dollars, is using my brain to think through things. I've been sitting downstairs trying to think about your problem in the same way I think about my work."

"This isn't the Civil War," I say. "It's bad, but it's not that bad."

"I guess you're right," he says. "But whatever happens to you or Olivia feels that important to me."

"Thanks," I say, and I mean it.

"When I try to solve a problem and something just doesn't add up, there are certain things I look for."

"Like what?"

"Okay, let's break it down. A lot of things are pointing toward Ron Hartman. He was harassing Chloe. He admitted that. And it makes sense that, if she was being harassed in that way, she would be distant and distracted in the weeks leading up to the dance. Hartman was in the parking lot that night, so he knew about Danny's movie and how it might make him look guilty. He'd have reason to go kill Danny and take the movie. He wanted to keep Chloe from telling anyone about the harassment because he knew he'd get fired. Or worse. All the arrows point the same way."

"So it was him. He just needs to admit it and…" The words stick in my throat like pieces of broken glass. "He has to tell the police where Chloe is."

"That would be the end of it."

"Yeah. The end of a lot of things."

Dad studies me. His glasses are once again pushed up on top of his head, reflecting the light above. There's more gray in the stubble on his chin than I've ever noticed before. "I thought you might be struggling to accept that all of this is the answer," Dad says. "Is it because Ron was your friend and mentor?"

"Of course it's that. But it's also…I'll say it, but I'll sound like a fool."

"I doubt it," Dad says.

He sounds so confident, so much like he believes in me. I'm willing to sound stupid.

"Okay," I say. "I believed Ron when he told me his story. When he said he didn't take Chloe. And I thought he was telling the truth when he said he went after us but then another car came along. I believed him, so…"

"You're saying why would he admit to all those horrible things, but not admit to the rest? If he really knows where Chloe is, why keep it a secret?"

"Exactly. He admitted a lot. He's going to get fired at the very least. He's going to lose his new job. Am I wrong to think that makes it look like he's telling the truth?"

"There's no way to know. Some people will say anything to save their hides. And this guy was clearly trying to fool everyone."

"And he succeeded."

"Maybe you need to just sit back and think about all this more. Look for the things I mentioned before."

"Look for what?"

"Contradictions, for one," he says. "Places where there are two facts that seem in contradiction to each other. If two things contradict each other, there's tension. It's a pressure point." He purses his lips and folds his arms. "Press on that point. Maybe something will shake loose."

"None of it makes sense, Dad. Sometimes I think there's not enough information to put it all together. All we know are scraps I can remember, and now what Ron has admitted. Other times I think there's too much information."

"Too much?" Dad asks.

"Too much," I say. "If we know so little, then the answer could be an infinite variety of things. Chloe could have been kidnapped. She could have run away. She could be pregnant. She could be living in the woods like Tarzan. She could have been taken by aliens. Anything goes because we know don't know anything for sure. It all makes me want to bang my head against the wall."

"I understand. I'm sure the cops feel the same way. But if everybody just keeps—"

"Dad, I'm sorry, but I don't see how any of this is helping. No one has figured out anything. We're no closer. And…" The words linger at the back of my mouth. If I give them voice, then they might become true. But more and more, it seems like that is the very thing happening right before our eyes. "Dad, I'm starting to think Chloe isn't coming back. That we'll never know what really happened to her. No one will ever know except for the person who took her."

Dad looks disappointed. He frowns, and some of the light goes out of his eyes. It's disappointment at the truth of what I've said. But also disappointment that I might be ready to give up.

What else I can say or do?

First, I thought it was Basher. Then, I thought it was Ron.

I've got nothing.

"Well," Dad says, "if you want to talk, just let me know. And if you don't, that's okay, too."

He stands up and walks to the door. As he's pushing the door shut again, I say, "Thanks, Dad," but I'm not sure I speak loud enough for him to hear me.

# SEVENTY-SEVEN

SINCE DAD LEFT THE ROOM, I'VE BEEN STARING INTO space. But then, without knocking, Olivia barges into my room.

"I need you to give me a ride to Gabby's house."

"Sure, you can come in," I say. "And, please?"

"Can you *please* give me a ride to Gabby's house? Halloween is next week, and we have to finish our costumes."

"Can't you walk?"

"Dad won't let me. Remember? There's a kidnapper on the loose? And now we're pretty sure it isn't you."

"Nice."

"Sorry." She smirks at me. "Not really, it was funny. But can you drive me? I don't want to bother Dad. When I ask him for a ride, he acts like I want a million dollars."

"Are you ready to go now?" I ask.

She nods enthusiastically. "I got ready because I knew you'd say yes."

"I'm glad you think of me as your chauffer." I grab my keys and wallet.

"Can I just say—"

I hold up my hand. "No. You can't."

"Shut up. I know you want to hear every thought I have."

"I think I do hear every thought you have."

She goes on, barely pausing, while I tie my shoes. "I never thought Basher was guilty. Do you know why?"

"Why?"

"Because he told you he kept wanting to go over to the house and work on cars or whatever stupid masculine shit he did over there. Why would he want to go over and hang out with Chloe's parents and work on cars and stuff if he'd hurt her? I mean, how much of a psycho would you have to be?"

"I went to her house. And *into* the house."

"And you're not guilty, either. Why would Basher want to go over there if he was guilty? See? He's a jerk, but not a killer."

I finish tying my shoes but don't get up.

"How did you know Basher wanted to hang out with Scott?" I ask.

"You said. That night you tried to kick his ass and failed epically, he told you. Don't tell me you don't remember this, either. How scrambled is your brain?"

"No, I do." I remember lying in the grass, waiting for my breath to return. That's when Basher said he offered to spend time with Scott and work on the Mustang to distract him from Chloe being missing, but Scott told him no. Scott said he hadn't been out in the garage at all.

In fact, Basher said that Scott acted offended at the suggestion. Like the last thing he wanted to think about was going into the garage.

"I can't give you a ride, Livvy."

"What do you mean?"

But I'm already up and heading for the stairs, ignoring Olivia who is following along and calling my name.

In the kitchen, Dad sits at the table with a thick book about Ulysses S. Grant open before him. He's using a highlighter to mark significant passages, but when he sees me, he pushes the book aside and caps the marker. "What's the matter?"

"I've got to go somewhere. And Olivia wants a ride to Gabby's. Can you take her? I'm in a hurry."

He steeples his fingers against his lips, nodding his head.

Olivia comes rushing down the steps and stands in the doorway. Watching.

"What are you in such a hurry to do?" Dad asks.

"I have to talk to someone. About one of those contradictions."

"Why don't I go with you? Or why don't you call Detective Haley? I'm worried that there's someone out there—"

"Thanks, but no."

"Hunter, this is dangerous."

"I've got this, Dad. I'm not doing anything dangerous."

"Okay," he says, clearly not satisfied. "Is there anything I can do to help? Besides driving your sister to Gabriela's house?"

"I don't know," I say. "Do you have any advice?"

"What's going on, Hunter?" Olivia asks. "Will someone tell *me* what's going on?"

But I ignore her. And so does Dad.

Dad's brow furrows. His lips purse. This is what he looks like when one of his students asks him a particularly vexing question during office hours. Finally, he says, "Be careful. And don't take any shit."

# SEVENTY-EIGHT

ONCE AGAIN, THE BASHERS' HOUSE IS LIT UP LIKE A LIGHT bulb factory.

Little tremors of anxiety flood through my body.

The chime of the doorbell echoes inside the house, followed by the high-pitched barking of a small dog. I hope Basher answers, but luck isn't with me tonight.

Basher's dad looks at me through the sidelight. He yanks open the door and steps outside. He's a shorter, squattier version of his son, but there's a resemblance in the heavy brow, the broad nose.

"What the fuck are you doing here? Are you looking for another ass beating? I promise this time no one's going to pull him off you."

One step back. And one only. I refuse to yield too much ground, even though it's his porch.

"I just want to talk to Mike. I want to ask him a question."

"Well, you can't. Now get out of here before I call the police."

"Can you just—"

And then Basher is there, appearing behind his dad and placing one hand on his shoulder. "Dad? *Dad?*"

Mr. Basher spins around like he's about to be jumped, but when he sees Mike's face, his posture relaxes. "What?"

"I want to talk to him, Dad," Mike says. "Just go back inside. Mom's starting that movie she wants you to watch with her."

"You come with me," Mr. Basher says. "There's only trouble out here. This loser couldn't even keep that perverted teacher away from his girl."

"Dad. Go in. I've got this."

Mr. Basher stares at his son for a moment, and then shoots me one more tough-guy look, the kind of thing intended to make me melt into the ground. My face flushes, but I don't move or flinch. Mom always said: *I've been barked at by bigger dogs than that.*

It's true. After everything else, Mr. Basher is the least of my worries.

When he's finally gone, Mike shuts the door and faces me. He's wearing a T-shirt and shorts, no shoes. It's a cool night and cloudy, with moisture in the air like it could rain at any moment. He makes no concessions to the weather, standing there like it's a hot day in July.

"What do you want?" he asks, his voice flat.

"I want to ask you something," I say. "And then I'll leave you alone." I turn and point to the yard, to the spot where he tackled me. "When I was here that night, when you threw me on the ground, you said something. You said you'd been over to Chloe's house and tried to help Scott with the car."

Basher sounds impatient. "Yeah. So what?"

"You said Scott told you he hadn't been working on the car. That he hadn't been in the garage since Chloe disappeared."

"Yeah. So?"

"When I was in their house on the night I took the journal, I overheard Laura and Scott talking."

Basher's face scrunches with disgust. "That's sick, dude. Why did you do that to them? They're such good people."

"That's not important. When they were talking, Laura was complaining about Scott going out to the garage every day. That he was spending all kinds of time out there. Something doesn't add up."

One side of Basher's mouth turns up. "That's what you wanted to ask me? That's the big deal? Scott didn't want me coming around and lied about it. So what? Go home, Hunter. I'm tired."

"Can the Mustang be driven? Does it run?"

Basher hesitates. "Like a dream. The body's a little rough in places, but the engine is sweet as hell."

"So…Scott could have driven that car the night of homecoming. And maybe now he doesn't want anyone to see it."

Basher grabs my elbow in a grip like an iron claw. He pulls me off the porch and into the yard. We stop twenty feet from the house. He leans in close—so close that some of his spit lands on my face when he talks.

"You're talking some serious bullshit," he says. "Are you really saying Scott ran you off the road in the Mustang? Are you sure you want to say something that freaky?"

"Maybe I am. But what else could have happened?"

"The cops searched the whole house. You know that. They only missed the journal because it was in the wall."

"Maybe they didn't even look in the garage. Why would they? They searched the house because they wanted to find anything that was related to *Chloe*. Her computer, her journal. Hair samples. Clothes for those scent dogs they used during the searches. But it was all Chloe's stuff. Why would they look in a place that belongs to Scott? Chloe never went in the garage. She didn't keep anything in there. And Scott was never a suspect."

"No," Basher says, shaking his head. "No. Not this. You can't say this."

"Just tell me how you get into the garage, Mike," I say. "I know there's a code. I've seen Scott use it. If you tell me that, I'll leave."

"You're going to break into their house again?"

"I didn't break in. And this is just the garage. I want to look at the car and then leave."

"How do you know I wouldn't give you the wrong code? Or maybe Scott changed it? He changes it every couple of months. How do you know I won't give you the code and call the police?"

"I don't know any of that," I say. "But I'm willing to risk it."

He studies me in the darkness, his eyes looking down on me.

"Look, I know you care about Chloe, too," I say. "I know that. You wrote that poem about her. You want to know what happened. All I'm doing is trying to eliminate this…contradiction. Once it's cleared up, I'll never think about it again. I'll move on."

Basher's still staring at me, and I can't read the look on his face. I expect him to grab me again and drag me back to my car. But he stands still while the clouds rush by overhead.

"You're an idiot, you know that," he says.

"I know."

"I mean, really. There's something wrong with you."

"There is. You're right."

Basher turns and starts back for the house.

"Is that it?" I say. "You're not going to help?"

"Get in your car," he says. "I have to get my shoes."

# SEVENTY-NINE

WE PARK IN THE SAME SPOT AS THE NIGHT OF THE GREAT journal heist.

It's getting close to nine, and the neighborhood is quiet. Our mission is easier. We're just going into the garage, not the house. Basher and I dash across the grass like overgrown trick-or-treaters. We move through a few neighbors' yards until we reach the Summerses' property. Mike is ahead of me, and he presses his body against the side of the garage, so I do the same.

There are two lights on in the house—one in Chloe's room and one in the kitchen. But we can't see anyone. Both cars are in the driveway—Laura's and the rental I saw at the accident site.

"The door's on the other side," Mike says, gesturing with his head. "I say we go around the back instead of crossing in front of the garage."

I give him a thumbs-up. We walk the perimeter—first along the side of the garage we're on and then around the back. We move carefully. Three garbage cans and an old wheelbarrow make it an obstacle course for us. At the far corner I peek around at the house. Still no movement inside. There's a light above the door to the garage, but it's turned off. A break.

"Why don't I go and open it," I say. "Then I'll signal you."

"Okay, Jason Bourne."

"What's the code?"

Mike's eyes get bigger. "Oh. It's Chloe's birthday. 0-2-1-8."

I remember Chloe saying it was a special birthday because she'd be turning eighteen on the eighteenth. "That only happens once."

Would she ever get to celebrate it?

I crouch again and slink along the side of the garage, keeping my eyes on the house. I reach the keypad and take another quick glance at the house. I drop flat on the ground.

Scott is in the large kitchen window. He's wearing a Garrett Morgan sweatshirt and carries a mug of tea or coffee. He pauses, presses his face against the glass, and looks outside.

Right at me.

I'm frozen on the ground, pressed as flat as my body can get. The grass is wet against my face. Scott continues to stare out at the night. Then he turns and walks away from the window.

Relief surges through me like cool water.

I push myself up, my fingers shaking, and enter the code.

The knob doesn't budge. I check the window, looking for Scott, and see nothing. I enter the code again, being more careful than ever.

No go.

I look down the length of the garage. Mike's head appears. I shrug. He shrugs back.

If it's not Chloe's birthday, it could be anything. It could be Scott's best friend from kindergarten's birthday. It could be four random numbers.

Laura's birthday was in August. I went to the party along with a million other relatives and friends. August 16.

So I try that: 0-8-1-6.

Nothing.

I look at Basher again. He leaves his position behind the back wall of the garage and rushes over to me. We speak in whispers so low I can barely hear him.

"What's Scott's birthday?" I ask.

"How the hell do I know? I say we leave. Abort mission."

"No, Mike. Think. When's his birthday?"

"I don't know." His forehead wrinkles. "Wait. He went to a car show on his birthday last year. He offered to take me, but I had practice."

"April then?" I ask.

"Yeah, April. April 4. Or maybe it's the twentieth. Shit. One of them is my mom's birthday, and one is Scott's."

I try the first one and enter it. 0-4-0-4.

The knob turns easily. And we're in.

# EIGHTY

BASHER CLOSES THE DOOR BEHIND US.

There's one window on the back wall of the garage that lets in a little light. It's even darker inside the garage than outside. The air smells like oil and grease and rubber. I sense more than I see the Mustang in front of us—a dark, sleek presence in the enclosed space.

Basher speaks in a hissing whisper. "Okay, do your thing, Gifford. You said the car came at you from the driver's side, so that means any damage would be on the passenger side of the Mustang."

The front of the car faces the large garage door, so we squeeze our bodies around the front bumper and reach the far side of the Mustang. We both crouch down next to the fender.

"I can't see a thing," Basher says.

"I'll use my phone's flashlight."

"They'll see us."

"No. The window's in the back. And this light isn't that bright."

The flashlight beam passes slowly over the fender. I know nothing about cars, nothing about body work. The fender looks clean and unblemished to me.

"Well?" I say.

"I'm not an expert," Mike says. "But I don't see any damage."

"Could he have fixed the damage?"

"Of course. But the whole car's been worked on. Just about every inch. It's hard to tell when any one part was restored. Maybe a professional could."

"Okay, let's look at the side."

"No, put that out first." He nods at my phone. "They'll see."

"Just look here first," I say, moving the light down the side of the Mustang. "Any part of the car could have hit us."

We crouch along the side of the car with my light glowing the whole way. Some small dings and scratches, but nothing big. Nothing that would have come from a collision. But the police haven't said that they know the other car hit us or just came close enough to force us into the tree.

I straighten up and click off the light. It feels darker now than ever.

"Okay," Basher says. "That's it. You did what you came to do. Now let's get out of here. If I get arrested, Coach won't let me start on Saturday. And there are going to be some college scouts there. I have to play."

But I don't move and wait for my eyes to readjust.

Basher puts his hand on my arm. "Come on."

"What about the trunk?" I ask.

"You think Chloe's in the trunk? It's been almost two weeks. It would stink. Come on, Gifford. We need to go."

Something has to be there, something we haven't thought of. But Basher's right—every moment we're in the garage is another moment of greater risk. And if we get caught…it's not going to be good. Not for me anyway…

But my eyes are seeing more. Tools on the wall. Shelves and cabinets. Saws and hammers.

And something in the corner, something I didn't know was in the garage…

"Hunter," Basher says, pleading. "Now."

"Wait," I say.

My mind hears the door opening but doesn't process it fast enough.

"Shit," Basher says. "Holy shit."

The overhead lights come on, freezing us in place like a couple of scared kids.

# EIGHTY-ONE

THE LIGHT IS BLINDING.

Laura stands in the entrance to the garage, her eyes moving from Mike to me and back again. I can't tell if she looks calm or angry about finding two people in her garage who aren't supposed to be there.

"Laura," Mike says, "let me explain what we're doing here. We were walking by, and we thought we saw someone trying to break in—"

Laura reaches behind her and eases the door shut. We're still standing at the rear of the car, its entire body a buffer between Laura and us.

"Don't lie to me, Michael," she says. "You're not very good at it."

"Don't blame him," I say. "This was all my doing. I brought Mike into this. I'm the one who wanted to come here."

Laura takes a step forward. "Why?"

Would a lie do us any good?

"We wanted—*I* wanted to look at the car. To see if it had

damage on it. Mike said Scott didn't want to work on the car, but I overheard the two of you talking about how much time Scott's been spending out here. So I thought…I'm just trying to figure out where Chloe is."

"What did you see when you looked at the car?" She lifts her chin as she continues. "Did you see anything?"

"Nothing," Mike says. "I mean, Scott's still restoring it, but the fender on the passenger side looks great. No damage. Nothing."

"And does that satisfy you, Hunter?" she asks. "Do you now believe that Scott isn't the guy who ran you off the road?"

I'm about to step onto a tightrope, and I'm not sure there's a net to catch me.

"I guess I'm just wondering…"

"Easy, dude," Basher whispers. "Chill."

"I'm just wondering if Scott found the journal and read it when he went to fix the wall. Maybe he saw what Chloe wrote."

"*You* found it when you broke into our house," Laura says.

"But there were pages missing, especially at the end," I say. "Maybe Scott tore them out to cover up what happened. Maybe he learned what was really going on with Chloe." I swallow hard and say it. "Maybe he found out Chloe was pregnant."

Laura's shaking her head. "She wasn't pregnant."

"How do you know?" I ask.

Laura shakes her head with more force. "Because I'm her damn mother. And I helped her dress for homecoming. And I know what time of the month it was. She *wasn't* pregnant. You claim to know Chloe so well. You know she was a perfection-ist. We saw the journal. She said she ripped out pages when she didn't like the writing."

"Yeah, I know. But maybe there was stuff about Ron. Maybe she named him. And when Scott went to fix the hole, he found it. And read it." I take a step forward. I feel like I'm on firmer ground now. "Laura, what would Scott do if he found out someone was sexually harassing his daughter? Would he just let it go?"

Basher's staring back at me, his eyes as big around as grape-fruits. But he doesn't say anything. He doesn't move a muscle.

"Or would he confront the person?" I ask. "Would he go after the guy?"

"He'd absolutely have the right to," Laura says.

"Yes, he would."

"So is that what you think he did?" Laura asks. "You think Scott found the journal, read about Hartman, and went off to the school to confront him? And instead of confronting Ron Hartman, he decided to run you and Chloe off the road? Does that make any sense?"

When she says it like that, it doesn't. It's like being in school when I give a wrong answer.

"Unless..." Mike says next to me.

His voice makes me jump. He hasn't said much yet, but...

"Unless he didn't know what Hartman's car looked like. And he was so pissed off he went flying up to the school, and he saw

Chloe's car leaving...and he just thought...or assumed...if he was really pissed off."

I jump in and finish where Basher leaves off. "He'd just read the journal, so maybe he assumed it was Chloe and Ron in the car going off somewhere. To do who knows what. And he wanted to stop them and..."

Laura starts to move.

I turn back to her.

She has a gun out, and it's leveled right at Mike and me.

"I don't think I can let you boys leave," she says.

# EIGHTY-TWO

THE BLACK METAL OF THE BARREL SHINES UNDER THE bright garage lights.

Mike and I lift our hands, and as he does, Mike says, "Laura, you don't have to do this. We don't really know what happened."

She turns to me. "Have you shared this theory with anyone else?"

"No, I haven't. We literally just figured it out."

"We're moving, you know," she says. "Too many bad memories here. Too many good memories as well. Everywhere we turn we're reminded of Chloe. It's too much. Scott went to talk to his boss today about a transfer. People will understand. They'll think it was just too painful to stay—and that's true. Just not for the exact reasons people think."

Laura starts walking down the driver's side of the Mustang, the gun in front of her. Mike and I shuffle down the passenger side, keeping the car between us.

"We won't tell," Mike says.

"Tell what?" she asks.

"Whatever happened," Mike says. "Shit, I don't even know what happened, Laura. But we won't say anything. I promise."

She stops directly across from us, raising the gun above the roof of the car. "A man has to protect his family. That's what a man does. If someone threatens his family, if someone harasses his daughter, he has to do something about it. And if things go too far when he protects that family, then he has to clean up that mess, too."

"Did you do something to Chloe?" I ask. "Were you the one driving the car that night?"

She closes her eyes. I'd charge her, but the distance is too great. When she opens them again, she says, "I wasn't, but I might as well have been. Whatever Scott did, he did for me. And for Chloe. He was trying to protect us, but he drove too fast. His emotions got the better of him. That happens, right? He didn't tell me the truth right away because he wanted to protect me. She's our only child, one we tried so hard to have."

"But it was an accident then," Basher says. "Why not just tell the cops?"

"Scott thought it was better if I believed Chloe had disappeared or been kidnapped than to think her own…"

Her eyes glisten with tears under the overhead lights. She uses her free hand to wipe them away.

"Scott planned to tell me someday when everything calmed down. When Chloe was presumed dead. But he couldn't wait once Hartman got arrested. You see, Scott was afraid Hartman would identify his car and then it would all come out. That's why he tore out the pages of the journal that mentioned Hartman. If people saw those, they might put it together that Scott went after him the night of homecoming. But he couldn't bear to get rid of the whole journal. Not when Chloe was gone. We wanted to cling to anything that belonged to her. And Scott wanted me to hear it from him and not the police. That's why he told me earlier today." She closes her eyes for a moment and takes a deep breath. "Let me tell you boys something. I was angry. Very, very angry. This is my child we're talking about. My only child."

"We hear you," Mike says.

"And it's been very hard for me to learn what happened. To accept Scott's role in it. I came very close to calling the police myself. And he knows it. In fact, he told me I could if I wanted to." She sniffles. "But I've had to accept it. And understand. He's my husband. He's my life, too. It was an accident. Just an accident. We've got a long road to travel together. But I couldn't lose everything. Not my husband on top of my daughter. Do you know how much worse it is for Scott? He has to live with what he did to Chloe for the rest of his life. Causing her death was an accident. And he also has to live with what he did to that boy who made the movie."

"Why did he do that?" I say, my words just above a whisper. "Why would he hurt Daniel? That movie pointed the finger at Ron. Not Scott."

"Scott knew that if the police talked to Ron, they'd find out there was another car," Laura says. "That boy, Daniel, kept calling here, trying to interview us. He wouldn't stop looking, and it would eventually lead to Scott. So Scott had to silence him."

"He needs to go to prison for all of this," I say.

"This has been worse than prison, knowing he caused his daughter's death."

"Where is Chloe? Where's her body?"

"We'll take Chloe with us," she says. Her eyes dart to the corner of the garage. "Don't worry. We're a family. We'll always be together, like we are now."

My eyes follow Laura's to the rectangular object I'd seen earlier. I can hear it humming. One of those giant freezers.

"Oh, God," I say.

Basher moves. He grabs a metal gas can from the floor and throws it over the Mustang at Laura. It flies right at her head, and she ducks and fires the gun at the same time.

# EIGHTY-THREE

MIKE GRUNTS AS I DROP TO THE FLOOR.

My face presses against the smooth cement. Mike falls to the floor next to me, moaning in pain. I can see underneath the car to the other side. Laura is on the floor, too.

The gun is out of her hand. It slid under the car about two feet, leaving it closer to her but not too far from me.

I scuttle crablike, slipping my body under the car. My left hand extends as far as it will go, reaching for the gun. Laura grabs for it from the other side, but I get it first.

Laura's hand clamps over mine. I try to pull away, but she's surprisingly strong. I pull and pull and can't seem to shake her. Laura uses her free hand to start clawing at my face. Her nails rake against my skin like talons, and I tuck my head down to protect my eyes. Blood trickles down my face.

I almost let go. Almost lose my grip.

She'll use the gun. I know.

She'll use it again.

Footsteps slap against the concrete floor of the garage. Shoes move toward Laura.

Is it Basher, up off the ground? They're not his shoes, not his legs.

"Stop it. Stop it."

It's Scott. He's down on the floor now, wrapping his hands around her waist and pulling her back. My hand comes free, and I slide out from under the car, holding the gun.

I've never held one before. It's heavy. Dense. I'm afraid if I move, even the tiniest bit, it will go off.

But I have to go to Mike. He's on his back. His left hand is clamped against his right bicep, which is gushing blood. He's been shot. He looks ghostly pale, and I set the gun carefully on the floor next to him, removing my jacket and using it as a tourniquet.

"My right arm," he says, his voice faint. "I won't be able to throw. For the college recruiters…"

"Maybe you'll throw better," I say.

One side of his mouth goes up, but his eyelids flutter and then close. I take out my phone to call 911.

"Think about this, Hunter," Scott says from the other side of the car. He has Laura on her feet, his arm around her. Her head is slumped against his shoulder, her eyes closed.

"I have to call them. He's losing too much blood."

"I know, Hunter," Scott says. "But we're going to leave. Laura and I. Okay? And you need to just forget all of this. You don't understand it."

"I understand it. I really do."

Scott starts toward me. "Just listen, Hunter—"

But Laura places her hand on Scott's arm. "Stop," she says. "Scott. Just stop. It's over, okay? Just…I'm so damn tired…"

Laura starts to sob. She collapses or faints, and Scott eases her out of sight behind the car. Before I dial, a siren sounds in the distance, drawing closer and closer.

Had a neighbor heard the shot and called for help?

I pick up the gun and stand, walking around the car and over to the corner where the freezer sits. It's not locked. Anyone could open it. Scott must have been doing that very same thing on those lonely, guilt-filled nights when he came out here, pretending to work on a car or a table or a lamp.

"Don't look in there, Hunter," Scott says. "You don't want to."

But I do.

I have to.

My free hand lifts the lid. Cold billows out, puffing around my head.

And I see Chloe. One more time.

The blue dress. The bloodstain…

And I'm back in the car. On that night.

I'm not imagining. *I'm remembering.*

I push the airbag down, out of my face, and wipe blood out of my eyes.

On my right. Chloe.

She's slumped over, still restrained by the seat belt.

Blood on her face. Blood on the dress.

Broken glass on her body.

I reach over. Touch her. She's not moving. Not breathing.

"Chloe! Chloe!"

And I'm alone. Very alone.

"I'll get help… I'll get help…"

Someone opens the passenger door.

A voice. Scott's voice: "Oh, God. Oh, God. What have I done?"

I push open my door. I can't find my phone.

I don't know what I'm doing.

It's getting black. I'm fading…

And that's where my memory ends.

I don't know how long I stand at the freezer, staring at Chloe one last time, before the police come in and pull me away.

# THE FINAL VIDEO

THE CAMERA AND TRIPOD ARE READY IN MY BEDROOM. For the last time.

It's been a few weeks since everything happened. I'm not sure I've processed it all, but I'm trying. I'm seeing the therapist Dad found. And I'm back in school and spending time with my friends when I feel up to it.

But I don't know if anything will ever really feel normal again. Maybe it shouldn't.

And I don't want to make any more videos. I just need to say one last thing.

The red light glows.

I may not be ready, but I start talking anyway. And I know I'm going to share this one:

"I don't think I need to tell you my name by this point. You know who I am, and you've read about me. A lot of people have even been sending me messages telling me how sorry they are about Chloe. And Daniel. And part of what I want to say here is I'm really grateful for all that."

"My family's been incredible. And all of my friends. I'm really happy to be back in school and acting like a normal kid again. I never thought I'd appreciate that, but I do. After the last month or so, all I want is for my life to be normal."

I remind myself not to ramble. No one has a long attention span anymore. Even me.

*Get to the point, Hunter.*

"Chloe's dad is going to jail for a long time. A long time. If he'd just told the truth about the accident that night, he likely would have been put on probation. And then Daniel...all of it would have been avoided. But Scott couldn't imagine telling Laura that he'd caused their daughter's death. He thought that was worse than anything."

"And Ron Hartman is never going to teach around here again. I wish I could say he's never going to teach anywhere again, but we know that may not be the case. That's just the world we live in. A lot of people have been talking about Scott and Ron and how they could do the things they did. And sometimes it feels like no one is talking about Chloe. Or they're not talking about her enough. I started wondering what I could say about her and... I couldn't really come up with anything that felt right. It was either too many things or not enough things. So I decided I'd just tell a story."

I take a deep breath. And try to keep my shit together.

"At the end of last August, Chloe and I went to the mall together. It was a Saturday, and the place was packed. Back to school shopping and whatever. Chloe needed clothes, so we went to a few stores. After we shopped for a while, we sat down in the food court to get something to eat. And, as usual, the two of us just started talking about everything—the upcoming school year, college applications, our friends. As far as I was concerned, the rest of the world—the mall, the food court, the other shoppers—had all disappeared."

"All of a sudden, someone flopped down into a seat at our table. The person sat down so fast that I jumped. It was a girl, about fifteen, and I'd never seen her before in my life. But she sat down like she belonged there and started talking to us like we knew her."

"'I've been looking all over for you guys,' she said, 'and here you are in the food court.'

"I thought she was confused. That she'd mistaken us for other people. Or had something wrong with her. But Chloe didn't act that way at all. Chloe just went along with it."

"'Yeah, I'm so sorry we didn't see you sooner,' Chloe said to the girl. 'But you're with us now, so it's all good.'"

"And then Chloe went ahead and pushed her french fries over to this girl. And then offered her half of her sandwich. And all the time, I was wondering who she was. I assumed she must have been a friend of Chloe's, but Chloe hadn't introduced me yet. The two of them talked for a few minutes, even though the girl was acting kind of anxious and looking over her shoulder all the time, like someone was following her."

"Finally, Chloe asked her, 'Is someone going to pick you up? Or do you need a ride?'

"And the girl said, 'I texted my mom. She's meeting me outside. She should be here by now.'"

"'Why don't you walk out with us?' Chloe said."

"And I was thinking that I wasn't finished eating yet, but Chloe grabbed her bags and stood up. And she looked at me and nodded, so I stood up, too. And the three of us walked out of the food court and over to the doors leading out of the mall."

"As we walked, I heard Chloe say something to the girl in a low voice. 'Do you see him?'"

"And the girl said, 'No, I don't. Thank God.'"

"When we got outside, an SUV pulled up, and it was the girl's mom. The girl ran over and opened the passenger door and climbed in. She looked back once, tears in her eyes, and said to us, 'Thank you, guys. So much. Thank you.'"

"And Chloe just waved, and we watched them drive off.

"We started walking to our car, and as we did, Chloe could tell I was clueless, so she explained it to me. She said that the girl was being hassled by some creep. He was probably following her around, trying to talk to her. Maybe he even offered to buy her something or take her somewhere."

"'She was probably alone,' Chloe said to me. 'But girls are taught that if they're ever in that situation, they should go up to another girl and act like they know each other. Just start talking. And we're all supposed to know to play along, because then the creep will think the girl is with other friends, and he'll leave her alone. That's what that girl was doing.'"

"'And you just knew what to do?' I asked."

"'Women have to know how to do those things, Hunter,' Chloe said. 'We're always in those situations where we have to deal with that crap. I just did my best for her. That's all I could do. No, I had to do it.'"

I swallow hard. I'm almost finished with the video.

"I guess I'm not sure what to do next. I don't know what my life will be like. But I'm just going to do what I have to do and hope it works out."

"And I'm never going to forget Chloe. I hope none of you do, either." I try to think if there's anything else to say, and there's just one more thing. "I love her. I really do. Still. And that's all I've got."

I reach out and click off the camera.

The red light goes out.

And I begin the rest of my life.

# ACKNOWLEDGMENTS

Thanks to Kara Thurmond for her web prowess. Thanks to Samantha McAllister and my nieces, Emma and Melanie Brandt, for their thoughtful insights along the way. Thanks to all of my writer friends, especially the very supportive community in SCBWI Midsouth.

Thanks to everyone on the talented team at Sourcebooks. Big thanks to my editor, Steve Geck, for his guidance and wisdom. And special thanks to Eliza Swift for taking a chance on this book in the first place.

Big thanks to Laney Katz Becker for her relentless work on my behalf. And big thanks to my agent David Hale Smith and everyone at Inkwell Management.

Thanks to my family and friends.

Thanks to all the readers!!!

Thanks to Molly McCaffrey for everything.

# ABOUT THE AUTHOR

DAVID BELL is a USA Today bestselling, award-winning author whose work has been translated into multiple languages. He's currently a professor of English at Western Kentucky University in Bowling Green, Kentucky. She's Gone is his YA debut.

**#getbooklit**

Your hub for the hottest young adult books!

Visit us online and sign up for our
newsletter at FIREreads.com

 @sourcebooksfire

 sourcebooksfire

 firereads.tumblr.com